PD

A CLANDESTINE EXIT

Ryan chuckled. "Are you suggesting I allow the servants to see me leaving your bedroom?"

"Sir?"

He grinned and walked over to the fireplace. "Fortunately, I have a solution, thanks to my father's feat of engineering." Manipulating the latch, he opened the hidden door, then gave Miranda a playful smile. "There are secret passageways connecting virtually every room in this house. Amazing, isn't it?"

"Everything about this house amazes me," she answered carefully.

"If you're certain you're feeling better, I'll make a clandestine exit. But first, let me show you how to lock the door behind me."

"I'm quite certain that isn't necessary," she murmured, wondering what he'd do if he noticed that the locking pin was missing.

He arched an eyebrow. "I'm shocked, Miss Kent. I would have imagined you'd be asking the butler to nail this door shut. . . ."

THEN HE KISSED HER

Kate Donovan

Lori Handeland

Julie Moffett

ZEBRA BOOKS
Kensington Publishing Corp.
http://www.kensingtonbooks.com

ZEBRA BOOKS are published by

Kensington Publishing Corp.
850 Third Avenue
New York, NY 10022

First Printing: May 2003
10 9 8 7 6 5 4 3 2 1

Printed in the United States of America

CONTENTS

LOVE PASSAGES

Kate Donovan

One

As Ryan Collier studied the young woman seated across from him at his desk, he knew he was scowling and didn't much care. After an exasperating week with his rambunctious cousins—an exasperating *month* if one also considered the antics of his spendthrift sister!—he had no desire to engage in so useless a pastime as interviewing a governess who was little more than a child herself.

To her credit, the prospective employee met his annoyed gaze without any sign of unease. From the poised set of her shoulders to the delicate way she kept her hands folded in her lap, she exuded a quiet sort of confidence that had thus far kept Ryan from summarily sending her on her way.

Glancing one final time at the letter in his hand, he said, "The unfortunate truth, Miss Kent, is that Emmaline Weston has wasted *your* time as well as mine. I specifically asked her to recommend a mature, seasoned governess. It was my belief that as headmistress of the Somerset Academy for Girls, she might have come into contact with one or more suitable candidates. Instead, she inexplicably chose to send me one of her students."

Miranda Kent flashed a reassuring smile. "Mrs. Weston knew you'd be curious at first, but was confident that, after reading her letter of reference, you would see that I am well-suited to this position."

"I see nothing of the sort. You're neither mature nor experienced. You're a naive young girl."

The candidate's expression didn't change, but Ryan noted her left hand, which had been folded in her lap, move almost imperceptibly, tapping fingertips on fingertips, once and then again.

Before he could guess at the meaning of the gesture, Miranda said, "Your reaction is understandable, Mr. Collier. But I assure you, I've had extensive experience caring for and instructing the younger girls at the Academy."

"Yes, yes. Mrs. Weston insists you have an amazing aptitude in that regard. Unfortunately, aptitude is no substitute for maturity, especially when the situation is as dire as this."

"Dire?" Miranda inclined her head slightly, as though fascinated. "I'm aware that your cousin's children—two boys and a girl, isn't it?—were abandoned here without warning. It must have been quite disconcerting for them."

"For *them?* They're fine. *I'm* the one who's been disconcerted," Ryan retorted. "You may well have had experience with children at the Academy, Miss Kent, but my cousin Nick O'Hara did not produce normal children. They were raised to say and do whatever they please, and what pleases them most is mayhem. It's as though a horde of miniature barbarians has descended on this household."

Miranda's soft, bubbly laugh interrupted his diatribe. "How dreadful. I assure you, sir, I shan't tolerate barbaric behavior in any charge of mine."

"You find it amusing? Believe me, I'm not exaggerating. The boys in particular are shockingly undisciplined. The little girl is not completely hopeless, but even she has no idea how to behave in a civilized household."

"How old is she?"

"Amy? Just three years, I believe. Young, but not too young for a few simple rules, wouldn't you agree?"

"Yes, sir. Wholeheartedly."

Pleased by the unequivocal validation, Ryan gave her a measured smile. "Would you like an example?"

"Yes, sir."

"From the moment Amy arrived, no matter how often I asked her to play in the nursery or on the sunporch, she insisted upon arranging her dolls and sundry paraphernalia on the staircase, completely oblivious to the fact that adults were trying to navigate around her."

"Oh, dear."

"To be fair, I eventually learned that she had a reason for her misbehavior."

"Oh?"

He nodded. "When I finally demanded to know why she seemed to play everywhere but the nursery, she told me she was afraid of the lions."

Miranda's green eyes widened. "I beg your pardon?"

Chuckling at the predictable reaction, Ryan explained. "We finally realized Amy was referring to the carved lion heads mounted on the nursery mantel. And, of course, I immediately had the carvings removed. So that problem, at least, is behind us. Now if only the boys could be handled so easily."

"It's been disconcerting for you." Miranda nodded sympathetically. "But also for the children, wouldn't you say? Mrs. Weston mentioned that their father's hasty departure had something to do with—well, with—"

"With the fact that he's wanted by the authorities?" Ryan hoped she noticed the sarcasm dripping from his voice. "Further proof that the children were raised without scruples. My cousin Nick apparently stole a diamond necklace, then absconded without having the decency to take his children with him."

"The poor little dears," Miranda murmured, adding quickly, "and how unfair to *you* as well."

He winced, realizing that she somehow saw him as unsympathetic to the children's plight. Worse, she clearly perceived him as self-involved, when nothing could be further from the truth. "I haven't for one moment shirked my responsibility to my cousin's children, nor shall I ever do so. Is it too much to ask in return that they respect my home and my rules?"

"Of course not, sir."

Massaging his eyes in a futile attempt to vanquish the headache that had accompanied the children's arrival two weeks earlier, Ryan continued, "My frustration is compounded by the fact that I need quiet in order to pursue my livelihood. I assume Mrs. Weston told you I'm a essayist?"

"She didn't need to tell me that, Mr. Collier," the candidate assured him, her tone unexpectedly eager. "I've read everything you've written—most particularly *The Necessary Quest for Utopia*—with great admiration and interest."

"I'm delighted you approve."

He regretted his patronizing tone, especially when he realized she was again tapping her fingers in her lap. Still, her pretty face showed nothing but respectful interest as she assured him, "I can only imagine the depth of concentration necessary to produce such compelling essays."

"The irony is brutal, is it not?" He smiled in spite of himself. "After years of contemplating and championing Utopia—the highest form of civilized society to which man can aspire—and after establishing for myself a personal sanctuary that reflects those lofty qualities—"

"You're subjected to a barbaric invasion?" Miranda's green eyes twinkled. "It's almost absurd, is it not?"

"It is *fully* absurd," he corrected her. Then he grinned in apology. "Do you see now why I need a more mature governess? If these were ordinary children, a pretty candidate straight out of Somerset Academy might be perfectly suited to the task. But these children are less disciplined than most, and my requirements are admittedly stricter than might be found in the average household. I want order restored. I want my solitude respected. In fact, I want it guaranteed. It will require a grim-faced, experienced disciplinarian to accomplish that."

"And yet, in your essays, you place such profound reliance on intelligence and imagination. If I'm not mistaken, you value them far above experience."

"But not above discipline."

Miranda nodded. "That's true. Fortunately, I am a highly disciplined person. It's the way I was raised, but also my natural temperament. If anyone can teach those children the value of structure and discretion, it is I."

Ryan rubbed his eyes again, his frustration returning. What possible purpose could be served by this conversation? To be sure, the girl was intelligent and collected, but she was hardly up to the challenge at hand. Keith and Brandon would take one look at her, realize how outmatched she was, and proceed to dismantle the Collier mansion brick by brick.

Unless, of course, they were old enough to notice how pretty she was, in which case perhaps she *could* exert some influence over them. Keith in particular was almost ten, which seemed time enough to start noticing attractive females. Ryan grinned at the thought, then almost immediately found it annoying. Miranda Kent was undoubtedly closer in age to ten-year-old Keith than to Ryan himself! Did she honestly think she would be able to succeed where a grown man had failed?

"How old are you, Miss Kent?" he demanded. Before she could answer, he added, "I see here that you have only recently completed your course of study at the Academy. My sister was sixteen when she left Mrs. Weston's tutelage. Am I to presume—"

"Certainly not," she interrupted, adding quickly, "My circumstances are unusual, sir. My father was an aficionado of all things Roman and Greek, and so in addition to the regular course of study at the Academy, he asked that I be immersed in the classics to every extent possible. Even when I had exhausted Mrs. Weston's curriculum, I continued my study under the guidance of a professor at Twin Oaks, a neighboring school for boys. You've heard of it, I'm sure."

Ryan nodded. "I'm impressed. And a bit surprised. Isn't that an elaborate education for a woman who intends to spend her life teaching elementary lessons to young children?"

"My father never intended for me to spend my life as a governess, sir, and I doubt that I shall do so. It suits my purposes for the moment, and I only hope it suits yours as well."

"You don't intend to pursue a career as a governess?" Ryan eyed her sternly. "May I ask, then, why you're here?"

"My father's untimely death left me in financial straits. The compensation you're offering for one year's service is exceedingly generous. It is my hope that it will enable me to embark on the life I wish for myself."

"Which is?"

She flushed. "Surely that can't matter to you as long as my service is satisfactory."

Was she daring to reprimand him? Or worse, attempting to make him feel guilty for interrogating a penniless orphan? Arching an eyebrow, he reminded her,

"As you said, I am offering generous compensation in hopes of employing a professional governess. Your lack of both experience and, apparently, *interest* in such a profession seems eminently relevant to this inquiry."

Her green eyes held his gaze without wavering. "You're correct, of course, and so I shall explain myself. I can think of no higher calling than raising children to be intelligent, responsible citizens. I believe I am well-suited to such an endeavor, and believe further it is the most agreeable way for me to support myself until I am fortunate enough to marry and have children of my own to raise."

"In other words, the generous compensation you would receive in this position might enable you to find a suitable husband? That's what you meant when you said it would allow you to embark on the life you wish for yourself?"

The young woman hesitated, then sighed. "I can't imagine a better future than that, sir."

The simple statement touched him, and he had to remind himself that his purpose in all this was to solve his own problems, not those of a lovely stranger.

She seemed to read his mind. "In addition to my other qualifications, there is the fact that I am here, ready and willing to assist you. It might take weeks to arrange for another candidate. Couldn't we give it a try, for just a while?" Before Ryan could protest, she added, "If at any time—after one hour, one day, one week, or even thereafter—I fail in any way to perform to your satisfaction, you may dismiss me without any obligation to compensate me for one minute of my time here."

"That's a rather drastic offer," he protested.

"A confident one," she replied. Her gaze warmed. "I understand your misgivings, sir. But surely Mrs. Weston would not have recommended me if I didn't have some small talent. She is a perfectionist at heart, and profoundly protective of her reputation for excellence. I'm proud to have her endorsement in this matter, and determined to prove myself worthy of it."

He eyed her with reluctant amusement. "After an hour with my cousins, you may well terminate this arrangement yourself. And as for my sister—" He grimaced, remembering his hope that a stern, matronly woman would be a good influence on Stephanie as well as on the children. But this girl was too young, and clearly too inexperienced, for such a task.

Miranda pursed her lips. "Mrs. Weston spoke of your sister with great fondness. *And* great exasperation. It's my understanding that you hope to instill in her a sense of financial responsibility and an appreciation for the arts and other cerebral pursuits. I don't mean to sound presumptuous, sir, but mightn't my own tendencies in that regard serve as something of an example?"

Ryan grinned. "You underestimate my sister. She's not yet twenty-four years old, but has already set Europe on its head, married twice, and exhausted the fortune my father left her in his will. I sincerely doubt whether an innocent girl of your age—" He interrupted himself to ask once again, "What age exactly is that?"

"I'll be nineteen before the year's end."

Ryan chuckled at her persistent evasion of the fact she was a mere eighteen years old. Then he stood and came around the desk, motioning for her to rise.

As she stood, her gaze never left his, and he was impressed anew by her direct, confident manner and the softness underlying it. It was a reassuring combination, and for just a moment, he allowed himself to believe that she could actually tame his wild cousins, so that in a year's time, or even less, he could pack them off to boarding school.

As had happened more than once, she seemed to sense his thoughts, and told him simply, "This study will be your sanctuary again soon, Mr. Collier. I'm certain once the children understand how important your work is, and how pleasant a home can be when all participants respect one another, we will establish an atmosphere in which the children can thrive and be happy with no inconvenience to you."

"Well, then . . ." He cleared his throat before opening the door and gesturing for her to precede him into the hall.

Miranda greedily studied the walls of the Collier mansion, enchanted by the graceful beauty and strength of the arched doorways, vibrant murals, and intricately carved molding. Having spent most of her childhood in cramped quarters aboard her father's sailing ship, she imagined that the little O'Hara cousins simply couldn't resist running and jumping through such spacious halls, or raising their voices just to hear them echo off the twenty-foot ceilings. Even the best-behaved child would be tempted to do so.

Of course, the man following so closely behind her would disagree with that assessment, and while Miranda was disquieted by his use of such terms as "the horde" or "barbarians" to refer to little children, she wasn't about to sit in judgment of a brilliant philosopher, especially when that brilliant philosopher might just provide a means of extricating her from her unfortunate debt-ridden state.

Then her lean, dark-haired host took her by the elbow, guiding her toward a huge circular staircase, and she almost jumped at the unexpected contact. Eight years at an academy for girls hadn't prepared her for the feel of a man's hand, even when that touch was as impersonal as this.

Her thoughts turned to her predicament with Armstrong Hemmingway, a man with plans to touch her in ways that were far from impersonal. *Don't think about him right now,* she pleaded with herself. *Concentrate on Mr. Collier's needs, which are much more benign and much, much less depraved.*

"I'll ask Simon, my butler, to show you to your room so that you can settle in," he was saying in his clipped, no-nonsense tone. "Dinner will be served promptly at six-thirty. You can meet the hellhounds then."

Miranda gave him a perfunctory smile. "I look forward to it."

"The dinner hour is the portion of my day I have chosen to devote to the children and Stephanie—whether they wish it or not. One of your duties will be to make that experience as painless for me as possible."

"Of course, sir."

"Your other duties will revolve around keeping the children quiet and *away from my study.* To the extent you can educate them, all the better. But I predict you will have your hands full simply ensuring they don't destroy the premises."

"Yes, sir."

"When you meet the boys—oh, *fine!*"

Startled by his tone, which was almost a growl, Miranda followed the direction of his annoyed stare and was startled anew at the sight of a little girl sitting on the staircase, just two steps below the first landing, carefully arranging her dolls. She was a tiny child with golden hair and delicate features, so unlike her guardian that Miranda almost couldn't believe they were related.

"Amy?" He was clearly trying not to raise his voice. "What are you doing on the stairs?"

"Pwaying wif my dolwies," she explained.

Miranda almost giggled at the adorable yet confounding announcement.

"Why aren't you playing in the nursery?" Ryan asked.

"It's too wonewy there."

"Wonewy?"

"Lonely," Miranda whispered, adding so that the child could hear, "Do you miss your brothers when you're alone in the nursery, sweetheart?"

"No," the girl explained. "I miss the wions."

"You *what?*" Ryan demanded.

Miranda had to bite her lip to keep from laughing at his outraged roar. "I have a suggestion, Mr. Collier. Why doesn't Amy take me upstairs and show me the nursery?" Stooping slightly to meet the child's gaze, she murmured, "How does that sound, Amy?"

"It sounds nice."

"Let's gather up these pretty dolls first, and you can show me where they belong."

Ryan cleared his throat. "I'll leave the two of you, then. And I'll direct my driver to deliver your bags to your room. Amy, perhaps you could show Miss Kent to her room after she has seen the nursery?"

Amy nodded. "I will, Uncle Wyan."

"Thank you." He gave Miranda an amused smile. "The children have always addressed Stephanie and me as aunt and uncle."

"It's charming, sir," she assured him.

"And it reinforces my authority. To the extent they're capable of respecting authority."

Miranda kept her face expressionless, while silently observing that Amy seemed extremely respectful, and not at all barbaric or uncivilized. If Ryan Collier's criticisms of the boys were as unwarranted as those of this darling little girl, Miranda had no doubt she could make a success of this venture.

More confident than ever, she dared to assure him, "I shall do my best to further reinforce your authority at every opportunity, sir."

"Thank you." He hesitated, then bowed slightly. "You're undoubtedly fatigued from your journey. Please use this opportunity to rest before dinner. You can meet the boys and Stephanie then."

"At six-thirty sharp." Miranda nodded. "I look forward to it, sir. Thank you again for this generous opportunity. I shan't fail you."

"We'll see." With another, more dismissive bow, he disappeared back down the hall toward his study.

Miranda sat on a step and flashed a warm smile. "We're going to be spending quite a bit of time together over the next few days, Amy. Mr. Collier has brought me here to act as your governess. Do you know what that is?"

"Uncle Wyan told us we have to do whatever you say. And if you teach us something, we have to wearn it."

"All of that is true. But I'll also care for you, and listen to you, and have lovely talks with you. It is my sincere hope that we'll have a lovely time together."

"Keif said you'd be mean and ugwy. But you're not. You're pwetty and nice."

"As are you." Miranda slipped her arm around the girl's shoulders and gave her a reassuring hug, then adopted a brisker attitude. "We'd best gather up these toys without further delay. It wouldn't do for someone to trip on them, would it?"

"No."

With a teasing smile, she added, "You don't really miss the lions, do you?"

"I miss my papa."

Humbled, Miranda gave her another, more loving hug. "I'm certain he misses you too."

Amy shrugged.

"Is that the reason the nursery seems lonely to you?"

The girl nodded again. "Papa pwayed wif me and my dolwies evewy day. They miss him, too."

"Poor dears." Miranda scooped up most of the toys, leaving two for Amy to carry. Then she helped the child to her feet and guided her carefully up the graceful curved staircase until they'd reached the second floor, at which time, Amy scampered ahead, passing two rooms before darting through a doorway and out of sight.

Hurrying to join her, Miranda stepped into the nursery and smiled with relief. Having feared Ryan might have housed "the barbarians" in a dungeon or otherwise foreboding chamber, she saw that her employer had transformed an elegant, richly furnished room into a haven for a little girl by means of such frilly touches as a pink coverlet draped over lacy white eyelet linens, a tiny table and chairs topped with a miniature tea set, and baskets brimming with toys.

Setting her armload of dolls on the window seat, Miranda announced, "There. Now the dollies can see what a beautiful day it is."

"They want to sweep wif me," Amy told her, climbing up into a lacy canopy bed as she spoke.

"To . . . oh, I see. Is it time for your nap?" Miranda stretched, admitting to herself that a nap sounded wonderful. "Shall I tell you and the dollies a story while you fall asleep?"

Amy nodded, snuggling into her pillow. "But not the one about the giant."

"Certainly not," Miranda agreed, launching instead into a soothing tale of a land where the houses were made of gingerbread and the clouds were spun from sugar. Within minutes, her new charge was asleep.

Patting the child's shoulder, she turned toward the doorway and was startled to see a beautiful young woman, who announced mischievously, "You cannot possibly be the new governess. You must instead be an angel, come to rescue the children and myself from my evil brother."

Miranda bit back a smile. "Stephanie Collier, I presume? I'm Miranda Kent, recently of the Somerset Academy. Mrs. Weston sends her warmest regards."

"Look at you." Stephanie crossed to stand in front of her, her blue eyes twinkling. "How I wish I'd seen Ryan's reaction. Was he furious? Or simply speechless at having his wishes so openly defied?"

"Mr. Collier was expecting a more seasoned candidate," Miranda admitted. "But he has agreed to trust Mrs. Weston's recommendation, at least for a few days. After that, he will make his final decision."

Stephanie giggled, then tugged at Miranda's hand. "Let's talk in your room, shall we? Have you seen it yet? It's even gloomier than this one. Of course, the entire mansion is hopelessly forbidding. A tribute to its owner."

Miranda followed Stephanie into the hall and past several more doorways. "It's a somewhat daunting atmosphere for a child," she told her hostess. "But otherwise, I truthfully find your home enchanting. I can't imagine how it must have been, growing up here. I lived on a ship until I was eleven, and then went to live at the Academy. These spacious halls and opulent furnishing are glorious in comparison to either."

"A ship? How exciting." Stephanie pushed open the last door on the right, then grabbed Miranda's hand again and pulled her into a large room dominated by a stone fireplace. "Ghastly, isn't it?"

Miranda studied the rich blue velvet drapes, mahogany furniture, and dark-paneled walls for a long moment before admitting, "I adore it."

"Well, perhaps you *are* the ideal candidate after all," Stephanie said with a shrug. "Did you bring any belongings, or are you as penniless as I?"

"The butler will be bringing my bags momentarily," Miranda explained, resisting an urge to add that she was indeed penniless, but, unlike Stephanie, had no wealthy brother to whom to turn to remedy her plight.

She has no idea how fortunate she is, Miranda decided with a soft sigh. *It's just as Mrs. Weston said. Stephanie is charming and good-hearted, but also somewhat frivolous to have exhausted a generous trust fund by the age of twenty-four, with the assistance of two husbands, yet to still not appreciate the circumstances into which she was born.*

Not that Miranda would have traded her own childhood for Stephanie's. She was quite certain that until the day her father died, she had been the most fortunate girl in the world. Still, a trust fund or a wealthy older brother would have helped fill the void, both emotional and financial, left by her father's passing. At the very least, they would have prevented her from falling prey to Armstrong Hemmingway's dastardly manipulations.

Shaking away such gloomy thoughts, she asked, "How long has your family lived in Bridgehaven?"

"Father and Mother built this home thirty years ago, soon after they married." She smiled at Miranda's surprised reaction. "From the look of this place, one would guess it's much older, which was exactly Father's intent." Settling into an overstuffed chair by the fireplace, she explained, "It's a replica of the manor house in England where he was raised. Some of the carvings were actually taken from the carriage house on that estate and transplanted here."

"It's remarkable."

"I've visited the original, and aside from the fact that it's much larger, they are identical in almost every detail. Father even included the secret passageways that made the manor house so fascinating. Let me show you." She jumped up, then ran her fingertips along the molding that surrounded the stone hearth.

To Miranda's amazed delight, an entire section of wall swung open. "Oh! How wonderful!"

"These passageways run all through the house. By day, there's enough light from the glass blocks hidden in the roof to allow one to easily find one's way. But at night, it's somewhat treacherous, so be very, very careful."

Miranda laughed. "I'm quite certain I won't step one foot in there. Unless the children . . . oh, dear. They don't play in the walls, do they?"

"If those rascals knew about these passageways, they surely would. Fortunately, the secret has been closely guarded. Other than Ryan and myself, I can think of only one or two persons who know about them. Even the servants don't."

"And yet you told *me?*"

"We're confidants." Stephanie crossed to Miranda and gave her an effusive embrace. "I'm so very relieved you're young and personable. I insist we become the best of friends immediately."

"I'd like that," Miranda admitted. "I only hope we have the chance. Your brother has not yet made his final decision—"

"If you're a good influence on *me,* he'll beg you to stay. And I'll convince him that you are. I'll pretend to read the most ponderous books in his collection. I'll even dress like you, although I can't imagine how your poor breasts survive under that harsh bodice." Her blue eyes twinkled as she tugged at the low neckline of her own dress. "As you can see, mine enjoy fresh air."

Miranda bit back a smile. "I suspect your brother will not be fooled for long."

"No?" Stephanie grinned. "You might be surprised at how easy it is to fool Ryan. He's really rather naive, in a boorish, unforgivable way. Was he beastly to you when you dared be young and pretty rather than meaty and unpleasant?"

Miranda laughed again, but insisted loyally, "It was an honor to meet such a highly respected philosopher and author. And it was good of him to give me this chance, even though I didn't fit his requirements."

"No one fits Ryan's requirements," Stephanie assured her. "Least of all me. But, like you, I intend to impress him. Do you know why?"

Miranda winced. She had heard the details of the arrangement, and knew Ryan had agreed to create a new trust fund for his sister if she spent a full year under his roof, improving herself, learning to handle her own finances, and eschewing the company of lovers—all three of which went against the very grain of her character, if Mrs. Weston's account was at all accurate.

Then Stephanie surprised her by murmuring, "It's not the money, Miranda. It's my desire to earn his respect. He's so much like Father, and when I see disapproval in his eyes, it breaks my heart. If Father had lived, I wouldn't have dared behave as I have these last few years. And while I don't regret most of it, I know I embarrassed the family—Ryan in particular. I'll never forgive myself if I can't find a way to remedy that."

"Then don't just pretend to read the books," Miranda advised.

"I don't care about such things," Stephanie said with a shrug. "But I do agree with Ryan on one score. I simply *must* learn to handle my own finances. It was humiliating to wake up one morning and realize I had squandered a fortune. All my friends and lovers turned their backs on me once the money was gone. And the ultimate humiliation was returning here and enduring Ryan's high-handed lectures. I will never, *ever* allow myself to be in that position again."

Miranda patted the sister's arm. "I understand more than you might suspect. My own father died when I was fourteen years old, and I was consumed with grief over the loss of his love and guidance. What I didn't know was that his business affairs were in a precarious state. Then his business manager came to the school and told me—" She stopped herself, embarrassed at the trembling of her voice. Shaking her head, she added more brightly, "If I'm able to perform to your brother's satisfaction, I'll be paid generously. We have that in common, it seems."

Stephanie grinned. "There's only one way to succeed with those boys: bribe and threaten them. I'll do what I can to help you."

"Wouldn't it be better if I actually taught them to behave?"

"It can't be done. It's unreasonable of Ryan to ask it of you. Just as it's unreasonable of him to ask *me* to live like a nun." A sly smile spread across her face. "Shall I tell you another secret?"

"Perhaps not," Miranda replied, only half teasing. There was something about the sparkle in Stephanie's eyes that told the young governess she was about to hear something scandalous.

"Do I have your promise never to reveal a word of this to Ryan?"

Miranda hesitated, but only for a moment before nodding.

Stephanie glanced toward the closed bedroom door, as though expecting her brother to burst into sight. Then she revealed with breathless delight, "I'm in love with the most wonderful man. Ryan doesn't suspect it, and he mustn't ever know. But it's so perfectly glorious! The instant my year in this mausoleum is ended, Harry and I are going to be married. Isn't that wonderful?"

"Yes," Miranda admitted. "It must be difficult, not being able to see him or correspond with him."

"To the contrary, I see him almost daily."

"Oh?" Miranda bit her lip. "Is he one of the servants?"

Stephanie burst into laughter. "Do you suppose I could have an affair with one of the servants right under Ryan's nose? He's naive, but ferociously suspicious. Not that any of the servants is attractive in any case. No, Miranda, Harry Anderson is no one's servant. He lives in Bridgehaven, and has a lucrative law practice."

"He's Mr. Collier's attorney? That's how you and he see one another? When he visits on business?"

"His visits are for pleasure only," Stephanie corrected her with a giggle. "He uses the passageways, Miranda. Isn't that romantic?"

"Oh, dear."

"Harry hates having to sneak about just to see me. If he had his way, I'd walk out the front door and into his arms and we'd marry today. But I want to earn Rye's respect. And I want to have enough money to support myself should the worst happen. Even though I know in my heart that Harry and I will be in love forever, I've learned bitter lessons, Miranda. Still, I'm happier than I've ever been."

"It really is romantic," Miranda admitted. "But aren't

you afraid Mr. Collier might discover the two of you together?"

"That's why we never meet in my bedroom. We meet here, in this room."

Miranda gasped.

"Isn't it shockingly brilliant? And now that *you're* here, it's even better. Rye would never dare enter without knocking—"

"You can't intend to continue meeting in my room," Miranda protested weakly.

"You'll be with the children. I promise we won't inconvenience you."

Shaking her head, the young governess crossed to the open wall that led to the passageway. Pushing it closed with a firm shove, she examined the mechanism that served as its latch. "Is there a way to lock this?"

Stephanie sighed. "Please don't do that. We'll be discreet, I promise. When you meet Harry—"

"I don't want to meet Harry. And I most particularly don't want Harry to step foot into this room again. I'll keep your secret, Stephanie, but please don't involve me in it. Mr. Collier would have every right to dismiss me if he suspected I was helping you defy him."

"He won't suspect," Stephanie began, but seemed to read the determination in Miranda's expression, and added quickly, "I'll speak with Harry about finding another place to meet."

"Thank you."

Stephanie patted her shoulder. "You should rest before dinner. My brother will undoubtedly interrogate you, as he does all of us every night. The best tactic is to simply agree with everything he says, no matter how unreasonable or insufferable."

"I appreciate the advice."

"Poor dear. You're honestly shocked by my affair with

Harry, aren't you? You spent too much time at that awful Academy. It's not a normal life for a pretty girl like yourself. I remember how I was when I left, so starved for male attention I literally fell into the arms of every man I met." She smiled grimly. "Ryan won't want you socializing too much, but certainly you'll be allowed a day in town occasionally. Harry can introduce you to some of his friends—"

"That won't be necessary," Miranda said sharply. Then she glanced toward the hall. "Do you hear that commotion? It's either the boys or my luggage. Shall we see which?" Without waiting for a response, she bustled past Stephanie and opened the door just in time to admit the driver, who was loaded down with her threadbare bags.

Relieved by the interruption, she waited until the servant had departed, then encouraged Stephanie to leave as well, insisting she needed to rest for a while. Not that it would be easy to do so, knowing there was a strange man lurking in the walls!

That isn't any of your affair, she reminded herself once she was alone. *As long as you're not an active participant in the deception, Mr. Collier can't hold you responsible for it, even if he discovers the intrigue.*

Still, she couldn't have the lovers meeting in her room, so she again examined the paneling, and was intrigued to find that two of the tiny wooden rosettes decorating it could be easily pulled free. Each was attached to a slender metal rod, one of which was much longer than the other. She had simply to switch their locations, so that the long rod was positioned right above the latch, and the door no longer budged when the mechanism was manipulated.

Smiling with relief, she thanked her father and Mrs. Weston for teaching her to be resourceful and logical, then slipped out of her traveling outfit and into a soft dressing gown. Her confidence, while slightly shaken due to Ryan Collier's disparaging interview and Stephanie's scandalous revelations, had not deserted her. In fact, she was more determined than ever to take advantage of this opportunity to free herself once and for all of all obligation to Armstrong Hemmingway.

Which meant she needed to be rested for her first meeting with the boys. Her employer would be watching the encounter closely for signs of inadequacy on her part. With a mischievous smile, she rummaged through her valise until she found the copy of Ryan Collier's *The Necessary Pursuit of Utopia* that Mrs. Weston had given her for her journey. She had always enjoyed reading the school's copy of Collier's brilliant essay. Now she would study it for another purpose—to learn *about* the author, rather than from him.

Ryan sat at the head of the dining table and surveyed his household grimly. It had been folly to allow Miranda Kent to stay, even for a day, not only because it was unfair to raise the poor girl's expectations, but because it had clearly raised the hopes of the children and Stephanie as well. In the case of Amy and Stephanie, there seemed to be instant and genuine affection for the newcomer.

Keith and Brandon seemed pleased as well, although Ryan suspected their reaction was somewhat less honorable, stemming undoubtedly from a belief that they could dominate and frazzle this slender, soft-spoken female. In the meantime, they were openly ogling her bosom, despite the fact that she was dressed primly, having changed out of her stiff, lackluster traveling outfit and into a stiff, lackluster cotton dress.

"Miss Kent?" the elder boy demanded suddenly.

"Yes, Keith?"

"Have you been married as many times as Auntie Stephanie?"

Brandon howled with laughter, and Ryan shot them each an angry glare. He would have reprimanded them aloud, but wanted to see if the governess would have the poise to do so herself.

Unfortunately, Stephanie commandeered the situation by saying cheerfully, "Didn't we warn you, Miss Kent? They're unforgivable brats. You mustn't try to teach them or even tolerate them. Just punish them daily, and hope Nick returns for them before too long."

Ryan noted that the governess's fingertips tapped the tabletop gently, in much the same way that they had done when resting in her lap in his study. What did it mean? He had taken it as a sign of disapproval that afternoon, but now wondered if it indicated discomfort or a momentary lapse of confidence, both of which would be perfectly understandable under the circumstances. And while he suspected it was painful for her to discover that she was simply not up to this particular challenge, it would make Ryan's job easier when he dismissed her.

"I'd like to hear about him," Miranda said quietly.

"Him?" Ryan frowned. "Are you referring to Nick? You'd like to hear about *him?"*

"Yes." She turned to Keith. "Just as you are understandably curious about me, I'm curious about *your* background. For example, is your father tall?"

Keith's expression hardened. "Yes."

"I thought so. Because you're tall for your age, as is Brandon. My father was tall as well. Would you like to hear about *him?"*

"Yes," Keith said quickly.

As Miranda launched into a breezy description of her

father the sea captain, Ryan had to admit that she had accomplished a fairly interesting maneuver, illustrating to Keith how an inappropriate dinner topic could make a person uncomfortable, and then rescuing him with an appropriate topic, thereby fostering an appreciation for civilized conversation.

Or more likely, she hadn't executed a maneuver at all, but had simply stumbled onto a solution for the boy's gaffe. That seemed more likely, given her age and inexperience. Still, Ryan was impressed by her poise. Aside from a finger tap or two, she had shown no reaction to the scandalous question Keith had posed.

So intent was Ryan on listening to the ensuing conversation, he almost didn't notice Brandon's furtive movements as the younger boy scooped a piece of bread from the breadbasket and secreted it under his shirt. Again! After Ryan's instructions on two separate occasions not to engage in such uncivilized conduct!

His patience snapped, and he was about to rebuke the child when he realized Miranda had noticed the bad behavior too.

Let's see how you deal with this, Miss Kent, he challenged her silently.

But to his chagrin, she simply said, "I can't remember when I've had a more enjoyable meal. Thank you all for making me feel so welcome."

"We're just so very glad you're here," Stephanie responded heartily.

"And we're so *very* glad you're not ugly," Brandon added. Then he dissolved into laughter that was echoed by his brother.

"That's enough," Ryan informed them sharply.

"Aren't *you* gwad Miss Kent isn't ugwy, Uncle Wyan?" Amy asked in a sweet, innocent voice.

The questions prompted a renewed spate of guffaws

from the little boys, and to Ryan's annoyance, even Stephanie joined the hilarity.

The only thing that kept Ryan from barking his disgust was the slight furrow in the brow of Miranda Kent. For a moment, he allowed himself to enjoy the fact that for once, someone else in the household was offended by bad behavior. Then he reminded himself that it wasn't enough for her to be offended. She was the governess. It was her job to *correct* bad behavior.

"Miss Kent?" he said, prodding her gently.

Her fingers tapped the tabletop twice. Then she smiled and said simply, "I believe I have been complimented, children. Thank you. In time, I intend to teach you to offer less controversial observations, but for the moment, I must admit I'm pleased you don't find me ugly. In fact, I'm inspired to tell you a special bedtime story. About an ugly duckling. I think you'll enjoy it."

"Tew it now!" Amy pleaded.

"I'll tell it as soon as you're ready for bed."

"Us too? Not just Amy?" Brandon asked.

"I can't imagine anything nicer than telling my story to three such charming children."

Ryan pushed his chair back so abruptly, it made a grating sound, but he didn't care. This was simply too much. Was this to be her tactic? Pandering to the horde? "Excuse me, Miss Kent. Stephanie. Children. I'll be in my study if anyone needs me. And Miss Kent?"

She met his glare with her insufferably sanguine smile. "Yes, Mr. Collier?"

"After you've told the children the story of the ugly duckling, would you be so kind as to join me in my study?"

"Certainly, sir."

"Ryan?" Stephanie's tone was guarded. "What are you going to do?"

"I'm going to have a conversation with Miss Kent."

"I'd like to be there when you do."

"Perhaps another time," he said with a pointed growl.

"I agree with Mr. Collier," Miranda interrupted. "I hope you don't mind, Stephanie, but I'd really prefer to speak with your brother alone."

Stephanie eyed her in disgust. "If you insist."

"I'm afraid I must."

"So, Ryan." Stephanie pushed back her chair as forcefully as he had, then rose to her feet, muttering, "I see now why you allowed Miranda to stay. The poor girl is so desperate for this position, she'll tolerate your worst behavior and agree with your most absurd positions. How wonderful for you." Without waiting for a response, she swept out of the room.

Shaken by the observation, Ryan turned to Miranda and insisted, "My sister is mistaken."

"I know that, sir. She's a generous person who wants to help me. It will take time for her to realize that I need no protection. And . . ." She glanced toward the wide-eyed children, then back to Ryan. "In time she will learn that when I agree with you, it isn't simply because you are my employer, but also because you are correct. This household needs order and discipline, so that every member can begin to thrive, intellectually and socially. It's what you wish for the children, because you love them. And it's what I want for them, because I am their governess."

"Thank you, Miss Kent."

Miranda smiled. "Perhaps we should have our discussion now while the children are preparing for bedtime."

"Yes. I think that would be best."

She turned back to the children. "Shall we meet in the nursery in one half hour for our story?"

Her charges nodded soberly.

"Fine. You are excused from the table."

Without hesitation, the threesome scooted out of their chairs and bolted for the hall.

Two

"Sit down please, Miss Kent." Ryan watched as the governess took her seat across the desk from him, her confident expression never wavering. Then he took his own chair and murmured, "Thank you for joining me."

"Of course."

He was rarely at a loss for words, and realized now that perhaps pacing was in order, so he stood and began to do so. "I made no secret this afternoon of the fact that I had misgivings over this arrangement."

"Your reaction was perfectly understandable, given my lack of experience as a governess."

He groaned inwardly. Was she actually making his argument for him? Didn't that prove Stephanie's claim that this poor girl was so desperate she'd say or do anything to please him?

For just one instant his thoughts took an unexpected turn. How far *would* she go to please him? Then he forced himself to focus on the prim dress rather than the graceful body beneath it. No, there was no question of *that.* Not that he'd ask, of course, but it was reassuring to know she'd say no even if he did. Which he wouldn't. It was absurd even to entertain such a fanciful notion! And an insult to the girl, who was pretty, but certainly not a seductress in any sense.

Aren't you gwad Miss Kent isn't ugwy, Uncle Wyan?

He chuckled despite himself. At the moment, he might have preferred an ugly governess, if only to keep his thoughts from straying.

"Is something comical, sir?"

"I was thinking about Amy."

"She's darling."

"I agree."

"She looks up to you," Miranda added softly. "On the way down to dinner, she said it was her favorite meal because Uncle Ryan is always there."

"Don't you mean Uncle Wyan?" he asked with a grin.

The governess didn't answer, but there was no mistaking her response: two quick, condemning taps of her fingertips.

The reaction infuriated Ryan. Did she dare imply that he had misbehaved? That an innocent, loving observation on his part was suddenly unpardonable? "Do you have something to say, Miss Kent?"

"Yes, sir."

"By all means, then. Proceed."

She gave a hearty sigh. "I may well be inexperienced, but I know enough to be shocked at the sorry state of your cousins' deportment. I now understand why you felt as though your household had been turned on its ear. You are the champion of all that is civilized and enlightened in our society, and you can expect nothing less from your own family. I was raised with exactly those expectations. They are as natural to me as breathing. Together, I am convinced we can teach these children to behave—you by your example, and I by my instruction."

"You're a penniless orphan so desperate for employment that you'd agree with me at any cost," he countered.

"Am I?" She rose slowly to her feet, then challenged him with her emerald stare. "Is it so impossible to believe that a penniless orphan can be well-bred and intelligent?"

"I didn't say that." He coughed lightly. "If I implied it, I apologize."

"And if I appeared to parrot your beliefs, *I* apologize. There is no doubt in my mind that we disagree on several collateral issues. Still, on the whole, our positions are similar."

Several collateral issues? Ryan grinned angrily. She was as much as admitting that she felt he had mocked Amy's immaturity of speech. And that she disapproved of his use of the term "horde" to describe innocent children.

Frustrated, he decided to change the subject. "Did you see Brandon hide a piece of bread under his shirt?"

"Yes."

"Yet you said nothing?"

"I intend to discuss it with him in private, Mr. Collier. I didn't want to embarrass him by bringing it up at the table."

"I see." Ryan grimaced, acknowledging that she was absolutely correct, and admitting further that it didn't seem fair to dismiss her yet.

And since he prided himself on being fair at all costs, the dismissal would have to wait for another day. "I continue to have misgivings, Miss Kent."

"That's understandable, sir. Either I will allay them, or you will eventually dismiss me. That is our arrangement, is it not?"

"It is."

Miranda smiled. "The children are awaiting their story, sir. Is there anything else?"

He studied her for a moment, then almost chuckled. Why was he concerned? The children—specifically, Keith and Brandon—would do his job for him in short order. If she truly cherished civility, she would run screaming from the mansion after a few days with those boys. And if she was simply desperate for employment, she would quickly learn that there were easier avenues and would tender her resignation before long. Why should he be drawn into the distasteful act of dismissing her when the situation would resolve itself of its own accord?

Smiling, he told her, "If for any reason in the next few days you decide you acted rashly in accepting this position, you have only to come to me. I'll compensate you well for the time you spent here and transport you in comfort back to the Academy."

"It's little wonder you are regarded as a pillar of civilized society, Mr. Collier. Since I can't hope to adequately express my gratitude, I'll simply leave you to enjoy the remainder of your evening. Good night, sir."

"Good night, Miss Kent."

Even after the bedtime story was finished and Miranda was finally alone in her room, she still seethed with frustration over the conversation with Ryan Collier. Had she honestly admired him for nearly a year? How could she have been so naive?

She still remembered the night she had first stumbled onto a collection of his essays in the Academy's library. Every word had transfixed her. Every sentiment had seduced her. Here was a man who understood her craving for civility and respect. This author, this Ryan Collier, had been a hero to her, combating the forces of brutality and baseness that had dared enter her world in the person of Armstrong Hemmingway.

But Ryan Collier was no longer her hero. He wasn't even her ally. He was her adversary. Her detractor! Her nemesis, second only to Hemmingway. Could that be possible? Could life dare to be that unfair to her?

It's you who's being unfair, she chastised herself as she slipped under fresh linens and snuggled into bed. *Mr. Collier is correct. The behavior of those boys is abysmal. And he's correct to want a governess who has proven her ability to civilize such children. He has just met you, and he sees an inexperienced girl who will say anything to keep her position. How can he be expected to know that you sincerely and wholeheartedly embrace his philosophy?*

A soft, scratching sound from the vicinity of the fireplace startled her out of her reverie, and she shrieked under her breath as her accusatory gaze fixed itself on hidden passageway door. The thought that an amorous man name Harry Anderson lurked behind it was more than she could bear. Was Stephanie deranged? Was Miranda herself deranged for not running to Ryan Collier with this information?

Jumping to her feet, she scurried to the hinged wall and quickly ascertained that the lock was still in place. Then she forced herself to take a deep, calming breath and returned to bed, determined to be rested for her next encounter with Ryan Collier's rambunctious cousins.

"Miss Kent?"

"Yes, Brandon?"

"What does the word 'coitus' mean?"

Miranda eyed the boy coolly. "Brandon?"

"Yes, Miss Kent?"

"Please go and play with your brother for a while. I need to check on Amy."

The boy gave her a brilliant smile, then dashed off to

join Keith, who was ruthlessly knocking ripe cherries out of a tree with a branch he'd found on the ground.

You owe Mr. Collier an apology, Miranda told herself unhappily as she made her way into the mansion, up the stairs and into the nursery. *They truly are a horde of barbarians!*

After three days and nights in the company of Keith and Brandon, Miranda's nerves were in shreds. Worse, her confidence was decimated. How could one be expected to guide and educate creatures who lived only to pillage and destroy?

To her credit, she had managed to keep them from disturbing their Uncle Ryan, but for how long would that last? They were ultimately uncontrollable! And *she* was literally exhausted, having been unable to relax her vigilance for even one minute.

Even nighttime offered no relief, thanks to Stephanie and Harry. Miranda was acutely aware of the fact that they were still using her room for their trysts. She knew from the subtle wrinkles that appeared out of nowhere in her bedcovers and from the fact that someone kept removing the slender iron rod from the lock in the paneling.

Men in the walls of her room! How could she be expected to sleep under such circumstances? And how could she be expected to discipline the boys when she hadn't been able to sleep for three nights straight?

Just think about Armstrong Hemmingway, she counseled herself as she stared down at Amy's sweet, slumbering form. *With the money Mr. Collier will pay you, you can be free of that fiend forever. Without it, what will you do?*

Settling into a rocking chair, she allowed herself to daydream of the time, one year away, when Ryan would send Keith and Brandon off to boarding school. At that time, according to Mrs. Weston, he planned to find either a school or a new governess for Amy. Perhaps he'd even offer Miranda that position, but she would decline. Armed with her wages, she would return to Armstrong Hemmingway's town house and fling the money in his face. Then, with grace and dignity, she would begin the difficult but rewarding task of building a new life for herself.

But that could only happen if she succeeded here and now, which meant she'd best continue to keep a close eye on the boys. They had been alone for almost half an hour, more than enough time for barbarians to bring down civilization. She simply had to be more vigilant somehow, despite her overwhelming urge to curl up beside Amy and whimper herself to sleep.

Hurrying down the stairs, she was heading past the study doorway when an angry voice called to her.

"Miss Kent!"

Miranda almost groaned aloud. *Not now.* Not when her defenses were so weak. Arguing with Ryan Collier was a sport for the well-rested, not an exhausted young woman. She had been fortunate enough to survive their last private encounter, and since then her only exposure to him had been at the dinner table, where, blessedly, the boys had been subdued. With any luck, Ryan believed it was because of Miranda's skill, rather than the truth—Keith and Brandon had been so relentlessly engaged in misbehaving during the day, they simply had no energy left to disrupt the evening meal.

"Is something wrong, sir?" she asked, hoping he hadn't heard the worry in her voice.

"Frankly, yes. Please join me."

She wanted to scream "No!" but dutifully entered the room instead, sensing from the rigid set of his shoulders that he was in a foul mood. And while she tried to assure herself she was a fine governess, part of her had come to agree with the philosopher—an inexperienced, sheltered woman, however intelligent, was simply no match for horrid boys like Keith and Brandon O'Hara.

Ryan stepped aside, indicating with a sweep of his arm that Miranda should proceed past him. Inhaling deeply, she squared her shoulders and did so, then gasped to see two gleaming swords lying haphazardly across his usually uncluttered desktop. It simply wasn't like him to treat such valuable—and dangerous!—artifacts with such little regard.

"Those swords have been in my family for twelve generations," he growled from behind her. "For twelve generations, they have been treated with respect bordering on reverence. Now, thanks to you and Emmaline Weston, they have become playthings for unruly children who are able to invade my study at will due to the inattention of their governess."

"I'm so very, very sorry, sir. I pray no damage was done. How did they manage . . . oh, I see." She bit her lip as she noted the footstool that had been pulled up to the wall just under the glass case in which the swords had been displayed.

Then she turned back to Ryan and murmured, "I take full responsibility, of course. And I give you my solemn word it won't happen again."

His blue eyes glinted like the steel in his swords. "I wanted a governess who could impart knowledge and discretion to those boys, but I would have settled for one who would simply keep them out of this room. Did I not make that clear?"

"Yes, sir. Abundantly clear. As I said, I take full responsibility."

"On the contrary, the fault is mine, for allowing you to stay for even a few days. Not to mention Emmaline

Weston, who showed the poorest judgment of us all." His jaw tightened visibly. "I swear, there was a time when I admired that woman for having managed to keep Stephanie out of harm for as long as she did. But she has certainly failed me—and *you*—by suggesting this unworkable arrangement."

Miranda's chest tightened with despair. "You mustn't blame Mrs. Weston! Blame me, of course—it is outrageous that I could not meet even the most basic standard you set for my performance here. I have failed you, but I have also failed Mrs. Weston. You see that, don't you?

"She was so kind to recommend me for this position, knowing how desperate I was to earn money quickly, and under safe conditions. She trusted me not to let her down, and I can't bear the thought her reputation might suffer because of me. Please, Mr. Collier?"

She could see he was embarrassed by her outburst, but couldn't stop herself. She simply had to ensure that Emmaline Weston's standing in the community was not damaged because of misplaced generosity and trust. Grabbing Ryan's hand and pressing it between her own, she insisted, "Do you remember when you said girls usually leave the Academy at the age of sixteen, or seventeen at the very latest?"

He nodded warily.

"I did in fact take my leave of the place at seventeen. I was sad, as it was the only home I'd known for six long years, but I was also glad that I would be able to repay the generosity of my father's business manager, who had paid for my education after Father's death. It was our arrangement that I would finish school and then come to work for him as his personal assistant to repay the debt."

Ryan frowned. "Your father's estate didn't provide for your education at least?"

"He intended to provide for me, but—" She paused to steady her voice, then dropped his hand and managed a halfhearted smile. "It was a shock to me as well. And to Mrs. Weston. I'll never forget the day Mr. Hemmingway came to the school to tell us about Father's last voyage. It was a month after news of the shipwreck had reached us, and I was only barely beginning to deal with my grief. It had never occurred to me, or to Mrs. Weston, that there wouldn't be money for my last three years of schooling, but we learned from Mr. Hemmingway that Father had invested everything he owned in that last voyage. When the ship went down, all was lost."

"That must have been devastating."

Miranda nodded. "Mrs. Weston was so kind. She had been almost a mother to me for so long. But I knew it put her in an awkward position. Then Mr. Hemmingway reassured us both, insisting that he and Father had been friends, as well as associates, and he knew how much my education meant to him. He insisted upon covering the cost with his own funds, promising me he'd f-find a way . . ." She stopped again to regain her composure, knowing if she said one more word she'd begin to sob.

"Miss Kent—"

"I'm fine." Miranda jutted her chin forward proudly. "Mr. Hemmingway said he'd heard from Father how intelligent and well-organized I was, and he suggested I complete my education, then come to work for him so that he could benefit from the education for which he'd paid. I was grateful, as was Mrs. Weston.

"And I was determined I would serve him well one day. And so, when that day arrived, I tearfully took my leave of Mrs. Weston and the Academy and traveled to Boston to start my employment. Hemmingway met my train and insisted upon taking me to his home, where he m-made it quite clear what my duties would be. I was shocked and frightened—"

"Miss Kent," Ryan murmured, resting his hands on her shoulders. "You needn't go on—"

"But I must!" She wiped furiously at a tear that had begun to travel down her cheek. "I must make you understand why Mrs. Weston sent me here. She knows how desperate I am to repay every penny that fiend spent on my education. She offered her own small savings to help me do so more than once, but she's a widow, and getting on in years, and it would be unthinkable to jeopardize her future. But when your request for a governess arrived, offering to pay a sum almost magically equal to the amount of my indebtedness—"

"I understand."

"I gave her my word I wouldn't fail her. Wouldn't fail *you*. But I've made a mess of it. I alône. You see that, don't you? Please don't allow *my* failure to lower your regard for her."

"My regard for her could not possibly be higher than it is at this moment," he said simply.

A flood of relief helped Miranda regain her composure at last. "The woman is nothing less than a saint, Mr. Collier. When I finally managed to evade Mr. Hemmingway's advances and rushed back to the Academy, she contacted him and told him quite simply that my contract with him was clear: my employment wasn't to start until my education was finished. And it was far from finished, she declared. I believe she would have found new lessons for me until I was old and gray if necessary. And in the meantime, I helped with the younger girls and earned a bit that way, which I saved toward my indebtedness. But it would have taken so long."

"And then my letter arrived, presenting a solution."

"But only because she honestly thought I could serve you well, sir. You believe that, don't you?"

"Yes, Miss Kent. I believe that."

"If she had known how miserably I would fail you, she never would have recommended me."

"What surprises me," he admitted, "is that you were comfortable coming here, to the isolated home of a strange man, after your experience with that bastard Hemmingway."

"But you weren't a strange man," Miranda reminded him. "Mrs. Weston knows you to be a man of principle. And I had read your essays. Had had a glimpse into the world you cherish. A world where everyone—man, woman, or child—is treated with respect." She stopped herself, alarmed that he might mistake her wistful tone for an attempt to regain his confidence, when nothing was further from the truth. She had to leave this place immediately. She knew that better than he. She had failed him. And worse, she had told him about Armstrong Hemmingway. She couldn't bear to stay for even one more hour under such miserable, humiliating circumstances.

"Miss Kent? Are you crying?" Keith asked from the doorway.

"Oh, dear." She turned to eye the two brothers with disappointment and regret.

Brandon's gaze was fixed on Ryan. "Why did you made her cry? She never does anything wrong."

"Unlike yourselves," Ryan said with a drawl.

Miranda wiped her eyes again, then stepped toward the children. "Do you remember what I told you about this room?"

Keith nodded. "It's a sanctuary."

Ryan arched an eyebrow. "Apparently, you don't know what the word means."

"Yes we do," Brandon retorted. "It's like a church. Even though *you* aren't *God.*"

"Brandon!" Miranda gasped.

Keith interrupted in a soothing voice. "Miss Kent explained to us that you're a philofficer, Uncle Ryan. And you need quiet and privacy to make your philofficies. She said people pay money to read what you think, so we have to let you think a lot. So that's why this is a sanctuary, like church. And we mustn't play in here."

Ryan seemed about to respond, when his attention was distracted by the appearance of the butler. "Simon? Did you need something?"

The old man grimaced. "I'll come back when it's more convenient, sir. Only mind those swords until I've finished polishing them. It wouldn't do for the laddies to make sport with them."

"Polishing them?" Miranda asked softly.

Simon nodded. "There are certain tasks I don't trust to the maids, and caring for these swords is one of those. I was in the middle of just that when I heard a commotion outside." He gave the boys a quick but meaningful glance. "I realized the young laddies were in danger and rushed to their aid –"

"That dog was in danger, not us," Brandon protested.

"Be quiet, dolt," Keith said, punctuating his warning with a quick shove. Then he added defensively, "We didn't tease him. He's just a mean dog, Uncle Ryan. Honest."

Miranda moistened her lips, not daring to look at Ryan. "It sounds as though everyone's had an exciting afternoon. Under the circumstances, Simon, would you mind asking the cook to do me the favor of serving the boys a nice slice of pie?"

"Pie?" Brandon's face lit up. "You aren't cross with us?"

"Actually," she murmured, "I'm rather proud that you remembered our little talk about respecting your Uncle Ryan's study."

"I agree," Ryan said with unexpected warmth in his voice. "I'm impressed that you've mastered the concept of sanctuary so readily. And . . ." He stepped up to the boys and rested his hands on their shoulders. "I owe you an apology."

"You do?" they chorused. Then Keith asked carefully, "Are you going to have pie with us?"

"Go along with Simon. Miss Kent and I need another moment."

"You aren't going to make her cry again, are you?"

"No, Keith. I give you my word I won't do that."

Embarrassed, Miranda edged away and, as soon as the children were out of sight, murmured, "If you'll alert the driver, sir, I'll go and pack my belongings. I'll want a few minutes alone with the boys and Amy—"

"You can't possibly believe you're dismissed," Ryan interrupted, shaking his head as he spoke. "I owe you an apology—"

"Don't!" She covered her ears and turned away from him. "Really, Mr. Collier, nothing could be further from the truth. It was a harmless misunderstanding, and if I had simply asked the children what happened rather than babbling on and on about my personal affairs, no harm would have been done. I don't know what possessed me, other than a sincere desire to protect Mrs. Weston's reputation."

"Miss Kent." He took her by the waist and turned her toward himself, then looked down at her with sorrowful eyes. "You haven't done anything wrong. It's I who misbehaved. I don't blame you for wanting to leave, but the children need you, and so I'm afraid I must insist that you stay."

She shrank from the pity in his gaze. "I am neither matronly nor experienced, sir. Which means your sudden reversal of attitude toward my fitness as a governess is based upon knowing my pitiable circumstances. I cannot possibly accept money from you under such conditions. Surely you can see that? Mrs. Weston will send another governess—"

"I'm not asking you to stay because of your personal circumstances. I'm asking you to stay because you somehow managed to explain the concept of 'sanctuary' to barbarians."

She felt her cheeks warm. "Nevertheless—"

"Are you intent upon arguing with me?" He grinned in evident frustration. "I suppose if I were to say you're the worst possible candidate and must leave my house immediately, you would insist that you are perfectly suited and intend to stay?"

"It must seem silly to you, sir, but—"

"It doesn't seem silly." His voice softened to a warm growl. "I'm ashamed of myself for the way I confronted you. And I'm furious with that bastard Hemmingway for taking advantage of you. And I want you to stay. It's that simple. There's no point in arguing with me, so please just agree so that we can go and have our pie."

Overwhelmed by the mix of amusement and sincerity in his brilliant blue eyes, Miranda dropped her gaze to the ground. "May I ask a favor?"

"Anything."

"Couldn't you please just forget what I told you? I don't think I could stay even for an hour knowing that you pitied me."

"It isn't pity. It's outrage."

"No one in the world knows about it, except myself and Mrs. Weston. And, of course, Mr. Hemmingway himself."

"The bastard."

She stepped back and shrugged her shoulders. "To hear *him* tell it, I am an ungrateful, scheming female who took advantage of his generosity, knowing full well what he expected in return. This matter is between him and me. I would appreciate—in fact, I must insist—that you put it out of your mind and never speak of it or think of it again."

Her bravado faltered and she added unhappily, "I really can't forgive myself for telling you. Would you excuse me, sir? I—I'd like to go to my room and compose myself."

"Certainly. Rest until dinner. I'll have Simon keep an eye on the boys, and if Amy comes down from her nap, I'll send her to have pie as well."

"Thank you." She stepped into the hall, then turned to flash him a tearful smile. "You'll put it out of your mind?"

"I'll do my best."

Without thinking, she curtsied slightly, then turned and sprinted for the staircase, mortified at having so completely lost her composure. What would her father think? Or Mrs. Weston? To have burdened a strange man with tales of her financial woes and compromised circumstances!

He'll never be comfortable with you again. Yet he'll be unable to dismiss you for fear of sending you back into Hemmingway's clutches. You've put the poor man in an impossible situation! If you had a decent bone in your body, you'd use one of those ridiculous passageways and leave without his knowing. You could send for your bags once you were far away, and that would be the end of it.

Half running back to her room, she threw open the door, then groaned in disgust at the sight of the wall panel just beginning to close. From the depths of the passageway she heard two voices, one giggly, one gruff, and knew Harry was scolding his pretty paramour to be silent. If Miranda needed further proof of her suspicions, she had only to glance at her bed—or, more precisely, its tousled bedcovers—to know she had interrupted a tryst.

This is madness, she told herself frantically. *How can you hope to earn Mr. Collier's trust, much less his money, under these ridiculous circumstances?*

Still, as Ryan himself had observed, the boys had apparently mastered the first rule of the Collier household: they understood that the study was a sanctuary.

Was it possible she could actually succeed here after all? Not completely, of course. No governess could. The boys were simply too rambunctious. But in a year's time, she could use a combination of threats and bribes, just as Stephanie had suggested, along with a judicious sprinkling of knowledge, and perhaps by the time Ryan sent them off to school, they would be ready for civilization.

Despite the distasteful condition of her bed linens, she knew she should lie down. But before she could do so, she checked the hidden door, only to discover that the long rod was missing completely. Frustrated, yet still resourceful, she tiptoed down to the nursery, where she had already identified a second mechanism, and borrowed the locking pin. Then she kissed Amy's cheek and returned to her room for a long nap and a chance to decide what to do next.

He felt sorry for her. She could see that in his eyes at the dinner table that evening. Even when the children peppered her with questions about her father's ship, Ryan never once arched an eyebrow in disapproval.

Of course, she was redeemed slightly when Brandon informed Ryan that her father's ship had been called the *Siren,* adding, "Do you know what a Siren is, Uncle Ryan? They sing to lure sailors onto rocks. One sailor from Greece put wax in his ears so he wouldn't hear them singing, but he heard them anyway and almost got killed. Then he almost got killed by a monster with one eye! He almost got killed *lots* of times."

Ryan smiled. "I see you've been learning in spite of yourself. A tribute to Miss Kent."

"Tomorrow we're learning a poem about an island."

"Oh?" Ryan turned inquiring eyes to Miranda.

She felt her cheeks redden. "The boys are at an age where declamation seems appropriate, don't you agree?"

"I despised declamation at the Academy," Stephanie interrupted.

Ryan scowled. "I can imagine. But Miss Kent is correct. There is no better intellectual training than to commit a great work to memory, thereafter to recite it with excellent diction and heartfelt emotion. I'll look forward to hearing each of you boys as soon as you're ready to recite something for me." To Miranda he added, "A poem about an island, is it?"

Not wanting to embarrass Keith by saying that the poem had little to do with actual islands, she explained carefully, "One of John Donne's devotional works, sir."

"An excellent choice." Ryan moistened his lips, then began to speak in a voice so rich and pure it melted Miranda's heart in her chest. "'No man is an island, entire of itself; every man is a piece of the continent, a part of the main . . .'"

Even Stephanie seemed transfixed as the diners listened in rapt silence, until Ryan finished with a flourish: "'And therefore never send to know for whom the bell tolls—'"

"It tolls for tea!" Brandon exclaimed. "You know every word, Uncle Ryan! I want to learn to do it just that way."

Ryan glared. "It doesn't toll for *tea,* 'it tolls for *thee,'* more so at the moment than you'd care to know."

Stephanie giggled. "Poetry at dinner. It's all so very sophisticated. Miranda has been such a wonderful influence on each and every one of us."

Ryan's eyes narrowed. "I haven't yet noticed any change in *your* behavior. In fact, I haven't seen much of you at all. How have you been spending your afternoons?"

Stephanie grinned. "Miranda knows. Shall I tell him our little secret, Miranda?"

Before the hapless governess could do anything other than cringe, Stephanie added brightly, "I've been reading *Paradise Lost* at Miranda's insistence."

"Oh?"

Stephanie shot Miranda another playful grin. "Today's episode was particularly exhilarating, even though it was interrupted before I reached the very best part."

Miranda eyed her sternly. "You should read in your bedroom, where you aren't so easily interrupted."

"The rare beauty of reading is that one can do it in all manner of different places. Isn't that true, Rye?"

"I'm just pleased you're reading at all," he told her with a shrug. Then he gave Miranda an approving smile, and she felt her cheeks warm again. Was it purely sympathy, or was he actually beginning to see her as competent?

Then, out of the corner of her eye, she saw Brandon snatch a small red potato from his plate and hide it under his jacket, and her last shred of confidence vanished. After her endless, albeit gentle, lecturing on the subject, the boys simply couldn't seem to alter their behavior.

Worse, she could tell from Ryan's expression that he, too, had noticed the transgression.

But rather than scowl, scold, or otherwise show his displeasure, he abruptly excused himself from the table, pausing only to nod respectfully in Miranda's direction.

Because to him you are now a pitiful waif, she told herself grimly. *And there is really only one way to dispel that misimpression—by becoming the quintessential governess, which is exactly what you're going to do, starting this very moment!*

As had happened more than once since Miranda's arrival, Amy's bedtime that night was a tearful affair, in part because the child was afraid of the dark, but mostly because her father's absence weighed so heavily on her. Miranda could remember all too well how her own grief over her father's death had been most overwhelming at day's end, so she indulged the child freely, this night more so even than the others, because she too felt so distressed over the day's events.

"Try to think about something else, Amy darling."

"I *want* to think about my papa!"

"Of course you do. How thoughtless of me to suggest otherwise." She pulled the child into her lap. "Tell me all about him. I want to hear every last detail."

Amy's blue eyes glistened through her tears. "Evwy night, he sang a song about me and mamma."

"How lovely." Miranda cradled her against her chest. "Would you like me to sing to you?"

"No! *I want my papa!*"

"Hush now, sweetheart. I know you miss him—"

"I wanted to go wif him! Why didn't he take me? I would've been a good girl. Not bad. I didn't mean to be bad—"

"Oh, Amy! You were never bad. I'm certain your father wanted to take you with him. I'm certain he misses you fiercely. He loves you—"

"*He doesn't wuv me anymore!*" the half-hysterical child wailed, burying her face against Miranda's chest.

"My God," came a gravelly whisper from the shadows, and for a moment, Miranda thought Ryan Collier had noiselessly entered the nursery. Then the speaker stepped into view, his handsome but unfamiliar face contorted with regret. "You don't really believe that, do you, pumpkin?"

"Papa!" Amy hurtled herself out of Miranda's lap and into the golden-haired newcomer's arms. "Papa! You came back."

"Shh . . ." He gathered her against his chest, then grinned tearfully over her head in Miranda's direction. "We meet at last, Miss Kent."

Miranda's own eyes were damp with amazement and delight as she slowly rose to her feet. "Mr. O'Hara? Thank God you're here. Does this mean—" She bit back her many questions, sighing instead. "Shall I go and fetch the boys? They'll want to know right away that you've returned."

"I never left," Nick O'Hara assured her with a wink, adding in a singsong voice, "I'd never leave my pretty little pumpkin, would I?"

"Yes, you did," Amy corrected him, pulling free to stare into his eyes. "I missed you. I'm angwy wif you."

"Forgive me or I'll tickle you into submission."

Amy giggled. "I fwogive you."

"That's better." He arched an eyebrow in Miranda's direction. "And you, Miss Kent? Can *you* ever forgive me?"

"Pardon?"

Nick flashed a mischievous grin. "I've been naughty,

haven't I? I can't think of a more tempting prospect than being punished by such a pretty nanny."

Miranda felt her cheeks turn scarlet. "Your reputation as a tease precedes you, sir, so I shan't take offense. But I *shall* take my leave, if you don't mind."

"Stay and visit." He grabbed her by the hand. "If you're going to raise my children, I'd like to know everything about you."

"Raise your children? Oh dear." Miranda pulled her hand free. "I had assumed your return meant that—well, that you had been cleared of suspicion and that my employment was ended." Faltering, she managed to insist, "How very brave and noble of you to return."

"I never left," he repeated, grinning again. "But I'm flattered you see me as brave and noble." Still holding Amy, he planted a kiss on Miranda's cheek. "From a distance, you were pretty. I see now you're positively ravishing."

"Mr. O'Hara!"

"Hush, Randi," he warned. "One never knows when Rye might be lurking about."

Miranda winced. "Are you saying Mr. Collier doesn't yet know of your return?"

"He never *left,*" an impatient juvenile voice reprimanded her, and Miranda shook her head, amazed that yet another person had managed to enter the nursery without her noticing. Turning toward Keith, she saw that the secret door beside the fireplace was half open, and groaned in confusion. "You know about the passageways?"

The boy nodded. "Sure. We use 'em all the time."

As though to confirm his brother's boast, Brandon stepped out of the darkness and into the room. "Don't tell Uncle Ryan, or he'll make another rule to spoil our fun."

The boys didn't seem at all impressed by their father's return. *Because he never left,* Miranda explained to herself uneasily. *And somehow, the boys have known all along. That certainly explains their stealing of food from the dinner table. But Mr. Collier doesn't know—*

She felt the room begin to spin, even as she whispered, "Oh, no."

"You'd best sit down, darling." Nick set Amy onto the ground, then guided Miranda to the foot of the bed. "I'll explain everything."

"Thank you." She seated herself as primly as possible, given the circumstances.

Nick met her inquiring gaze with quiet sincerity. "I didn't steal a diamond necklace. I don't believe anyone did."

"I don't understand."

He shrugged. "I was engaged in a harmless flirtation with a married woman in Bridgehaven. Her husband found out and wanted revenge. So he hid the necklace, then reported it stolen by me."

"Oh, dear."

Nick seemed encouraged. "The fellow is a doctor with considerable influence in town. I wasn't sure I could convince a judge of my innocence, even with Rye's help. My only hope was to find the necklace, either in the jealous husband's possession, or with the true culprit. I couldn't do that from a jail cell, obviously."

"You never left?"

Nick chuckled. "That's my girl. Take a deep breath, then give me a pretty smile."

Miranda scowled. "Mr. Collier knows nothing of this?"

"He'd turn me over to the authorities. It's the civilized reaction, you see." Kneeling down, he reached for his daughter and murmured, "Do you understand, pumpkin? We can't let Uncle Ryan know I'm here. He's a good man in many ways, but he can't protect Papa. If Uncle Ryan finds out I'm here, I'll have to go away again."

"No!"

"Hush now, or he'll hear."

Miranda struggled for a neutral tone. "You can't possibly believe I'll keep this from Mr. Collier."

"I *know* you'll keep it from him. Just as you've kept Stephanie's secret. If you'll deceive him to protect illicit lovemaking, you'll surely do so to protect an innocent man's liberty, not to mention the happiness of three precious children."

Miranda glared. "I suppose Stephanie has known all along that you're here?"

"No. I would have trusted her with the secret if it weren't for her brawny lover. But Harry Anderson is just the type of attorney to do something rash, like report me to the prosecutor." His dimples deepened. "You can't tell anyone, Randi. The boys and Amy, you and I—we're the only five who can know."

"This can't be happening." Miranda shook her head again. "I'm not comfortable with secrets. And Mr. Collier doesn't deserve such rampant disloyalty."

"It's only a matter of time before I find the necklace and clear my name. Rye will be deliriously happy to be rid of us all. You'll come and work for me. It will be much less taxing. Or at least"—his eyes twinkled—"in regard to the children. I'll have demands of my own, no doubt—"

"Mr. O'Hara!"

Nick chuckled. "Hush now, darling. Go on to your room and get some sleep. I'll put the children to bed. Once you've had a chance to think, we'll have another, longer visit."

Miranda wanted to assure him that there'd be no more visits. That she would report him to Ryan in the morning, then pack her bags and return to the Academy. But in her heart, she knew it wasn't so. It was just as he had said: she had deceived her employer to protect a love affair. Wouldn't she do the same to protect a man's freedom? A little girl's happiness?

"Just find that necklace quickly then," she muttered under her breath. But he was already singing Amy a charming lullaby about a little girl with golden hair just like her mother's.

And so with a reproachful glare toward Keith and Brandon, Miranda rushed back to her room, where the absurdity of her dilemma was heightened by the need to check the lock on the passageway door before she could even hope to find a few hours' rest.

Three

Three weeks later, as Ryan climbed the stairs toward his suite of rooms on the third floor, he noted with satisfaction that there were no dolls in sight. It seemed Miss Kent was succeeding at every turn. And unless his ears deceived him, she had somehow managed to convince Amy to actually play in the nursery! A singsong voice was emanating from the second floor, and he decided to pay a short visit for the purpose of praising his niece for obeying the rules.

And he had to admit he relished the thought of seeing the pretty governess at work. She had done such a good job of keeping the children quiet, he never saw any of them except at dinnertime. Even Stephanie had been quiet and out of sight, and he credited the governess for that amazing development, too. Had she honestly convinced his sister to curl up with a book?

He was smiling as he rapped his knuckles on the half-open door to the nursery. The singing stopped abruptly, but not before he heard something about a lion. Intrigued, he stepped into the room, only to frown slightly at the realization that his niece had been jumping on the bed in time to her nursery rhyme.

"Good afternoon, Amy. Where is Miss Kent?"

"She's in the boys' woom. Wistening to their decwa—de*cla*mation."

"And you're supposed to be napping?"

The little girl nodded, then gave him an apologetic smile. "Pwease don't tew Miss Kent I was jumping on the bed."

He cocked his head to the side. "What would she do if I told her?"

"She would be vewy, *vewy* disappointed."

"Well, we can't have that, can we?" he asked, charmed by the pronouncement. Reaching for the child, he lifted her down to the floor. "What were you singing?"

"I was singing my decwa—de*cla*—mation."

Ryan bit back a smile. "Aren't you a little young for that?"

"Miss Kent told the boys it would make their words sound cweawer. My words aren't cweaw, so I asked her to teach me, too."

"Oh, I see." He touched her rosy cheek. "I admire that, Amy. We must all seek to improve ourselves, mustn't we? Even a wonderful, intelligent girl like yourself."

The child beamed. "Do you want to hewr it?"

"Very much."

"Will you tap for me?"

"I beg your pardon?"

She pointed to a chalk board that had been propped on a shelf. "Miss Kent taps for me, so I don't fwoget to say my words wight."

He smiled at the poem that had been neatly lettered on the board:

La La
Ra Ra
La La
Ra Ra

"What is it you'd like me to do?"

Amy picked up a long, slender pointer and tapped the first line, while chanting carefully, "La la lion."

"I see." Charmed again, this time by the fact that his niece had pronounced each sound so perfectly, he dropped to one knee and looked her into the eye. "That was excellent, Amy."

"Thank you, Uncle Wyan," the little girl cooed.

"Well, hello you two," came an even sweeter voice from the doorway, and Ryan jumped to his feet, then grinned at his own behavior. Was he suddenly a schoolchild himself?

"Good afternoon, Miss Kent. Amy was just giving me a demonstration of her latest lesson."

"Oh?" Miranda gave him an uncertain smile, then turned her attention to her student. "I thought you'd be asleep by now."

"Uncle Wyan visited me, so I couldn't."

"Hmm."

Ryan chuckled. "I apologize, Miss Kent. But since I've already interrupted your routine, could I ask further indulgence?"

"Sir?"

"Amy was just telling me about the tapping. Since I know it's a specialty of yours, I was hoping I might have a demonstration."

"A specialty of *mine?*" Miranda frowned. "Whatever do you mean?"

"He wants to heaw my dec-*la*-ma-tion," Amy translated.

"Oh, dear."

Ryan savored the crimson blush spreading over Miranda's face. He wouldn't have thought she could be any prettier, but as she moistened her lips and seemed to search for a proper response, he was quite certain he'd never seen a more attractive sight.

Then she explained, with evident wariness, "Amy's

declamation isn't something from a famous speech or verse. It's something I myself composed for her. You'd be disappointed, I assure you."

"I'm quite certain, Miss Kent, I could never be disappointed by you."

She eyed him sternly, and he could almost hear her long, slender fingers tapping against her skirt in disapproval. Daring to grin in her face, he pulled up a nearby rocking chair and deposited himself in it. "Amy? I'm ready for your performance."

Miranda hesitated, then turned to the little girl. "Your uncle is enjoying himself at our expense, I'm afraid. Would you like to recite your poem?"

"What about the tapping?" Amy asked.

The governess winced but nodded. "I'll do that, of course." To Ryan she added defensively, "It's a way of reminding her to concentrate, and it works quite well. Although I'm certain it will seem silly to you."

"Nothing you do could seem silly to me, Miss Kent."

Her green eyes flashed more brilliantly than any emeralds Ryan had ever seen, and he was sure he was about to hear her raise her voice for the first time, but she collected herself quickly, then reached for the pointer. Without allowing time for further mischief, she nodded to Amy, then spoke clearly, saying "Once there was a—"

"La la lion," Amy chanted, enunciating perfectly as Miranda gently tapped the syllables on the chalkboard.

The governess gave Ryan an embarrassed glance before saying, "and his name was—"

"Ra ra *Ryan*," Amy announced with an impish grin.

Ryan chuckled. "I'm honored."

"It's not over," Amy complained. "Now I have to start again."

"By all means."

He struggled not to laugh as he listened to the entire poem, tapping and all:

Once there was a la la lion
And his name was Ra Ra Ryan
His mighty tail was la la long
And he was never ra ra wrong.

"Brava!" Jumping to his feet, he applauded briskly. "Amy, that was excellent. I can't remember when I've felt so proud."

The child beamed, then turned to Miranda and said happily, "Thank you for teaching me."

"Oh, dear." Miranda dropped to one knee and embraced her student. "You are so very welcome, sweetheart. Now climb into your bed, won't you? I'm sure your uncle has to be going. And I have some mending to do before dinner. So up you go."

"Here." Ryan lifted the little girl onto the bed, then kissed her cheek lightly. "Sweet dreams. And thank you again for the performance."

To his surprise, the girl hugged his neck with almost fierce affection. "I wuv you, Uncle Wy—I mean, Uncle Ryan."

"I love you, too, Amy," he whispered, touched by the gesture. Then he urged the child down onto the bed and pulled the coverlet up over her.

Turning to face Miranda, he was pleased at the soft glow in her eyes.

"What a lovely treat for Amy, Mr. Collier," she murmured. "You must visit the nursery more often."

"I intend to do just that. I would have come sooner had I known I had been memorialized in verse."

Miranda's smile was wistful. "I'm sure you realize I only used your name because Amy is determined to begin pronouncing it correctly. She's been working so hard, even though I've assured her it will all fall into place in time, with or without practice."

"Don't underestimate the power of your tapping, Miss Kent. It provides one powerful incentive to improve oneself."

She flushed and backed away from him, then arched a disapproving eyebrow. "I'm afraid your mockery is lost on me, sir."

He stepped up to her again, then leaned his face closer to hers hoping to feel the heat radiating off of her crimson cheeks. "It's true, then, Miss Kent? You honestly don't know about the tapping?"

"Really, Mr. Collier! I must ask you to stop teasing me this instant. What will Amy think?"

"Amy is sound asleep. Observe for yourself."

Without glancing toward the bed to confirm his statement, she adopted a cooler expression. "If you'll excuse me, then—"

Catching her by the arm as she started to turn away, he asked, "Wait just one moment, won't you?"

He thought he might see another blush, but was almost as pleased at how quickly she regained her poise. Had he ever thought her too young for this position? "I apologize for teasing you, Miss Kent. And I also apologize for my behavior on God knows how many other occasions."

"That's not necessary," she protested uneasily.

"I'm afraid it is. Unlike the lion in your charming verse, I'm afraid I have been ra-ra-wrong."

"Mr. Collier!" She tried to spin away from him, but again he caught her by the arm.

Trying not to grin at the alarmed look on her face, he insisted, "I was wrong in thinking I needed a strict, matronly woman to help me with the children. I see now that sort of governess never would have succeeded. Everything you said to me in my study that first day was true: You are by nature discreet and disciplined, and those qualities permeate my household due to your presence. The children are behaving and learning, and Stephanie is reading books—"

"You mustn't thank me for any of that," Miranda protested, tugging free of him. Then she hurried to the door, turning only to inform him apologetically, "I have mending to do, sir. I'll be in my room until dinnertime. Thank you again for visiting the nursery. I'm quite certain it meant the world to Amy."

Before he could respond, she bolted into the hall.

Ryan grinned proudly. So, the prim and proper Miss Kent could actually be made to stammer and swoon. It restored his faith in his ability to seduce a female. Not that he had been trying to seduce the governess, of course, but it was nice to know she wasn't completely immune to his charms.

What would she do if he followed her to her room and tried to kiss her? He chuckled softly at the thought. She would tender her resignation, of course, and not just as an idle threat, so he'd best be content with this one unexpected flirtation.

Miranda's thoughts and emotions were in turmoil as she hurried down the hall to her bedroom. She had never seen her employer in so jovial a mood. Laughing at the use of his own name in that silly lion verse, praising Amy without restraint, and, of course, teasing Miranda without mercy. Why couldn't she have responded in kind, with a witty observation? Or, short of that, why couldn't she at least have responded with a good-natured smile?

Instead, she had scolded and scowled and taken offense. And why? Because he had stepped so close, spoken so intimately, and teased so impishly. And with every word, her temperature had climbed, while her senses reeled with confusion.

She only prayed he hadn't noticed, or if he had, had attributed her reaction to the confused ignorance of a schoolgirl. That was how he had viewed her until today, was it not? And apparently he had been correct. She was far from equal to the task of managing this household. She could barely manage her own emotions! Even now, her breathing was shallow and uneven, and when she closed her eyes, she could feel him towering over her, his lips so close to hers that their breaths mingled together.

Forcing herself to inhale and exhale deeply, she reminded herself that she was a governess, being paid by this man to keep order in his household. His behavior just now had been his bizarre way of complimenting her for a job well done, when of course nothing was further from the truth.

The children are behaving and learning, and Stephanie is reading books . . .

But the children *weren't* behaving. They were simply responding to bribes and threats, as any barbarian might. Even Amy, while darling, was still oblivious to all rules, scattering her dolls about and jumping on the bed despite Miranda's every stern glance and lecture. Thank goodness she hadn't been doing *that* when Ryan appeared in her doorway!

And what on earth had he meant by all of those references to tapping? She was almost certain it was something scandalously improper, and if only she had had some small measure of experience with gentlemen, she might have understood and could have reprimanded him sharply. Perhaps even slapped his handsome face.

Yes, a slap had clearly been called for, if only she had known what "tapping" meant.

Anger at his misbehavior flooded through her, and she welcomed it as it cleared away her confusion and self-doubts. It was Ryan who had misbehaved, not she. He was nothing more or less than another in a growing group of males intent on mischief at her expense, and she simply wouldn't allow it.

Shoving open her bedroom door, she shrieked in startled disgust at the sight of one of those very males naked and entwined with Stephanie, his bare haunches exerting themselves in the most primitive of ways. Darting back into the hall, she slammed the door shut, then leaned her forehead against it, trying desperately to quell her pounding heart.

Miranda had never even kissed a man, other than a friendly peck on the cheek. Even Armstrong Hemmingway, with all his disgusting suggestions, hadn't been able to paint so shocking a picture as Harry and Stephanie had just provided. Was it too much to ask that she be protected, for just another year, from such information, until she was ready to find a loving, civilized husband to slowly introduce her to it all?

"Miss Kent? Are you ill?"

"Oh, no." She didn't want to open her eyes. Didn't want to see that lean, handsome face. Not now. Not when she couldn't speak. Not when the image of a naked man yet lingered in her tortured imagination.

Still, she couldn't just will Ryan away, so she took a deep breath, then met his brilliant blue gaze evenly. "I hope I didn't alarm you, Mr. Collier. I'm quite fine, thank you for asking."

"You screamed."

"I believe I gasped."

Ryan studied her intently. "What made you gasp?"

"It's been a trying afternoon," she informed him, hoping he might understand that he had contributed to her distress. Perhaps then he'd go away and allow her to collect herself.

"You're as pale as a bedsheet."

"Am I?"

He rested his hands on her shoulders. "I've asked too much of you, haven't I? You do your job so well, I forget how atrociously those boys can behave. And as if that weren't enough, I've had the audacity to ask for your help with Stephanie. Can you forgive me for being so demanding?"

Miranda stared into his eyes and almost drooled with adoration. He could be so gentle. So considerate. Yet there was such strength in his voice. And in his hands. His arms. His lean, powerful body.

She almost shrieked again, this time at the image of muscular, thrusting haunches that had invaded her thoughts. Jumping away from Ryan, she stammered, "I'm f-fine now, sir."

"You're exhausted," he corrected her. "Let's get you into bed."

Before she could stop him, he grabbed the doorknob and pushed open the door. Then, with great solicitude, he cupped his hand under her elbow and led her into the room.

Scarcely daring to look, Miranda forced herself to confirm the fact that Harry and Stephanie were blessedly nowhere in sight. They had done their best to straighten the covers, but still Miranda was sure Ryan would notice the mess, so she asked him quickly, "I'd like to just sit by the fire for a few minutes. And . . ." She dislodged her arm from his hand, then smiled in apology. "You're being so wonderfully kind, but honestly, I'm fine. You really ought to leave, for any number of reasons."

Ryan chuckled. "Are you suggesting I allow the servants to see me leaving your bedroom?"

"Sir?"

He grinned and walked over to the fireplace. "Fortunately, I have a solution, thanks to my father's feat of engineering." Manipulating the latch, he opened the hidden door, then gave Miranda a playful smile. "There are secret passageways connecting virtually every room in this house. Amazing, isn't it?"

"Everything about this house amazes me," she answered carefully.

"If you're certain you're feeling better, I'll make a clandestine exit. But first, let me show you how to lock the door behind me."

"I'm quite certain that isn't necessary," she murmured, wondering what he'd do if he noticed that the locking pin was missing.

He arched an eyebrow. "I'm shocked, Miss Kent. I would have imagined you'd be asking the butler to nail this door shut."

She adopted her strictest expression. "Clearly, the door has been there since my arrival, and I have been quite safe. That's all I meant."

"And you're not curious about the mechanism?"

"I intend to study it in detail as soon as you've gone. And please," she added quickly, "you mustn't leave through the wall. It's completely unnecessary. It must be awfully dusty in there. Use the hall, won't you?"

"I don't mind. It's been years since I've even thought about these old passages," he confided. "My sister and I used to enjoy them so much."

She still does, Miranda told him silently. *And for all we know, she's enjoying them with a naked man at this very moment, so please, please don't go in there!*

The thought of his encountering the amorous couple—

or, worse, some sign of Nick's presence—alarmed her, but Ryan seemed intent upon entering the passageway, so she resigned herself, saying simply, "Thank you again for your solicitude. I'm sure I'll be well rested by dinnertime. I look forward to seeing you then."

"Come here."

"I beg your pardon?"

"You must be curious," he insisted. "Don't be afraid. There's nothing in here that can harm you."

"I'm not afraid," she corrected him, but she could see he was determined, so she walked over and stepped into the passageway beside him.

There was surprisingly little dust, and an amazing amount of light, courtesy of the glass blocks imbedded in the roof. The floorboards were more solid than she had pictured, as was a narrow iron staircase a few yards from her wall.

"Those steps lead to my rooms," Ryan told her.

"Well then, it does seem convenient for you to use the passageway, just this once," she replied coolly. "Watch your step, won't you?"

He caught her by the waist as she started to step back into her room. "May I ask your advice on something, Miss Kent?"

Warming instantly under his hands, she could barely keep her breathing even. "Certainly, sir. But can't it wait until after dinner? I could join you in your study then, and we could have a nice chat."

"I like it here," he replied. "Have you ever been to a dance, Miss Kent?"

"I beg your pardon?" Miranda stared in disbelief. Was he flirting again? Here, in a dark passageway outside her bedroom? What on earth was she to do under such compromising circumstances? Especially when her body was surprisingly ready to surrender to any and all advances.

Ryan smiled. "An invitation arrived today for Stephanie and myself to attend a party at the home of a local doctor. My immediate reaction was to turn it down, but now I'm not so certain. I've been so impressed with her progress—"

"Oh!" Miranda brushed his hands from her waist and smiled in embarrassed relief. "Of course you must take your sister to the dance! Despite all her mischief, I honestly believe she has been trying to earn your respect, Mr. Collier. A party would be the perfect reward."

He hesitated, then said quietly, "I agree that Stephanie deserves a reward. But it's you who deserves the credit—"

"That's not true," Miranda protested. "She had already made up her mind to try and please you before I arrived. She told me so on my first day here."

"Did she?" He smiled again. "Thank you for telling me that."

"I can only imagine her face when you give her the news," Miranda assured him happily. "She's been so patient, despite her yearning to shop and visit and mingle with her friends in town. How delighted she will be at an opportunity to wear a beautiful gown and dance the night away!"

"And would *you* enjoy wearing a beautiful gown and dancing the night away?"

Miranda gasped. "I hope you don't think I was suggesting *that!* I can't imagine anything more inappropriate." She shook her head, disgusted with herself for having raved about the prospect of a dance, giving him no choice as a gentleman but to invite her. "May I ask your indulgence, sir? I really do need to rest before dinner, or I shan't be a match for the children. Would it be terribly rude of me to ask you to leave immediately?"

"Not at all." His entire tone had shifted, as had his

posture, which was now stiff and formal. Then, as if to accentuate the effect, he bowed slightly. "Once you're safely back in your room, I'll close the door securely. After that, you have only to switch the position of the rosettes under the latch, and no one will be able to enter your room."

Forcing herself to echo his impersonal manner, she thanked him, then stepped back through the passageway, not daring to turn around again until she had heard the door swing solidly into place. Then she sank into the chair by the fire and struggled to understand what had happened between them.

As much as she wanted to blame herself completely—after all, she *had* overstepped the bounds of his harmless flirtation by implying he should escort his governess to a dance!—it was clear he was equally to blame. He never should have flirted with her at all, knowing she was inexperienced at such matters.

Still, the poor man must have been shocked to the bone when his flirtation had gone awry. She could only imagine how her eyes must have sparkled as she talked about beautiful dresses and dancing. In her heart, as she had spoken those words, she had imagined herself in just such a dress, at just such a dance, in the arms of Ryan Collier. Being a perceptive man, Ryan had read that in her expression and had been duty bound to extend the invitation, knowing that his own casual but effective seduction had inspired her foolish dreams.

You will find him before dinner and apologize, she instructed herself briskly. *He too will apologize, and perhaps the atmosphere between you will be strained for a day or two. But then it will return to what it was. What it should be. A professional relationship, nothing more.*

That would be a relief, she decided as she curled up in her chair, trying not to remember how it had felt, for just a few precious moments, to imagine something more.

It was with bittersweet relief that Miranda learned her employer wasn't dining with them that night after all. The butler explained that the master had been called away on an errand and wouldn't be back before the week's end. Miranda suspected Ryan was simply so uncomfortable at the thought of contending with his amorous nanny that he had decided to take a room in town for a few days, allowing her time to abandon her foolish notions and rededicate herself to her duties as governess.

And that's exactly what she did over the next three days. No more bribes for the children to behave. Instead, she lectured them sternly, insisting they attend to their lessons before venturing outside to play. They would have rebelled, she knew, if it weren't for Nick's intervention.

With Ryan out of the house, Nick appeared more frequently in the nursery, in the boys' room, and even in Miranda's own bedroom. She did her best to ignore the amorous father, concentrating instead on her agenda, which was to become the governess Ryan believed her to be. She would no longer tolerate foolishness, especially from Stephanie or Nick, and so she adopted a new tactic with them. She simply stopped speaking to them.

"I know you aren't really cross with me," Stephanie would wheedle. "I give you my solemn vow Harry and I will find a new room for our lovemaking. We'd do so in any case, since all your interruptions are becoming a nuisance."

Miranda's only response would be a cool stare and dismissive shrug of her shoulders.

"I'll do whatever you ask, Randi," Nick would whisper

in her ear during the children's lessons. "Do you want me to turn myself over to the authorities and go to prison? I'll do that gladly. All you need do is ask."

But Miranda would just glare at him, relying instead on Keith or Brandon to remind their father, "She wants you to stop calling her 'Randi.' And stop kissing her neck and popping out of the wall without knocking first."

Finally, she seemed to be making some progress with them. Nick visited as often as ever, but made an effort to call her Miranda and to sit quietly, rather than inciting mischief during the lessons.

And Stephanie actually began reading *Paradise Lost*, proving it to Miranda by reciting long passages from memory. Better still, Stephanie and Harry began meeting elsewhere, although she wouldn't tell Miranda where, other than to promise it wasn't in Ryan's deserted bedroom.

"Now will you be my friend again?" Stephanie pleaded over and over, and finally Miranda relented and gave her a sheepish hug.

"What a relief," Stephanie said with a hearty sigh. "Now I can share my wonderful news with you."

"I can only imagine what *you* consider wonderful news."

Stephanie laughed. "You'll agree, I assure you. Ryan has done something wonderful."

"I didn't realize he had returned," Miranda murmured.

"Don't look so alarmed. He's still miles away, I assume. But before he left, do you know what he did? He accepted an invitation to a gala at the home of a local doctor. And he's bringing me with him! Isn't that grand? Harry says the entire town is abuzz with the news."

"I'm glad for you, Stephanie. You deserve it."

"I've earned it," she agreed. "I only wish you could

come along. Harry could introduce you to some of his friends—"

"It would be inappropriate."

"Why? Rye's the only person in Bridgehaven stuffy enough to make such fine distinctions. Harry says you'd be very popular with the men in town. He claims one of them would steal you away from us and marry you within a month."

"I don't want to discuss it. Is that clear?"

"You have almost as many rules as Ryan," Stephanie complained. "It's a wonder he doesn't appreciate you more."

Miranda pursed her lips. "He has shown his appreciation by allowing me to keep this position despite the fact that I had no experience."

"That's true." Stephanie eyed her soberly. "Are you happy, Miranda?"

"Yes," Miranda assured her. "Run along and find Harry now. I'm sure he's lurking in the walls somewhere, pining for you."

"He was here all afternoon and is playing cards tonight. But I'll leave you alone, before I say something to make you cross again." She hesitated, then gave Miranda another, more emotional embrace. "I'm just so very glad we're friends again."

"As am I." Miranda hugged her in return, then smiled wistfully as her friend sauntered across the room, blew her a kiss, then disappeared into the hall.

Slipping out of her robe, Miranda climbed into bed and turned down the lamp, then thought about the question Stephanie had asked.

Are you happy, Miranda?

Happy? She wasn't sure she even knew what that meant any longer. Thanks to Ryan, she had found a way to free herself of her obligation to Armstrong Hemmingway, and so in that sense, she was happier than she'd been in more than a year. And she was living in a beautiful home, surrounded by paintings and books and elegant reminders of mankind's most lofty achievements.

So why was she so miserable? Because she was living a lie, and, worse, betraying the trust of the man who had rescued and sheltered her.

Lovers using passageways for trysts . . . suspected criminals using them to evade the authorities . . . Ryan would be so furious if he knew. And if he knew Miranda was privy to it all, he'd dismiss her without hesitation. His sympathy over her plight with Hemmingway, even his guilt over having been too harsh with her at times and too flirtatious at other times would evaporate into righteous outrage.

Did she honestly think she could participate in this deception for a full year? It wasn't in her nature. For all that Ryan craved order and civility, she herself craved it even more. And trust—she had learned a painful lesson about that when she was betrayed by the man she thought was her father's friend. Now she was betraying her employer. A man she respected. A man she adored . . .

"Wake up, darling."

"Nick!" Miranda pushed his nuzzling face away from her neck and glared in disgust. "Get out of my bed this instant."

"I have to talk to you, darling."

"Stop calling me that." Forcing herself to take a deep breath, Miranda readjusted the bodice of her nightgown, pulled her covers up over it, and repeated primly, "Get out."

"This is important, Randi. Vitally important."

His silver gaze was so sincere, she found herself relenting. "Say it quickly, then."

He flashed a roguish smile. "Do you see why I love

you? You have the sweetest heart. And as I only just discovered, the pinkest breasts—"

"Nick!" She gathered the bedsheet up to her chin.

He chuckled fondly. "Don't be such a prude, darling. We're practically engaged. And if my plan succeeds, we'll be able to marry before Christmas."

"Your plan?"

"It's brilliant." He slipped his arm around her shoulders. "When I overheard Stephanie talking about the party at Bentley's house, I knew just what we were going to do."

"You were listening to our conversation?"

"Pay attention, darling. Don't you see? Bentley is the fellow I supposedly stole the necklace from."

Miranda bit her lip. "I'm surprised he invited your cousins to his home."

"He invited the entire town. And he bears no grudge against anyone but me. I'm a little surprised Rye accepted, though. I'd have thought he would be more loyal than that."

"If you had stayed and defended yourself, rather than running off, perhaps he would have been."

"I didn't run off," Nick reminded her. "In any case, I'm glad Rye decided to attend the party. And I agree with Stephanie. You should go along."

"You want me to go to a dance with Mr. Collier?"

Nick chuckled. "As his governess. And I forbid you to dance with anyone. But once you're there, you can help me learn the combination to the safe. Do you see?"

"That would be so wonderful," Miranda admitted. "But why would this doctor tell me the combination?"

"He wouldn't. But if my plan works, he'll open the safe while you're in the room. And I'll be hiding behind the drapes, watching his every move. Do you see?"

"Why will he open the safe?"

"Because you'll flirt with him—"

"Nick O'Hara!"

He caught her face between his hands. "Nothing will come of it, darling. I promise you that. You'll flirt with him. Admire the emerald stickpin he invariably wears at social occasions. Tell him how much you adore jewels. He'll take you to his study and open the safe, intending to show you his collection of priceless gems, in hopes it will inspire you to be naughty. But once he has worked the combination and is rummaging in the safe, you'll run back to the party."

Miranda shook her head. "I can't possibly do that, Nick. I wish I could. Perhaps we could ask Stephanie."

"We can't trust her with this secret, darling. If she knew I was here, she might tell that beefy lover of hers. It has to be you."

"I'm not invited to the party."

"Tell Stephanie you want to go. She'll shame Rye into taking you. It's the least he can do, after forcing you to slave away in this gloomy house." Grasping her by the shoulders, he whispered, "Don't you see, darling? If you do this for me, I can find proof that the necklace was never stolen. I can be free again. My children can have a father again. You and I can marry or, at the very least, have a scandalous affair—"

"Hush. Let me think." Miranda jumped out of bed and began to pace.

Wouldn't this be for the best? she asked herself warily. Nick would take the children away, Ryan would have his sanctuary back, and Miranda would return to the Academy to painstakingly earn the money to repay Hemmingway. No more deception. No more men popping out of the walls. No more Ryan . . .

"Will you help me, Randi?"

"I don't know." She gave Nick an apologetic smile. "Part of me wants so desperately to help, but I'm not sure I could flirt successfully with this doctor."

"Of course you can. If you can convince a brilliant man like Rye that he's the master of an orderly household, you can convince Bentley you're attracted to him."

"That's true," Miranda murmured. "I'm so much more deceitful than I'd ever guessed."

"That's not what I meant, darling." Nick crossed to her and stroked her cheek. "You're the most honest woman in the world, and I adore you—"

"Don't!" She jumped free of him and began to pace anew. "This is madness, Nick. I honestly don't know if I can do it."

"Miss Kent!" Ryan's voice from the far side of the hall door was accompanied by loud knocking. "Miss Kent, is anything wrong?"

"Oh, dear!" Grabbing her robe, Miranda pulled it over her nightgown, took a deep breath, and hurried to open the door just enough to allow her to slip into the hall. Then she turned her face upward, intending to give Ryan a reassuring hello.

But her throat was too tight with amazement at the sight of him, even handsomer than she remembered, as he towered over her, his blue eyes vibrant with concern for her peace of mind. She could imagine how it might feel were he to lean into her, lowering his mouth to her own—

"Miss Kent? Did you have a nightmare?"

"A nightmare?"

"I heard your voice. You sounded distressed."

Miranda coughed lightly. "I didn't know you had returned."

"I'm only just back." It was his turn to clear his throat. "I suppose you're wondering why I was standing outside your door."

Miranda felt her cheeks redden. "You were standing here? For how long?"

"I was in the process of mustering my courage," he explained with a smile.

"Pardon?"

"I wanted to see if you were awake. So that I could apologize for my conduct in the passageway. And in the nursery, for that matter. And everywhere else, of course. My general conduct from the moment you first arrived."

"And shall I apologize for my various gaffes also?" she asked softly. "Or shall we simply decide to begin anew?"

He smiled in relief. "I'd like that."

"Then it's decided," she said, believing for one moment that it was actually possible. They would start over, slowly becoming acquainted with one another, respectfully exploring this undeniable attraction—

While you deceive him at every turn, just as Nick said? she challenged herself with unexpected ferocity. *Men in the walls, children on the rampage—and Mr. Collier all the while praising you for restoring his Utopian bliss? Have you become such a liar as all that? And with the man you admire and adore above all others?*

"Miranda? Is something wrong? You're pale again."

She licked her lips, seduced by the simple fact that he had finally called her by her given name. Seduced also by the way his eyes blazed with concern for her. There was such honest emotion in those eyes, as there was in his heart. Wasn't it time she repaid it with honesty of her own?

Tell him everything, she advised herself boldly. But then what? Would Nick be sent to prison? Would Stephanie be expelled from the house, never to win Ryan's respect? She couldn't be honest at their expense.

But perhaps she could find a way to be both honest and loyal, thanks to Nick's inventive plan.

"Mr. Collier?"

"Yes, Miranda?"

"The other afternoon, when you invited me to attend the party with you and your sister . . ."

"Yes?"

"I know it's awkward, but I believe I truly would enjoy an evening away from this house, as lovely as it is. Would it be terribly forward of me to belatedly accept your kind invitation?"

Surprise registered in his blue gaze. Then he stepped back from her, bowing as he'd done in the passageway. "I would be honored to act as your escort, Miss Kent."

"Thank you."

"Until tomorrow, then?"

"Yes, sir. Until tomorrow."

"Good night, Miss Kent."

"Good night, sir," she murmured as he retreated down the hall, apparently desperate to escape the clutches of an overeager female.

If only you knew, she told him in wistful silence. *If this plan succeeds, Nick will be cleared of all charges. He'll take his children away. Your sanctuary will be restored. And you shall be rid of this overeager, deceitful female forever.*

Ryan did his best to avoid the governess during the days leading up to the Bentley party. If he appeared too eager, he was certain she would cancel their plans. After all, she simply wanted a respite from the demands of the house and the children. If she suspected the demands Ryan was aching to place on her, she'd be aghast. And even if he could pretend to be calm and collected, he might say something to offend her, and again their plans would be ruined.

She seemed determined to avoid him, too, and he had to smile at that. Given her fondness for rules and proper behavior, she undoubtedly felt embarrassed over having accepted his invitation, feeling it was somehow inappropriate or unbecoming. Ryan, on the other hand, was not about to allow civilized society to interfere with the intensely enjoyable—and admittedly primitive—urges the proper governess could arouse in him. In fact, he was determined to corrupt her at the party—a secret he didn't dare reveal until she was safely out of the house, waltzing in his arms.

She wouldn't approve of your keeping secrets from her, he told himself with a chuckle. *I have a feeling our Miss Kent prizes honesty above all other virtues.*

The thought reminded him of the *other* secret he was keeping from her—a secret that might anger her more than his lustful intentions. If she knew he had taken steps to deal with that bastard Hemmingway on her behalf, she'd be outraged. After all, she had explicitly asked him to put all thoughts of that nasty business out of his mind.

Rubbing his bruised knuckles, he remembered sheepishly how good it had felt to smash his fist into that disgusting lech's face. Miranda would simply have to understand. Ryan had had no choice but to avenge her, not only because he was a gentleman, but because he had become hopelessly enamored of her.

Surely she would at least be flattered. She might even be relieved to hear she no longer owed Hemmingway anything! Ryan smiled, remembering the proud glint in her tear-filled eyes that day in the study when she'd told him of her predicament. No, she wouldn't be relieved, nor would she be flattered. She'd be furious.

But it had definitely been worth it.

Four

"Miranda, you look like an angel! Don't you dare dance with my Harry tonight looking so beautiful."

Miranda fluffed the skirt of her gauzy pink ruffled gown. "He'll have eyes only for you, Stephanie. You're ravishing."

"I am, aren't I?" she said with a grin. "Still, there's a radiance to you that I envy. I wonder if I had that glow when I was a virgin. Oh for heaven's sake, stop tugging at that neckline! It's modest compared to mine."

Miranda laughed. "I've never worn anything quite like this dress. Thank you again for lending it me."

"It's yours to keep. I'd never dare wear it now, for fear it would remind Harry of how beautiful *you* looked tonight." She turned and ran to the door. "Is that Ryan, bellowing for us? Has he no patience at all?"

Miranda felt a shiver run through her at the thought of wearing so frivolous a gown in Ryan's presence. Would he be shocked? Not that it mattered, of course. She had apparently shocked him down to his bones by inviting herself to the party. He had barely spoken to her the entire week, and even at dinnertime had focused his attention on the children, with hardly a glance in her direction.

Isn't that better? After tonight, he won't need a governess any longer and you'll never see him again. Be glad you didn't use this week to grow closer to him. It would just have made the parting all that much more difficult.

Following after Stephanie, she tried for a sedate smile, hoping Ryan would be so distracted by his sister's scandalous décolletage that he wouldn't even notice Miranda.

Waiting until Stephanie had almost reached the bottom of the stairway, Miranda stepped into view, then felt her confidence waver at the sight of Ryan, so dashing in his finely tailored black coat and trousers. He was addressing his sister, and for a moment Miranda was sure he wouldn't even glance up at her.

Then he raised his blue eyes and fixed her with a stare so openly admiring she nearly ran back to her room to hide. She had begun to think she had imagined that look that day in the nursery, but here it was again, so filled with mischief and desire her legs threatened to buckle under her from confusion.

As though sensing her predicament, he took the steps two at a time, and within seconds had her elbow cupped in his warm, strong hand. "May I?"

"Thank you, Mr. Collier," she managed to whisper.

"Isn't Miranda beautiful?" Stephanie demanded from the foot of the staircase. "Don't you wish now you'd treated her better? But it's too late, dear brother. She'll fall in love with one of her dance partners, and you'll have to send to Mrs. Weston for a new governess. And this time, it will be some horrid old maid barking orders at us night and day. What do you think of that?"

"I think you're mistaken," Ryan told her with a shrug.

"Excuse me?"

He slipped his arm around Miranda's waist, then leveled a stare at his sister. "I am Miss Kent's escort for the entire evening. There will be no other dance partners for her. Am I making myself clear?"

Stephanie gasped. "But what if Miranda *wants* to dance with someone else?"

Both brother and sister turned demanding gazes to Miranda, who was suddenly finding it hard to take a breath. But Ryan's piercing eyes helped her steady herself, and she managed finally to admit, "I won't want to dance with anyone else."

"Good Lord!" Stephanie wailed. "He doesn't *own* you, Miranda."

Ryan gave his sister a triumphant grin. "If you'd rather not accompany us, Stephanie, we'd understand perfectly."

"You'd what? Oh, for heaven's sake!" She stomped her foot, then spun away from them and headed for the entry doors, adding dryly over her shoulder, "I hope you're not going to make a fool of yourself at the party, Ryan."

"I just might," he told her. Then he offered his elbow to Miranda and murmured seductively, "Miss Kent? I am at your service for the evening."

Miranda wasn't sure exactly how to behave during the carriage ride, but to her frustrated amusement, her behavior didn't seem to matter at all. For the entire ride into town, Stephanie and Ryan chatted as though nothing at all unusual had taken place. In fact, they had a lively intellectual debate on their respective interpretations of *Paradise Lost,* turning to Miranda only briefly and casually when one of them needed affirmation of a particular point.

And Miranda knew exactly what was happening. Stephanie didn't dare antagonize her brother by questioning the existence or wisdom of his sudden interest in Miranda, so she was simply pretending it didn't exist.

And Ryan? He was roguishly enjoying Miranda's distress. He undoubtedly knew from her blush, her stammer, her shy smile, that he did in fact own her, body and soul, and he was biding his time before taking her into his arms and consummating his perfectly executed seduction.

They were quite a pair, this brother and sister. And Miranda had to admit she adored them both. They had given her her first real taste of family since the death of her father, and whatever happened this evening, she would cherish that feeling forever.

"Why did you allow Rye to bully you that way? You can dance with whomever you please. You know that, don't you?"

Miranda nodded, her attention distracted by Ryan, who was ensuring that their wraps were being properly consigned to Dr. Bentley's staff.

"Harry has arranged for several dance partners for you. If we hurry, we can disappear into the crowd before Ryan realizes we're missing."

"Go and have a lovely time," Miranda told her friend with a smile. "I'll wait for your brother."

"Why? Don't worry about Rye! Women *love* him. He'll have more partners than you can imagine, all vying for his affections. He doesn't need a governess tonight." She tugged at Miranda's hand, and when she didn't budge, stared in dismay. "Don't tell me you actually prefer my brother's company! Miranda? Is that it?"

Miranda patted the amazed sister's cheek. "I'll always be glad I met you. Go and have fun now."

"You sound as though you're saying good-bye," Stephanie whispered unhappily.

"I'm allowing this evening to be a moment in time, apart from all others."

"A moment in time? Oh!" Stephanie's blue eyes misted with tears. "With Ryan? Is that wise, Miranda? He'll be gentle, of course, knowing it's your first time, but—"

Miranda laughed lightly. "For me, a moment in time is a dance. And perhaps a kiss. Nothing more. Please don't worry. And please, please go and find Harry."

Stephanie hesitated, then pecked Miranda's cheek, wished her the best, and dashed into the crowd only seconds before Ryan returned.

Slipping his arm around Miranda's waist, he led her to the dance floor without saying a word. Then he took her into his arms and began to expertly waltz her around the room, his eyes blazing with admiration as he stared down at her.

"So," he said softly, "how does this feel?"

"Perfect," she admitted. "Except I can't breathe."

"Neither can I."

"Well then, it really is perfect," she told him in breathless relief.

As they danced, he trailed kisses along her neck, while his hands caressed the small of her back. "You're so beautiful. So irresistible," he murmured again and again.

"Oh, Ryan. I'll never forget this. Or you."

"I should think not," he said with a chuckle. "Who would have thought George Bentley would ever do me a favor, much less one of this magnitude?"

"Pardon?"

"Didn't you know?" Ryan grimaced. "Our host, Dr. George Bentley, owned the diamond necklace stolen by my cousin."

"Stephanie mentioned that."

"I see." Ryan frowned. "Was she surprised I accepted the invitation?"

"Surprised, but also pleased."

"I had my reasons." He flushed and added, "Not just romantic ones. The last exchange between Bentley and me was unpleasant. He had just accused Nick of theft, and I in turn threatened to sue him for slandering my cousin."

Miranda beamed with delight. "You defended Nick? How gallant."

"As always, you're easily impressed." Ryan's teasing gaze clouded. "After Nick ran away, I knew I owed Bentley an apology, but the words stuck in my throat. To this day, I haven't been able to bring myself to say anything."

"You had a perfect right to defend your own cousin."

"Still, before the evening is over—"

"No, Ryan. Please don't apologize to him."

He studied her with evident curiosity. "Why not?"

Their gazes locked, and she knew it was time for the truth, so she stroked his cheek and murmured, "I have so much to tell you."

"I forbid it, Miss Kent."

She caught the twinkle in his eyes just in time, and smiled in confusion. "I beg your pardon?"

His grin was sheepish. "You sounded so serious, and I want tonight to be—well, uncomplicated."

"Oh?"

"We have much to say to one another, and we shall. We'll share every secret tomorrow. But tonight, couldn't we just savor the miracle of finding one another?"

Miranda licked her lips, enchanted by his words.

His voice grew low and gravelly. "I never would have believed there was a girl in all the world as intelligent and beautiful as you, much less one who shared my craving for order and civility. And if your charming habit of blushing whenever I touch you is any indication, we share other cravings as well."

"Ryan!"

He nuzzled her neck, unrepentant. "Do you deny the heat between us? The giddy anticipation?"

"How can I?" she murmured, tilting her head back to allow him fuller access. "It's as you said—a night for miracles."

And not just for us, she added silently. *For Nick as well, if we're very lucky and if I can be clever and follow his plan.*

Catching Ryan's face between her hands, she whispered, "I would do anything for you. Would *you* do something for *me?"*

"Anything," he answered, his voice thick with desire.

"Would you see if there's some punch? I'm so very thirsty."

Confusion registered in his eyes, followed by amusement. "Not exactly the Holy Grail, but I shan't fail you, my love." Kissing the tip of her nose, he led her to the edge of the dance floor. "Wish me Godspeed."

Miranda laughed, then watched in spellbound delight as he ambled away. She was so close to heaven. Only one tiny detail stood in the way of their happiness, and she was going to take care of that right away.

Squaring her shoulders, she threaded her way through a group of partygoers until she was face to face with her host. Not pausing to think, she reached out her fingertip and tapped the jeweled stickpin that graced his lapel. Then she whispered throatily, "Your emeralds caught my eye from across the room, sir, and almost took my breath away."

Clearly startled, he seemed momentarily at a loss for words. Then a silly grin spread over his face. "Miss Kent, isn't it? I must say, my dear, the most beautiful jewels in the room are the ones sparkling in those magnificent eyes of yours."

* * *

It was even easier than Nick had predicted, and Miranda had to struggle not to grin at Bentley's willingness to be manipulated. Within minutes, he was leading her down a long, portrait-lined corridor, away from the party and toward his fabled emerald collection.

Her heart was pounding at the realization that Nick's reputation could be repaired before the night was through. And in the morning, as she and Ryan shared their secrets, there would be only joy in the knowledge that the children would be reunited with their father on premises a manageable distance from the Collier mansion.

"Here we are." Bentley steered her through a doorway and into a dimly lit room. As her eyes adjusted, she realized that the illumination came from a profusion of lanterns shining through the glass walls of what appeared to be a sunroom. There wasn't a drape in sight behind which Nick might be lurking, and only one solid wall that could possibly house a safe.

"This is an unusual study," she remarked uneasily. "But I suppose it's the perfect hiding place for your collection of precious gems."

"The only jewel that interests me at the moment is you, my beauty," he assured her, catching her by the waist and leering hopefully into her face.

"Oh, dear! *Don't!*" She batted his hands away, but he grabbed her again.

"Really, my dear. I only want to kiss you—"

"*Are you deaf, Bentley?*" roared a voice from the doorway, and Miranda spun toward it, expecting Nick O'Hara, but eternally grateful to see Ryan Collier, who advanced on Bentley with such ferocity the doctor seemed to lose consciousness even before a powerful punch ensured that result. Then without pausing for even a second, Ryan pulled Miranda into a frantic embrace.

"Darling, are you hurt? Can you forgive me for leaving you alone?"

"Ryan . . ." She wrapped her arms around his neck, hugging him gratefully.

"You're so trusting, Miranda," he murmured into her hair. "Promise me you won't go off with a stranger, not ever again."

"You don't understand," she insisted wistfully. "I was trying to clear Nick's name—"

"Nick?" Ryan stared in dismay. "Good God, Miranda, if I'd known *this* would be the effect, I never would have told you about my confrontation with Bentley."

"No, Ryan. You don't understand—"

"Not another word." Without further warning, he covered her mouth with his own, kissing her gently into silence.

Warmth spread through her, and in an instant, she had forgotten about jewels, Nick, and the other party guests. There was only Ryan, and she clung to him, allowing him to deepen the kiss until his hot, rough tongue was fully plundering her mouth, sending tingling waves of heat to every part of her love-starved body.

Then his mouth was on her neck again, tasting and seducing, and she wanted nothing more than to surrender to him. But the murmurs from the guests who had massed at the doorway, spilling into the room, brought her to her senses. "Ryan," she whispered. "People are staring."

He seemed confused for a minute, then turned his attention to the crowd. Scowling, he scanned the faces for a moment, then asked in disgust, "Where in blazes is Stephanie? Off with some fellow, I suppose. The minute my back is turned."

"What nerve," Miranda said, teasing. "Do you suppose she's off kissing someone?"

Ryan chuckled. "Touché, Miss Kent." Then he called out cheerfully, "Stephanie! Where in blazes are you?"

"I'm here! Stop bellowing." His sister pushed through the crowd, her wide blue eyes staring first at the still figure of Bentley on the ground, then at her brother and the woman in his arms. "What in the world happened?"

"Once again, Bentley has shown his true nature," Ryan told her. "First he accused our cousin of theft, now this! Daring to manhandle Miranda."

"*What?*" Stephanie pulled Miranda into a protective embrace. "Poor angel! I should have known better than to leave you alone." Glaring at Ryan, she reminded him angrily, "I entrusted her to you."

"Never mind. Go and fetch the wraps. We're going home."

"No!" Stephanie's voice was a plaintive wail. "You can't mean it. My first party in months—"

"We're leaving."

At that, Harry stepped forward, and before either Stephanie or Miranda could stop him, he insisted calmly, "I'd be more than happy to escort your sister safely home before midnight, sir."

Ryan scowled again. "What's your interest in my sister, Anderson?"

"Harry, don't!" Stephanie pushed her way between the two men. "I won't allow you to interrogate Mr. Anderson, Ryan. He's just trying to help. Miranda? Make Ryan behave."

"The host is unconscious," Ryan drawled. "You can't possibly think the party will continue under those circumstances, can you?"

"It will continue until I say it's over," a new voice announced, and all eyes turned to Sadie Bentley, a tall, voluptuous woman who seemed somewhat less than distraught over her husband's condition. "Mr. Collier, please feel free to leave your sister here. I promise she won't suffer the same fate your governess had to endure. My driver can take her safely home whenever she wishes."

"Ryan?" Miranda touched his cheek. "Mr. Anderson seems so sincere. Shouldn't you allow Stephanie to make this choice, as a reward for all of her hard work?"

He seemed about to scoff, then shrugged instead. "What about you, Miranda? What is *your* choice? Do you wish to go back to the mansion with me?"

She nodded.

His blue eyes began to twinkle. "Well, then . . . Anderson, have my sister home by midnight. Mrs. Bentley, thank you for your hospitality. Stephanie?"

His sister stared in guarded delight. "Yes, Ryan?"

"Behave yourself."

"Always," she assured him with a giggle.

Ryan shook his head, then grinned down at Miranda. "Shall we?"

Not wishing to give the governess a chance to change her mind, Ryan took off his coat and draped it around her shoulders, then whisked her outside and toward the carriage, ignoring the fact that her wrap languished in a wardrobe on the Bentley premises. Either Stephanie and her new beau would remember to fetch it, or they would not. Ryan didn't care.

He cared about only one thing—being alone with Miranda, if only for the precious half hour it would take to return to the mansion. Once there, the children might interfere. But for now, Miranda belonged to Ryan alone, and he intended to make the most of it.

"I have so much to tell you," she said breathlessly

when he had finally taken his seat beside her in the carriage.

"We agreed to talk tomorrow," he reminded her. "For now, I'd rather kiss you again."

Her lips parted slightly, and he thought she was going to protest, but instead she leaned into him and whispered, "Please do."

He kissed her gently, so as not to frighten her, but completely, so as not to leave any doubt. And to his relief, she welcomed him warmly, allowing his tongue to explore her mouth, while her hands slid up the back of his neck until her fingers were laced in his hair.

As she moaned with arousal, his own hands began to travel, stroking her back and shoulders, then tentatively cupping her breasts through the lacy fabric of her gown. When she moaned again, he felt a burst of impatient need, and urged her back onto the seat until she was semireclined. Then he loomed over her, grinning with fevered anticipation. "You're so beautiful."

"Ryan . . ." She pressed her hands against his chest, holding him sheepishly at bay. "I've been keeping secrets from you—"

"And I from you. For example, did you know I've never wanted a woman the way I want you at this moment?"

"Not that sort of secret," she said with a delighted blush. "You'll be cross—"

"With *you?* Never." Relenting in the face of her determination, he murmured, "I know you want to talk to me, but consider the consequences. If one of us says something impolitic, the kissing will stop. Is that what you want?"

"I couldn't bear it," she admitted.

Relieved, he arched an eyebrow in victory. "So?"

"Tomorrow will be time enough. But"—she caught

his face between her hands before he could lower it for another greedy kiss—"tomorrow, kisses or not, I'm going to tell you everything. I simply can't continue to deceive you."

"Neither can I," he admitted, brushing a hair from her cheek with his fingertips. "After tomorrow, we'll never have secrets from one another again. That will be our pledge. But for now, my only pledge is to shock you."

She laughed and wriggled, as though trying to evade him, but he sensed nothing was further from her true intention. Even when his rough hand slipped inside the low neckline of her gown, scooping one firm, soft breast free, she gasped but made no move to stop him. And when his mouth moved to her rose-hued nipple, teasing the hardened tip with his tongue, she repositioned herself with a subtle but clear intent to further accentuate her own enjoyment.

Inflamed, he stretched over her, crushing his mouth down to hers, savoring the taste and sound of her. It seemed she intended to place no limits at all on him, and while he knew he should forbear, he could not.

Then he slipped his hand low on her torso, gathering up the folds of her gown until he managed to slip his hand under the fabric, where he reverently stroked the soft, firm skin of her hip.

"Ryan!"

Cursing himself for his fumbling, he helped her back to a seated position. "I didn't mean to offend, Miranda. I was just—"

"As was I," she admitted, still gasping slightly through her arousal. "It is inexperience, sir, not lack of—well, of desire—"

"You don't owe me an explanation for resisting my misbehavior."

Gracing him with an apology-filled smile, she took

his offending hand in her own and kissed it, then studied the knuckles with evident distress. "I didn't realize you had bruised yourself on that awful doctor's jaw."

"It's fine."

"It's romantic," she admitted. "I never dared hope a man would ever care enough for me to fight for me."

"Oh?" Enjoying the easy shifts in her mood, he dared tell her, "You should have seen the bruises from my visit to Hemmingway."

"Excuse me?"

Cursing himself for falling into her unintentional trap, he smiled weakly. "Don't be angry, darling. I couldn't stomach the thought that you felt indebted to him. I went there to give him a piece of my mind. And his accursed money. The thrashing was completely unplanned. Exhilarating, but unplanned. Can you forgive me?"

"You hit Armstrong Hemmingway with your fist?"

Ryan nodded, wary.

"And I no longer owe him any money? None at all?"

"Not a penny. Nor do you owe me. I swear—"

"With this very fist?" She kissed his knuckles again, almost reverently.

Ryan nodded. Then, to his speechless delight, she guided his hand over her breasts, then her stomach, then lower still, while lifting her skirts high on her legs until he was once again in contact with her warm, moist skin, this time perilously close to her inner thigh. Then she laced her fingers in his hair as she had done before, dragging his face to hers, and in an instant, they had abandoned themselves to mindless passion so sweet, so complete, the rest of the world seemed to drop away, leaving only their love to blaze in its place.

* * *

"Let me walk you to your room, darling."

"What if one of the children saw?" Miranda blushed, knowing this belated concern for her reputation must seem laughable. But Ryan wasn't laughing. His eyes still sparkled with devotion and respect from the aftermath of their lovemaking, and she almost couldn't bear to step away from him—to begin the long walk down the hall to her lonely bed.

But if Ryan came with her, they would end up in that bed together. She had no doubt about that. Unless, of course, Nick was there—

"Morning will be here before we know it, Ryan. I need some time to rest. To think. To dream about you."

"I like the sound of that," he admitted, brushing his lips along her jaw.

"And tomorrow—"

"Tomorrow all secrets will be revealed," he assured her, chuckling fondly. "Sweet dreams, darling."

Floating on air down the hall, Miranda savored his words. All secrets *would* be revealed. She intended to see to that. She would give Nick an ultimatum: *Go to Ryan yourself, tell him everything, and know that he loves you and will believe you and will help you fight Bentley's accusations.*

Stephanie would receive a similar lecture, although in her case, there was no need to reveal all details of the past. It would be sufficient if she simply talked to her brother, asking for more freedom in exchange for her complete cooperation in her education. In that way, she could begin to meet Harry in town while still ensuring that she would never again blunder into a penniless predicament.

Turning when she reached her room, Miranda blew a kiss to Ryan, then grasped the knob and pushed open the door, half prepared to see Nick standing there. What she couldn't have predicted was the circus that actually awaited her.

There was Amy, jumping on the bed, chanting, "Randi's home, Randi's home," in a soft, singsong voice. A few feet from the bed stood Stephanie and Harry, arguing in voices that were anything but singsong. If they noticed Miranda's arrival, they showed no indication.

And Miranda barely noticed them either, so stunned was she by the sight of Brandon and Keith, sitting on the floor directly in her path amidst a pile of broken pottery. Horrified, she fell to her knees and began to frantically examine the scarlet and blue pieces, hoping against hope that these weren't the remnants of one of Ryan's priceless Oriental vases.

"We're sorry, Miss Kent," Keith told her mournfully. "We'll fix it. We promise. See? We found some glue."

"This can't be. Not tonight of all nights," Miranda whispered unhappily. "I was prepared for so much, but not this. Not tonight."

"Uncle Ryan won't be able to see the cracks," Brandon said with shaky bravado. "We'll work all night, and in the morning—"

"In the morning, your uncle will be furious. And rightfully so. This vase was in the drawing room. What could you have been doing in there that would result in this calamity? Never mind." She covered her face with her hands, miserable at the thought of Ryan's reaction to this latest, most irreversible insult. As prepared as she had been to tell him that the outwardly sedate household had actually been chaotic under her tenure, she hadn't dreamed of anything this extreme. This irreparable. This grotesquely unfair.

"Amy, *please* be quiet so that I can think," she begged the chanting girl. "And come down from there before you hurt yourself. Didn't you promise your father you wouldn't jump on the bed anymore?"

Startled by her own statement, and noting Nick's apparent absence for the first time, she scanned the room quickly and was humbled to see him standing off by himself in the shadows, his posture dejected, his expression almost tearful.

You're so selfish, Miranda Kent! she accused herself as she jumped to her feet and ran to him. *This poor man's hopes rested on the success of tonight's plan, yet you haven't for one moment considered how disappointed he must have been when he didn't learn the combination that would free him.*

"Poor Nick." She wrapped her arms around his waist and hugged him gently. "I'm so very, very sorry our plan wasn't successful. But we'll find another way—"

"We?" He pushed her roughly away, then sandwiched her face between his hands and said with rough finality, "After what I did to you? The danger I exposed you to with my selfish, thoughtless, insane plot? When I heard Bentley tried to force himself on you, I despised myself—"

"Hush, Nick. I'm fine. Ryan intervened."

"I'm grateful to him. And sick to death of myself. There I was, perfectly safe and hiding in the study, while you were all alone and in danger. You, whom I love above all other women!"

"Hush," she repeated, stroking his anguished jaw. "I'm here, safe and unharmed. Poor Nick. Please don't be so distressed."

"What in God's name is the meaning of this?"

Miranda shrieked softly as she spun to face Ryan, whose expression was so contorted, so confused, yet so condemning, that it caused her chest to ache with undrawn breaths.

"Ryan . . ."

His steely eyes were scanning the room, taking in every damning detail before staring again in Miranda's direction. "I'll be in my study, Miss Kent, when you're ready to explain this—this *outrage* to me."

Before anyone could respond, he spun on his heels and stalked out of the room.

Frozen to her spot, Miranda listened in miserable confusion as his footsteps faded down the hall. Even then, she wasn't quite sure what to do. What to say. What to think.

"Miranda?" Stephanie patted her on the shoulder. "Stay here. I'll go and explain everything to Ryan."

"I'll go," Nick interrupted. "This is all my doing. It's time I started accepting responsibility for it."

"How is it *your* doing?" Stephanie complained. "You had no idea until just a few minutes ago that I was seeing Harry—"

"We *all* knew, Auntie Stephanie," Brandon corrected her. "Except Amy, that is."

"I knew too, I knew too, I knew too," Amy chanted, until Nick strode across the room and grabbed her up into a hug, murmuring, "Not now, pumpkin."

Miranda shook her head. "I appreciate all the offers, but Ryan—I mean, Mr. Collier—asked for me, and I will be the one to explain. I'll do my best," she added lamely, struggling against the tears that were stinging her eyelids.

"Randi—"

"It's fine, Nick. I was going to tell him everything tomorrow in any case. And I've p-practiced this speech so many times, I know it by heart. If only I'd delivered it this evening, when I h-had the chance . . ."

"Poor Randi." Nick pulled her into his arms, but she wriggled away, suddenly furious with herself. Such self-pity, when it was Ryan who had been deceived. *He* was the injured party. And he was waiting for an explanation.

She had been unable to conduct herself with honesty or loyalty. The least she could do was be punctual.

He was standing with his back toward the doorway, staring up at the antique swords that had been in his family for so many generations. Was he seeing them? Miranda wondered. Were they enabling him to dispel the images of deception and chaos that had presented themselves in her room? She could only hope they had provided a source of comfort in the face of her betrayal.

"Ryan?"

He turned slowly, his face unreadable, his tone hoarse and unfamiliar as he murmured, "Thank you for coming, Miss Kent."

"Ryan . . ." She choked back a sob, then walked over to him and insisted, "There's no excuse for my conduct. I don't pretend there is. But—"

"Wait." He held up his hand, dropping it only when she had nodded for him to continue.

His blue eyes began to blaze. "I can't even begin to recite all the atrocities that presented themselves to me in your room tonight. Stephanie, entertaining a gentleman without my permission *in the middle of the night*. Amy, awake at midnight and defying my instructions not to jump on the bed. Keith and Brandon . . ." He seemed almost to choke on the list, and visibly steeled himself. "Of all the strange and ludicrous things I saw, only one matters. I'm asking you now to be honest about that one single, unfathomable sight."

Miranda bit her lip, then guessed. "Nick?"

"Yes. *Nick*."

She winced at the misery in his tone. "He's innocent,

Ryan. I'm convinced of that. He shouldn't have deceived you—*we* shouldn't have deceived you, but—"

"Miranda!" His eyes flashed with frustration. "I'm asking you a simple question. Are you in love with my cousin?"

She gasped. *"Him?* Certainly not! I mean to say, he's sweet in his own demented way, and I suppose I love him the way I'd love any misbehaving child in my care, but—no! I'm not in love with him. I'm in love with *you."*

"Thank God." Grabbing her by the waist, he pulled her against him and buried his face in her hair. "I stood in that doorway listening to his declaration of love, watching you caress him, and I swear, darling, I thought I was losing my mind."

"Oh, Ryan, forgive me. For that and for everything else. Especially the vase."

"A reproduction," he assured her, nuzzling her feverishly. "Valuable, but hardly irreplaceable. You mustn't fret about it, darling. Nor about anything else."

Wrapping her arms around his neck, she blurted out, "You can't imagine how it's been! Every day. Every night. The secrets and the passageways and strange men popping out of walls at every turn. And you were right about those children! They *are* hellhounds! You were right about everything. I couldn't maintain order or teach them their lessons. There has been chaos and deception at every turn. Even in your wildest imagination you couldn't know how abysmal my performance has been."

"Darling!" He tightened his embrace. "You're trembling. What have they done to you? What have *I* done to you?"

"You've been my refuge," she told him gratefully. "My sole reminder that civilization and discipline still existed in this world gone mad."

Chuckling, he led her to a chair and urged her to sit. "It's all over now, darling."

Hopeful for the first time since the scene in her bedroom, she murmured, "Nick is innocent, Ryan. He believes Bentley still has the necklace in his safe."

"I'll arrange to have the premises, including Bentley's safe, searched tomorrow."

"You will?"

"Once Nick's name is cleared, he can take the children and go. You agree with that, don't you?"

"I crave it. Of course, they can visit—"

"Short visits."

"Ever so short," Miranda agreed.

"And my sister?" He dropped to one knee. "What shall we do about her?"

"She's hopeless too, Ryan," Miranda told him. "Forgive me for saying it, but it's true. In her own way, she's trying. I honestly believe she wants to learn to manage her own finances, and she sincerely wants to earn your respect. But when it comes to men, well, she's a grown woman, and an incorrigible one."

"Tell me what you want me to do and I'll do it."

Miranda drew a long, steadying breath, then dared to suggest, "Tell her she can stay here for as long as she likes, coming and going as she pleases. And if she decides to marry Harry, she has your blessing."

"Marry him? She only met him five hours ago!"

Stroking his face, she smiled as she crooned, "My poor, sweet, trusting Ryan. Promise me you'll never change."

He chuckled reluctantly. "They haven't frightened you out of your original plan, have they?"

"Pardon?"

"That first day, here in my study. You said you wanted children of your own, to guide and teach and raise as good citizens. Is it possible you might still consider that? With me as the father?"

Miranda gasped, then admitted, "I can't imagine anything more wonderful."

"Then we're agreed. We banish the horde at the first opportunity, then we restore civilization to every room in this house. With the exception of our bedroom, of course."

"Pardon? Oh!" She flushed with embarrassed delight. There was such a naughty gleam in his eye, a gleam she remembered from that afternoon in the nursery when he had made scandalous suggestions she hadn't begun to understand. "Ryan?"

"Yes, darling?"

"Do you remember how you teased me, a few weeks ago, about—well, about tapping? It sounded so—well, so provocative."

"Provocative? Yes, your tapping is that. It's also paradoxical, making me wish to improve myself and to misbehave simultaneously."

"Whatever do you mean?" she asked in confused delight.

"Shall I demonstrate?"

Miranda nodded, then shrieked with throaty appreciation when he tumbled her to the floor of his sanctuary and proceeded to show her exactly what he meant.

WHEN MORNING COMES

Lori Handeland

One

Several moments passed before Seth Torrance realized the pounding in his head was echoed by a pounding on his bedroom door. Groaning, he turned away from the sound, only to get a face full of blazing sunlight.

What time *was* it?

"Major?" The voice on the other side of the door was familiar. Nevertheless, four years away from home, combined with at least four glasses of whiskey, made Seth's mind a muddle.

"Sir? Your mother requests your presence at the dinner table."

Dinner? Damn. He'd slept through breakfast—again. His mother would not be amused. But she so rarely was.

Honoria Simons Torrance found precious little to laugh about in this world. Once, Seth had wondered why his mother never smiled. The war had changed that. Now he found precious little to smile about, either.

"Major?"

The identity of the speaker came to Seth with such blinding clarity he winced, or maybe that was just the sun in his eyes.

Beckworth. The butler.

Seth had known the man for years. Why couldn't he seem to recall anything clearly from the time before he'd put on the Union Blue? Perhaps because the four years he'd spent at war were so much more vivid to him than anything the present had to offer.

More horrible, true, but the shouting, the shooting, the crying, the dying still lived in his mind and in his dreams. Seth had hoped to recover at home, in a place that he knew, surrounded by those who cared about him. Instead, he'd only gotten worse.

"There's a letter for you, sir," Beckworth continued as if Seth had answered. "From Virginia."

Virginia? The only person he knew in Virginia was—

Seth sat up. The room spun. The cannons boomed inside his head. He wanted to lie down and stay there forever. But Beckworth had at last lit on the one thing that would get him out of bed so early in the afternoon.

Henry. His best friend from their days at West Point. When they'd graduated twelve years ago, Seth had returned to the North, Henry to the South. By then the tensions that would lead to the war had already begun to rear their ugly heads. Seth hadn't seen or heard from Henry since. He'd often thought of him, wondered where he was, how he was.

Now the war was over and Henry had contacted him. For the first time in years, Seth looked forward to something—opening that letter.

Gritting his teeth against the pain in his head, Seth stumbled across the room and opened the door. "Hand it over."

Beckworth's long nose twitched and his nearly nonexistent lips tightened. But he said nothing.

Seth hadn't shaved for several days; he hadn't bathed either. He'd slept in his clothes and fed his nightmares with whiskey. He must look as awful as he felt, and that wasn't easy.

When Beckworth continued to stare at him without moving, Seth snatched the missive from the gold tray perched on the butler's gloved hand. He wanted to sneer at the uselessness of it all, but he'd discovered one thing in the last four years. Sometimes honor and tradition were all that stood between being a man or a monster. Funny, but at times they were what made a man into a monster, as well.

Seth shook off the memories and glanced at the envelope. He frowned. The letter wasn't from Henry, after all, but from an attorney named Arthur Blair. Seth didn't know him. He had a feeling he didn't want to.

Ignoring Beckworth, who hovered in the hall waiting for . . . Seth wasn't sure what, he tore open the envelope. As if they had a premonition of the words contained therein, his fingers trembled as he withdrew the paper.

May 1, 1865

Dear Major Torrance:

I regret to inform you of the death of your friend, Henry Elliot, at Saylor's Creek.

However, I would not be writing you this letter had not his wife, Georgina, followed him to our Lord yesterday following the birth of his child.

Mr. Elliot's final wish was that you, Major, become the guardian of all that was his. His will and testament in this regard are in my keeping.

Please come posthaste to the Elliot farm outside of Winchester in Frederick County, Virginia.

Sincerely,
Arthur Blair
Attorney at Law

The trembling in Seth's fingers spread throughout his body. He collapsed into the nearest chair.

"Major? Sir? Bad news? Shall I—"

Seth slammed the door on Beckworth's questions. Blessed silence filled the room. Too bad his head still pounded with the force of Confederate artillery.

Henry was gone. Seth found the tidings hard to believe, despite the hundreds of thousands of casualties. But then his friend had always been so much more alive than anyone else.

Henry laughed louder, rode harder, shot straighter. At West Point, he'd been near the top of their class, while Seth had wallowed near the middle. Of course, when the call came to war, it hadn't mattered where they'd placed on the list. Hell, look at Custer. Autie had finished at the bottom of the pile and it hadn't hurt him any.

But to lose Henry at Saylor's Creek—a horrible battle so near the end of a horrible war.

Seth got to his feet, crossed the room and reached for the whiskey again. But instead of drinking, he peered out the window, ignoring the pain in his eyes and his head, intensified by the bright and shiny sun. He stared at the loud and boisterous streets of Boston; he didn't really see them.

He had been at Saylor's Creek, too. Had one of his bullets ended Henry's life? Seth would never know, so he would always wonder.

He thought back to the glory days before the war, back when everything had been simple, back when honor and duty didn't get men killed. He and Henry had been as different as two friends could be—one a Boston-bred, wealthy Yankee, the other a Virginia-born, land-rich, money-poor farmer—but they had agreed on two things: Duty raised men above the beasts and honor elevated mere men to heroes.

Did he still believe that? Seth wasn't sure. But there was something he did believe. True friends were forever.

Henry had entrusted him with his most precious possessions, his child and his farm.

Seth placed the bottle back on his nightstand untasted, then called for a bath. He couldn't very well go to Virginia like this.

"Seth, I forbid you to leave." Honoria Simons Torrance turned away, expecting her orders to be followed without argument. They always were. "It's time you took the helm of this family and the business."

Seth stifled a sigh. His father had died when he was ten, and his mother had taken control of the munitions plant that had been in her family for generations. She'd done well. But now she wanted Seth to assume her position, and he didn't think that he could.

Not because he didn't know the business. He'd spent several years learning it when he'd returned home from his extended tour of Europe, which had followed his graduation from West Point. But four years spent seeing what a bullet could do to a person had cured Seth of any desire to make them. Not to mention that the first time he'd set foot in the plant upon his return, the sheer volume of the noise had left him pale and shaking. He'd excused himself as ill, and he hadn't been back since.

"You've been doing fine, Mother."

"Of course I have, but what will people think? You come home, hide in your room, then abscond to Virginia. I can just imagine what they're saying about us."

His mother had always cared more for what people thought than what he needed. Seth couldn't really fault her for it. She'd been raised to look lovely, pour tea, and have children—then turn them over to others. Once his father had died, she'd had a business to run, and she'd done so with the same determination she did everything else.

Now she'd determined that it was time for Seth to assume his responsibilities. She'd even chosen him the perfect wife in the form of Sophie Beck, a Boston-bred heiress he'd had occasion to meet only once. He could barely recall Sophie's face, which didn't endear him to the prospect. He ought to remember the single meeting he'd had with the woman he was expected to marry.

"It's far too dangerous in the South," his mother continued. "Wait a few years until the army gets things straightened out. Then it'll be a fine place for a holiday." She returned her attention to the list of wedding guests.

With the war officially over but a month and certain Confederate stragglers continuing their lost fight in far reaches of the country such as Louisiana, Alabama, Mississippi, even Texas, Seth understood his mother's concern. For a former Union officer to travel alone into what had been so recently enemy territory was ill advised, to say the least. But then he hadn't exactly been a model of sanity since his return.

"I'll be fine, Mother. I managed to survive the war. I can manage a quick trip to Virginia."

Even if he hadn't been managing much but a bottle lately.

"Quick?" She frowned at him over the top of her spectacles. "How quick?"

"Only as long as it takes me to find out what I'm dealing with, then make some arrangements for the child and the farm. Shouldn't be more than a month all told."

"You're supposed to be married in two months."

Seth rubbed at the pain that had sprung up again behind his eyes. He had not agreed to marry Sophie, hadn't asked her, didn't know her. But typically his mother rolled right over any obstacle in her path by ignoring it.

She wanted him to marry Sophie and provide grandchildren, so she merely arranged the wedding.

And Seth, who couldn't bring himself to feel much of anything these days beyond panic, had let her.

"I am *not* marrying Sophie in two months, Mother."

She blinked. "What?"

"I'm not saying I won't get married. I'm not even saying I won't marry Sophie. But I'd like to have some say in the rest of my life. Right now, I have a duty to honor Henry's last request."

It felt good to say no. He'd have to try it more often.

Her lips pursed. "You have a duty to your father's legacy. Your loyalty should be to this family, not to some Rebel who got himself killed."

"I highly doubt he got himself killed. The Union army probably had a bit to do with it."

"So you feel guilty? That's foolish."

Seth did feel guilty. But that was beside the point. "I have a duty to Henry," he repeated. "I'm honor bound to go. I'll be back in a month."

By ignoring his mother and plowing ahead with what he meant to do—a trait he'd learned from the master—Seth was able to leave the very same day.

Since the railroad lines had been disrupted—a fancy word for torn apart and thrown away—throughout Virginia, Seth rode his horse toward Frederick County.

The roads were filled with soldiers headed for home in both directions. Seth was polite to those he met, but he didn't tarry to chat. As he continued south, the men he encountered were thinner, more bedraggled, less friendly. He couldn't say he blamed them, but he wasn't turning back.

Though he'd done his duty, Seth had never been able to see the Confederate Army as a true enemy. The faces on the other side of the war were just like his. One day they'd been countrymen, the next they'd been killing each other. He'd found it hard to fathom. As a result, any animosity he might have carried for "them" had faded with the treaty signed at Appomatox Courthouse. Sadly, he couldn't say the same for so many others.

Seth reached Winchester near dusk, considered staying in town and riding out to the farm the next morning. However, the narrowed eyes and murmurs of "Yankee" when he passed convinced Seth to continue on his way.

But which way?

Though asking directions was near the bottom of the list of things he wanted to do, getting lost in the countryside with a passel of gun-toting Yankee haters was even lower.

Seth stopped at what looked to be a general store, though no sign was visible. A young boy and an even younger girl stared at him with more curiosity than hostility—an improvement over the rest of the onlookers.

Seth adjusted his observation on their lack of hostility when the boy sneered, "Yank," in lieu of a greeting.

Seth decided to ignore that. What choice did he have? "Could you direct me to the Elliot farm?"

"Could," the boy said and fell silent.

"Would you?" he pressed.

"Whatcha want with them?"

"I'm a friend of the family."

The boy snorted. "Sure ye are."

Seth reined in his impatience. He would have to get used to being treated like the enemy. Here, he still was.

"Regardless," Seth continued, "I've been asked to come there. If you can't direct me, I'll find someone who can."

The boy smirked. "Nah. I can tell you where it is."

"But, Billy—"

The kid punched the little girl in the arm. They must be related. She swallowed what she'd been about to say.

"Go directly down this road." Billy gestured with a grubby finger, "'bout two miles and you'll see a lane to the right. That'll take you to the house."

"Thank you." Seth hesitated. "Out of curiosity, how did you know I was a Yankee before I even opened my mouth?"

Billy spit into the dirt directly in front of Seth's horse. "You got shoes and a horse that ain't been et."

Seth couldn't think of anything to say to that, so he nodded good-bye and headed out of town.

Things were worse in Virginia than he'd anticipated. Of course, being in the Union army was a far cry from being in the Confederate. As Billy had pointed out, the North had shoes and food. The men who'd worn the gray had run out of both long ago. So what did that mean for the civilians ravaged by two armies for so long?

By the time Seth reached the Elliot farm, the sun had disappeared. Stars sparked to life with a brilliance he had not seen since his nights in the field. That had been the only good thing about those times, the purity of the sky above the sacrilege below.

The outline of a large, two-story farmhouse appeared on the horizon. From their talks at West Point, Seth knew that Henry came from a long line of gentleman farmers. His family had never owned slaves, depending on their own hands and that of their many children, as well as hired labor and indentured servants, to do the work.

Despite Northern propaganda, a minority of Southern men owned other men. Slaves were expensive. A large plantation and centuries of family money were needed to warrant them.

The steady clip-clop of his horse's hooves down the dirt lane that led to the house became a soothing cadence at odds with the horrific sounds that too often lived in Seth's head.

In Boston, Seth had hoped to find solace. Instead, the loud city noises, the shouts, the startling bangs and bumps had made him more nervous than ever before. He was always waiting for the next cannon blast, even though he knew there would be none, and when something did blare unexpectedly, Seth was thrown back to a time he prayed to forget.

How could he assume the mantle of leadership his father had left behind? How could he marry a socialite wife and propagate the family name as his mother expected when he never knew if he might lose his mind in the middle of an important meeting or a simple embrace?

He had no idea. But for the moment he was at peace. He wasn't waiting for the next loud noise, expecting the next disaster. Therefore, when it happened, he wasn't prepared at all.

The distinct snick of a shotgun echoed loudly through the silent night.

Two

Gabriella Fontaine kept the shotgun aimed at the man on the horse.

"You better turn around and get, mister, or I'll shoot you right here and bury you over there."

"I'm looking for the Elliot farm."

Ella's eyes narrowed. Yankee. Carpetbagger. Damn. She *should* shoot him. But then she would have to bury him as she'd threatened, and she just didn't have the time.

As if to emphasize the point, the baby started howling in the house. Poor thing. She was hungry. Every time Ella picked her up she clawed at her shirt, needing something Ella couldn't give her. The cow was dry; the goat pert near. Ella was at the end of her tether. And now this.

A carpetbagger sneaking down the lane after dark. She really, really wanted to shoot him.

"You can't have this farm, Mr. Carpetbagger. It belongs to some fool Yankee major."

A man Ella never expected to see. No rich Union boy would come all the way down here and take responsibility for a failing farm and—

"I'm not a carpetbagger," he murmured.

His voice was the most annoying she'd ever heard. Even when he spoke soft, like now, the words were harsh, flat, just plain strange. Oh, how Ella missed the rolling tones of a southern man. But they were all dead and gone.

"If you aren't a carpetbagger, then who are you?" she demanded.

"I guess I must be that fool Yankee major you were talking about."

She couldn't see his face, but she heard the amusement in his damnable voice. Ella was of a mind to show him how well she could shoot this shotgun, but that would scare the baby, who was shrieking loud enough to raise the dead already.

Peering through the shadows, she took stock of his weapons and sighed. He wore Army Colts at his hips and carried a Spencer rifle in the saddle holster. She could probably blow a pretty big hole in him, but he still might shoot her back. She couldn't do that to the children.

"How do I know you're who you say you are?"

"I have the letter from the solicitor right here."

A pale glow of parchment hovered in the shadow of the moonlight, and she sighed. With great reluctance, Ella lowered the gun. "You'd best come to the house. I need to pick up that baby before she hurts herself."

"Yes, ma'am. Would you like to ride?"

Ella shot him a withering glare, then tossed her head. "I'd sooner crawl, Major."

To his credit, he said nothing in return. He even got off the horse and led it along, like a gentleman would, rather than ride while she walked, which was what she'd expect of a Yankee.

With him closer and the moon so bright, she could make out his features. He was handsome enough, for the enemy, tall and broad, with a certain gait and gentle hands on the reins of his horse. Ella forced herself to look away.

"You know my name, ma'am, but you have me at a loss for yours."

"Gabriella Fontaine," she answered shortly. "I live on the next farm east. Georgina and I have been friends since we were children. I've been taking care of the—the—"

Unexpectedly, tears filled her eyes and she choked. She missed her friend something awful—as much as she missed her mother, her father, her brother, and her fiancé. All dead because of men like him.

"The baby," he finished, seemingly oblivious to her heartache. "Is it—um, I mean he? Or she?"

Ella refused to scrub at her eyes and let him know of her weakness. Instead she cleared her throat and soldiered on.

"*She* is named after me. But we call her Gaby."

The wails grew louder as they ambled down the lane. "I can hear why."

Defensiveness rose in Ella. "She can't help it. She's hungry."

"Feed her."

"With what, Major? Are you hiding a wet nurse in your saddlebags?"

He coughed, shuffled his feet. He was no doubt blushing at her gauche reference to the realities of life. *Men.* They were no damned good at anything but killing each other.

"You said 'we,' " he blurted.

"What?"

" 'We call her Gaby.' " They reached the house, quiet except for the squalls of the baby. He tossed his reins over the porch rail. "Who else is here?"

Ella gaped. Could he be serious? The expression on his face said he was.

"What did your letter say?" she demanded.

"That Mrs. Elliot had died and I was to take care of the child and the farm."

"Child?"

"Yes."

Ella didn't know whether to laugh or cry. "You'd better come with me."

She led him inside. The farmhouse was large, airy, intact—one of the few left so in the region. Winchester had changed hands seventy times during the war. The fields were charred, the population devastated. No family had emerged unscathed.

The Elliots were no different. Even though their house still stood, the inside had been ransacked. There was little left to sell. The animals, but for two, were gone. The crops that weren't hauled away had smoldered.

Ella retrieved one of their last stubs of candle wax. She could find her way through the house just fine. But she didn't want a Yankee, friend of Henry or not, behind her in the dark. Besides, she had something to show him, and she wanted to see his face when she did.

While she lit the candle, the major stood in the hall, glancing right and left, taking in the bullet holes, the missing paintings, the lack of furniture. He made no comment. What was there to say? He'd no doubt done his share of pillaging while he wore the Union blue.

After removing his hat, brand new from the looks of it, just like his suit and boots, he set the thing on the sole chair that remained in the hall. His hair was as dark as a crow's wing, long at the collar and over his ears, as if he hadn't had time for a trim before he'd begun his journey. The lack of a barber made him appear younger than the lines on his face implied.

Ella led the way upstairs. At the first room, she handed him the candle, stepped inside and scooped the sweaty baby into her arms.

Gaby had worked herself into fine form. After tugging on Ella's bodice a moment, she went limp with exhaustion. In her sleep the child hiccuped, trying to catch the breath she'd lost by screaming.

Even though the baby appeared at rest, Ella knew better than to put her back in bed. Gaby would only wake right up and start screaming again as soon as her tiny blond head touched the mattress.

"Is this what you wanted to show me?"

"Shh," Ella admonished.

He had the grace to look sheepish. He didn't look that way for long.

Ella stepped inside the next bedroom. When he continued to stand like a lump in the hallway, she beckoned. He joined her and she lifted her hand to indicate that he should raise his. The warm, wavering light of the candle filled the room, illuminating two tiny forms on corn shuck mattresses.

"Elizabeth"—she pointed to the nearest lump—"is two years old."

The baby fussed, and Ella shifted so that she rested against her shoulder. Sometimes having her aching belly pressed to Ella's body helped Gaby's disposition. Sometimes.

"Delia," she continued, indicating the lump on the bed closest to the window, "is three. Henry and Georgina made the most of those quick visits home between battles."

Without waiting for the major to speak, Ella sailed past him and into the hall. He followed her meekly to the next room. There, two tousled blond heads shared a single mattress.

"Joshua is seven," she said. "Cal's the oldest at twelve. Georgina lost two babies between Joshua and Delia, and there was another sister born between the boys, but she died of a fever when she was three. Georgina couldn't bear to think about another baby for a while after that."

Ella smiled softly. She loved every one of these children as if they were her own—perhaps because she might never have any of her own.

Her smile faded and she preceded the major out of the room, then turned to face him. He appeared shell-shocked. *Good.*

"Five?" he whispered. "There are five of them?"

"You didn't know."

Though her words weren't a question, he answered anyway. "No." He shook his head, then repeated, "No."

"Henry never mentioned them?"

"What?" He blinked and at last recovered from the blow. "No, we haven't corresponded since we left West Point."

Ella frowned. Why on earth would Henry leave the care of his children to a man he hadn't spoken to in over twelve years and a Yankee at that?

Because Henry was a fool. Even if the major had once been someone to trust, the war could have ruined him as easily as it had ruined so many others. Though he obviously had money and could feed, clothe, and house them all, she didn't want him here. From the panicky, trapped expression on his face, he didn't want to be here, either.

"Never mind," she said. "You can just run along home now. I can handle everything. Don't worry your head anymore about us."

He had been staring into the boys' room, but at her words he turned that gaze on her. His eyes were blue, very light against the sun-bronzed shade of his face. Were the shadows from the flickering candle or the past?

Ella stiffened. What did she care about his shadows or

his past? They all had their problems. Hers was getting rid of him.

"You think I'm going to just up and leave?"

She shrugged. "You thought there was one child. You didn't know about the other four. No one would blame you." She lowered her voice to a conspiratorial level. "No one would even know."

His eyes, already cool with shadows, became icy with contempt. "I'd blame me, Miss Fontaine, and I would know."

Ella's heart began to beat faster. He wasn't going to leave. The baby, as if sensing her agitation, wriggled and mewed. Absently Ella patted Gaby's back while her mind scrambled for a solution.

If he stayed, she couldn't. Live in a house with a Yankee? What would folks say?

She knew what they'd say. She'd never be able to hold up her head in Winchester again. Not that she had any hope of marriage or family. Even if there were any eligible men left alive, which one would want to take on the burden of five children who weren't even hers? But, husband or not, she had to live in Winchester. She had nowhere else to go.

"You can head on back to your place in the morning, Miss Fontaine." He lowered his head in a formal dismissal that made Ella grit her teeth. "I'm sure you've neglected your duties since taking up mine."

She had no duties to neglect, no one to go home to. But she wasn't going to tell him that.

The candle flickered, dancing with the shadows in the hall. As if in answer to a prayer, an idea bloomed, so wonderful, so devious, so perfect, she smiled.

The major blinked and stared, which made Ella pause. She'd forgotten how it felt to dazzle a man. That he could be dazzled when she stood before him in a four-year-old gown, her feet bare and baby spit on her shoulder, told Ella one thing—Yankee women had to be dog ugly and fashion foolish.

"You're so right, Major. I've let my place go something awful. In the morning, I'll just be on my way home."

She'd leave, all right. But she wouldn't stay away. She didn't trust any Yankee as far as she could spit, and she certainly wouldn't trust this one alone with her children.

Ella left Major Torrance in the hall and returned to the baby's room, her smile widening on the way. She wouldn't have to do anything to get rid of him. There were five experts just waiting to do it for her.

Three

Seth was dragged from sleep by the thud of muted marching as the sun spread light and warmth across his face. At first he thought he was back at war, his men trotting off to die as he lay sleeping.

He leaped from the bed, forgetting it was merely a rough mattress placed on the floor of the room where Georgina Elliot had died. Misjudging the distance, he stumbled and smacked his knee against the wall. Cursing, he yanked open the door.

Four curious, yet hostile, pairs of brown eyes met his. The explanation for his marching dream stood in the hall in various states of undress—the little girls still in their nightdresses, the younger boy in pants but no shirt. The elder boy had both. None of them possessed shoes, which explained the muted nature of the marching.

"Uh, hello," he began.

"Ella says you're our new keeper." The oldest boy—Cal, Seth recalled—spoke for them all. "But I'm here t' tell ya, we don't need none."

Seth winced at the child's choice of words. One of his first duties would be to hire a governess. The Elliot children, as well as many others in the area, no doubt, had had their educations sadly neglected. He doubted schooling was high on the list of priorities when food was at a premium. But now that he was here, that would change.

He studied Cal. The boy studied him.

"I'm sure you don't need a keeper," Seth allowed.

"No nanny, nor governess neither. Not that you look like one."

Well, thank goodness for small favors.

The wail of the baby made all of the children flinch. Without further comment they turned tail and ran, thundering down the stairs with all the grace of wounded buffalo.

Figuring Ella would get the baby, Seth stepped into his room and quickly dressed in another of the new suits his mother had bought for him. When he'd returned from the war thinner at the waist and broader at the shoulders, none of his old clothes had fit, which gave his mother leave to order more new clothes than he'd ever need and twice as many as he'd ever want.

Seth scowled at the array he'd hung in the small armoire last night. His mother had planned for him to attend business meetings, balls, and other nonsense. So his selection of dark frock coats and morning jackets were woefully out of place on this tiny farm at the base of the Shenandoah Valley, but he had nothing else.

The baby continued to howl. Seth could bear the noise no longer and strode down the hall to her room. Ella was nowhere in sight.

Odd. She'd seemed very attached to the baby last night. Watching her hold the child had touched Seth as he couldn't recall being touched before. What would it be like to be held in someone's arms as if you were cherished and adored unconditionally?

Seth had never experienced such love. He wouldn't experience it with Ella Fontaine, either. She loathed him.

Not that he blamed her. He was sure she had her reasons, reasons he probably did not want to hear. Women like Ella loved with their whole hearts, which meant they hated with their whole hearts, too.

It was his misfortune to be drawn to her. Not Ella's fault that the generous curves outlined by the sheen of the moon had haunted him, making him dream of something other than death for a change. How long had it been since he'd had a woman? He couldn't recall, which was the *only* reason he'd found himself imagining things he had no business imagining.

The crying continued and Seth glanced into the baby's crib—such as it was—an old apple crate fashioned into a tiny bed. Gaby saw him and increased the volume of her wails. He was reminded of certain battles when the Rebels howled so loudly the Union lines trembled. He'd never heard anything like the Rebel yell—until now.

"Uh—um. Shh." He patted her head. She stopped wailing, squinted at him, then drew in a long, deep breath.

"Uh-oh," Seth murmured.

She released that breath on a shriek of such fury the house seemed to rattle. Without thought, Seth scooped Gaby into his arms, as he'd seen Ella do the night before, and settled her against his shoulder.

She was soaked from tip to toe. The scent of urine wafted over his face, even as warmth seeped through his new jacket and into his clean shirt. But she stopped crying, so Seth was loathe to peel her away.

"Now what?" he asked.

The baby merely snuggled closer, rubbing her wet body all over the front of his clothes.

"You gotta change 'er, then feed 'er."

Seth spun around to find Cal leaning in the doorway. The kid was too skinny, his pants too short. His long, thin feet were dirty. He appeared both younger and older than twelve, perched between a boy and a man. Seth was surprised Cal hadn't run off to war. Nearly everyone else had.

"Where's Ella?" he asked.

"Gone."

"Gone?" Seth repeated, dumbly.

"Yeah. She said you sent her on home." The boy's lips tightened mulishly. "Said we should mind you and our manners."

From his expression, Cal didn't plan on doing either one.

"You know how to change her?"

"Do. But won't. You wanna be our keeper so bad, be it."

"Why do you keep calling me your keeper?"

"That's what Ella said."

Unease pricked at Seth's spine. Why would Ella call him a keeper, as if the children were animals? He didn't like that one bit.

"I'm your guardian," he said. "Your father and I were friends, and he wanted me to take care of you. Didn't he ever mention Seth Torrance?"

"All the time."

Seth smiled gently. "He trusted me. Can't you?"

"Nope. Just 'cause Pa trusted the enemy don't mean I have to. We don't need you. We don't want you."

"You have no choice."

The boy lifted, then lowered one bony shoulder. "That's nothin' new to me."

Cal strolled out, then clomped back down the stairs. Interesting that he'd approached with all the stealth of a Rebel sniper, yet couldn't seem to return the same way.

Seth knew very little about children and even less about babies. But he could learn. Why he didn't just hire a nanny, a housekeeper and a governess, instruct that the bills be sent to him, and hightail it back to Boston immediately, Seth wasn't sure. He'd have to eventually, but right now he wanted to stay.

Ever since he'd returned from the war he'd felt adrift, as if he had no purpose and no future, even though he did. Or at least he'd had one assigned to him.

But the idea of making weapons sickened him. His mother thought he'd get over it. Seth wasn't so sure.

However, he was sure of one thing. His friend had trusted him with all he held dear. Everyone thought Henry had lost his mind. Seth wasn't going to prove them right by betraying that trust. Together he and Henry had learned about honor, duty, and friendship. They might have lost touch with each other, but they had never lost touch with that.

Three days later, Seth felt as if he'd refought the Battle of Gettysburg. He was hot and dirty; he smelled. He hadn't eaten decently or slept the night through since he'd arrived. How could five children get the better of a hardened Union officer?

He wasn't exactly sure when he'd lost control. Was it when he'd changed Gaby's diaper that first day, thrilled to have accomplished the simple task, only to lift the child and have the cloth fall to the floor? Gaby had giggled and promptly wet on his socks.

Or maybe it had been when he'd gotten them both cleaned and clothed, then hurried downstairs, intent on making breakfast for the rest of the children.

Entering the kitchen, he cheerfully called out, "What shall I have for breakfast?"

The two little girls had burst into terrified tears.

Seth fought the urge to run back the way he had come. "What did I say?"

Cal shrugged. Joshua appeared uncomfortable. The girls continued to wail. Gaby joined in.

"Are you ill?" he questioned. "Does something hurt?"

"N-noooo," Elizabeth cried.

"Then what is it?"

But the girls were too little to articulate what had scared them so badly.

"Ah, I'm gonna milk the goat," Cal snapped and disappeared.

After that, things really got loud. Seth had fought in many battles. He'd triumphed with death all around him. But the shrieking of the girls, which seemed to hit unknown levels of sound, made him more edgy than facing a Rebel charge.

"What is the matter with you?" he demanded.

They stopped crying, drew in deep, deep breaths. Seth learned quickly; he knew what was coming. Obviously Joshua did, too, because he clapped his hands over his ears seconds before the girls let out a full-bodied howl. For lack of anything better to do, Seth jiggled the baby. Joshua pressed on his ears harder. The girls kept screaming.

Finally, the boy opened one eye, then another. He stared at Seth with a pitying expression, then lowered his hands with a wince and climbed off his chair. After crossing the room, he tugged on Seth's trousers and beckoned him closer. Then he whispered in his ear, "Cal told them that Yankees eat little Reb girls for breakfast."

Seth straightened. Well, no wonder they'd started screaming the minute he'd asked what was for breakfast.

When Cal came back with the baby's milk, Seth made the boy set his sisters straight. Still they looked at him as if he were an ogre—or maybe just the enemy.

The rest of that day and the next passed in a blur of crying, cleaning, and chaos.

By the third day, they needed supplies. Since Seth

couldn't very well leave Cal in charge of the little ones—by the time he got back they'd think Seth was Satan himself—he loaded all five children into the wagon.

The trip wasn't one of his better ideas. Delia and Elizabeth couldn't seem to grasp that they shouldn't stand up in the wagon. They fell over and bumped various body parts several times. The rattling of the wagon kept Gaby awake—not that she slept much during the day . . . or any time, he was beginning to think.

Joshua was so excited, he couldn't sit still. His wiggling made Seth's horse more nervous than pulling the wagon already had. Cal just smirked the entire way. Seth soon found out why.

The girls had never seen a store before. They ran wildly through the aisles. Elizabeth knocked over a tower of tin cans. Delia yanked a sack of flower off the countertop before he could stop her. It exploded against the floor, covering her with white powder. She laughed and began to dance in the dust.

Joshua tried to help pick up the cans and dropped one on his toe. He didn't howl, but large, slow tears dripped down his cheeks.

Cal continued to smirk. Seth jiggled the baby. The storekeeper filled their order and hustled them out in a hurry.

Before the man could slap the rump of Seth's horse and send them on their way, Seth asked, "Do you know of a wet nurse I could hire for the baby?"

The storekeeper glanced at the children, then back at Seth. He spat into the dirt beneath the horse's hooves. Remembering the greeting he'd received from Billy the first night he'd ridden into Winchester, Seth wondered if that was the way folks in Winchester said, "Howdy."

"Can't say's I know of anyone who'd work for a Yankee," the man said.

Seth blinked. "But it's not for me. It's for the baby of Henry Elliot."

"Who was killed by such as you. No one's gonna come out there and help, 'specially a woman. You can put that right out of yer head."

"If you feel that way, then why did you sell me supplies?" Seth asked.

The man shrugged. "Gotta make a livin'. Only folks with money these days are Yankee scum carpetbaggers. Better the money's in my pocket than yours."

Cal snickered. Seth glared. The shopkeeper looked pleased with himself.

Seth drove home wondering what he'd gotten into. He needed help. He could not take care of five children alone. But if the storekeeper was correct, he wouldn't be able to get any help. If he couldn't, he'd have to take the children back to Boston with him.

Seth cringed at the thought of showing up on his mother's doorstep with five ragtag Rebel youngsters. She'd treat them like servants; she wouldn't be able to help herself. Their accents alone would ensure none of the children their age would play nice. They'd be clean, fed, clothed, and educated, but they'd be miserable.

He glanced at Gaby, sleeping momentarily in Cal's arms. He couldn't do that to her. He couldn't do it to any one of them.

They approached the farm, which was silent and still, empty but for the goat and the cow. Delia began to cry. "Want Ella!"

"Me, too." Elizabeth's lower lip trembled.

Joshua blinked, hard and fast, then ducked his head to hide his face.

Gaby awoke and began to wail. Cal dumped her in Seth's lap and took off. Seth sat on the buckboard with weeping children all around him and admitted defeat. He had to have help. No one would help him.

Except maybe . . . Ella.

He'd have to beg. Probably offer her the stars.

At that instant Delia, still covered with flour which had mixed with sweat from the long, hot ride, as well as her tears, leaned against his side. She stuck there like glue.

Suddenly the stars didn't seem too high a price to pay at all.

Four

Ella couldn't sleep. The moon shone directly into her eyes through the open roof of the barn. Not that she'd have been able to sleep even if the moon had been new. She missed the children so badly she ached with it.

Three days had passed. Three days! She hadn't believed Seth Torrance would last through one.

She'd crept over to the Elliot farm several times, careful to stay out of sight lest the children see her and cry. She didn't want to upset them, but she had to be certain they weren't hurt or worse. She had to make sure Torrance didn't pack them up and take them away. If he did, she'd follow and she'd take them back any way she could.

Ella stroked the barrel of the shotgun, which she kept by her side always. A woman couldn't be too careful.

As if in answer to that thought, footsteps dragged through the brush outside her resting place. Ella sat up slowly and, taking the gun with her, crept to one of the many holes in the side of the barn.

The moonlight revealed the waste that had once been the Fontaine homestead. The house had been burned to the ground soon after Chancellorsville, when Federal troops retreated willy-nilly across the state. Ella recalled watching it burn as her mother and her father mourned the loss of Stonewall Jackson in that very same battle. The great general had housed his headquarters at Winchester, and the townsfolk adored him. When he'd died after losing an arm, then succumbing to pneumonia, everyone had draped their windows in black for a month.

"The South has won a victory," her father said, "but the loss of that one man may prove too great."

He'd been right, but he hadn't lived long enough to know that. Thank goodness. He'd joined the army soon after, and within the year, both he and Ella's mother had followed General Jackson across the river to rest beneath the trees.

Their gravestones sprang from the ground behind the ruins of the house, a constant reminder of what Ella must never forget. They had died at the hands of the enemy, the same as her fiancé, Jamie McMurray, the same as Henry Elliot and countless others.

Perhaps even herself, if this heavy-footed intruder proved to be another foe. So far she'd been able to scare off the scum with the sight of her gun alone, but one day she'd probably have to shoot someone, and then she'd better kill him. She knew what happened to Southern girls when they crossed a Yankee these days. She'd rather die than be an enemy plaything.

Ella pressed her lips together and cocked her gun. A bird flushed from the trees, startling her. But she held steady on the trigger.

Unfortunately, the intruder shifted course and approached from the front of the barn. She heard the footsteps clearly, walking all the way around the structure, then advancing inside.

Ella held her breath. Maybe if she kept quiet, whoever it was would go away.

She waited, listening. No, the footsteps continued on—closer and closer. She carefully swung her gun away from the wall and aimed it at the top of the ladder that led to her home in the hay mow.

Sure enough, the ladder creaked. Her visitor started up.

A dark head appeared, the face one she knew. He saw the barrel of the gun pointed at his nose and froze.

"What do you want?" Ella demanded.

Seth Torrance scowled. "Do you greet everyone everywhere with that shotgun?"

"Only fool Yankees who walk through the woods like fat old mules." She pointed the weapon at the nonexistent ceiling and uncocked the thing. "How on earth did y'all win the war tramping around like that? Any Reb boy would have heard you coming for miles."

"I wasn't *trying* to be quiet. I want to talk to you."

The major pulled himself into the hay mow. In her tiny space, he seemed so much bigger than he had the other day. More dangerous; quite handsome.

Ella narrowed her eyes, annoyed with the thought and herself for having it. "You just stay over there," she ordered. "I can hear you fine."

He gave an impatient exhale. "You think I came over her to ravish you? I've got too much on my mind for nonsense."

Nonsense? Ella wasn't quite sure what to make of that. She was a bit insulted, and that was the most nonsensical thing she'd ever known.

"State your business, then." Regardless of his words, she kept her gun handy.

"I'd like you to come back and take care of the children."

She resisted the urge to smirk. Though he'd held out two days longer than she'd expected, in the end he'd behaved predictably. A man like him wasn't going to stay here and care for five children.

As if she'd refused his request, the major hurried on. "They miss you. The little ones call your name. I should have realized how attached they'd be." He shrugged and looked away. "I can't bear to hear them cry."

Knowing how loudly the girls wailed, Ella could imagine why.

Everything could go back to the way it had been before he'd arrived, which was just what she wanted. She'd still have the problem of making the farm profitable again. However, that was the same old problem—which she'd deal with another day.

"When are you leaving?" she asked.

"Pardon me?"

"You. Leaving. I'll come back and take care of the children then."

"Who said I was leaving?"

Some of Ella's joy faded. "You can't mean to stay."

"I mean exactly that. At least for the next month. I'd like to hire you to take care of the children."

"You want me to be a nanny?"

"And their governess, as well. I can tell by your speech you've been educated. The children need schooling. Can you do that?"

"I can, but I won't."

"Why not?" He peered through the holes in the barn, his gaze touching on the ashes that had once been her home, the gravestones, the empty barnyard, before coming back to her. "You have something pressing to do here?"

How ungentlemanly of him to refer to her reduced circumstances. But then, he wasn't a gentleman. And he was right. She had to eat. Nevertheless, she tried one more time to convince him to go.

"Major, I'm perfectly capable of taking care of the children on my own. You can run back to wherever it is you call home. I'll even write you a letter every month and tell you how they're doing."

"A letter would be lovely. Thank you."

Her heart lifted with hope. Then he dashed it with his next words.

"But I won't be needing one just yet. I plan to stay until I'm sure the children are settled and safe. Right now I need help. The children love you, and I thought you loved them."

Ella winced. Trust a Yankee to hit at her weakest point.

He kept pushing. "I can pay you. Cash money. From what I hear, that's slim in these parts."

Another rude comment, though no less than the truth. Ella bit her lip. She could go back to the children, sleep in a bed, have a roof over her head and food in her belly, even get paid for the privilege. Or stay here and . . . Ella glanced around the dilapidated dwelling. She didn't want to think about staying here.

Sooner or later the major would be called home to more important things. She'd be left with the children and his money. She could get the farm going again and keep them all together. Her reputation would be ruined, but she wasn't using it anyway.

"All right, Major. I'll come back for the children." He smiled. She continued, "And the salary of fifty dollars a week."

He stopped smiling. "But—but—that's outrageous!"

"Isn't it?"

Ella waited. She had him. After sending her away, he wouldn't have come begging unless he had no choice. She could well imagine the kind of response he'd received if he'd asked for assistance in the town of Winchester.

"All right," he conceded. "Fifty dollars it is."

Ella turned away so he couldn't see the triumph on her face. It appeared as if her years at Miss Duvray's School for Girls were going to be worth something more than the memories.

The first battle was hers. Ella planned on winning the entire war.

Five

Ella was thrilled to be back. The children were thrilled to have her. But life on the Elliot farm was not the way it had been. With the major there, how could it be?

Still, her days were so full taking care of the children, and teaching them, too, that she barely noticed Seth Torrance at all. Barely.

He spent the first week fixing the inside of the house. He patched the bullet holes, painted over them, brought in pictures from Lord knew where and hung them over the places paint and patch did not help.

The second week he worked on the outside of the house as wagons pulled in and out, bringing furniture, beds, clothes, and linens. He'd even ordered a hand-carved crib for the baby. No more apple crate for her.

Each child now had several sets of clothing for everyday wear, plus shoes, stockings, undergarments, and hats, as well as an outfit for special occasions. They were overwhelmed.

So was Ella, who was treated to the same gifts. Though she should refuse them, she found she could not. Having worn the same dress, in rotation with one other, for nigh on to four years, she couldn't keep her pride in place any longer. Wearing a garment that hadn't been hacked off at the ankle to keep it from dragging along the ground, since she no longer possessed a crinoline, was too wonderful to turn up her nose at.

She'd known the major was wealthy—his horse, his clothes, his boots, and his manner had all pointed in that direction—but she hadn't realized he was sinfully rich. To be able to order whatever he wanted and have it delivered wherever he chose on a whim seemed like magic.

The third week a heat wave descended. The baby developed an ill humor; Ella developed a headache. Several times each day she bathed Gaby with lukewarm milk and water, then sprinkled the heat-induced eruptions on her skin with rye flour. Nothing seemed to help until the middle of a very long night, when a cool breeze whispered in from the east.

Ella stepped onto the porch, Gaby in her arms. The baby gurgled with pleasure as the wind caressed her face. Even though she was in her nightdress and robe, Ella strolled to the lone apple tree at the far edge of a burned-out field.

There, beyond the remaining elms that shaded the house, the breeze blew strong and sure. The night was peaceful, until someone struck a match. The sharp snick, the sudden flare of light, the acrid scent startled her so much she gasped, whirled, and pointed the derringer she always kept in the pocket of her robe at the man who stepped from behind the apple tree. The flame touched the tip of a cigarette and illuminated a face she knew very well.

"Do you have to sneak up on me all the time?" she snapped, her heart thundering, and not just because the major had frightened her—again—but he wasn't wearing any shirt. Ella had never seen a man's chest before. She couldn't stop herself from looking at it now.

A curling mat of dark hair began just below his collarbone, growing finer and lighter as it dusted from chest to belly, then disappeared. The skin of his arms was smooth, the muscles rippling with every move that he made. The Colts slung low on his hips only emphasized the ridges across his stomach and the leanness of his thighs. For a soft Yankee major, he appeared awfully hard.

"I didn't sneak," he said. She yanked her eyes from his muscles and back to his face. "I was here all the time."

"Hmm," was all she could manage with him standing there half naked.

He drew in a mouthful of smoke, then set it free. "Out of curiosity, how many guns do you have?"

She still pointed the derringer at his chest, so she put it away. "Enough."

"For what?"

"To be safe."

"I'm here now. You don't need to worry."

She snorted. "You're one of the things I worry about."

He frowned, but he didn't argue. Instead he took another long pull on his cigarette, then gestured at the gnarled branches of the apple tree. "How did this survive?"

"I'm not sure. The damned Yankees—" she broke off, glanced at him, shrugged, and started over. "The soldiers spared the house but burned the fields. We're still not sure why. But this tree survived, and it produces. We'll have apples come fall. The resiliency of this land amazes me. When I think of all it's seen, all it's endured and yet it thrives, I'm stunned by the miracle."

He was watching her closely. "You love it here."

"Why wouldn't I? This is my home. I'm part of the land and the land's part of me. I never want to be anywhere else."

"Hmm," he murmured, echoing her, and continued to smoke as he contemplated the tree and the sky.

The night was enjoyable, the air between them cool and quiet—until Gaby lost her happy thought and began to cry. Exhausted, Ella nearly cried herself.

The major took one final draw on his cigarette, then ground the rest into oblivion with the heel of his boot before holding out his arms for the baby. "Hand the little creature over."

"You'd better put on a shirt first." Ella's face heated. "Skin to skin, she'll stick to you like a leech."

He glanced down, surprise lighting his face, as if he'd forgotten he was waltzing around in the night half dressed. Perhaps that was what Yankees did, and they never thought twice about it.

"Excuse me." He picked up the garment from the ground at the base of the apple tree and shoved his arms into the sleeves.

Gaby's breath started to hitch, the sure sign of a coming explosion. Before Ella could object, or he could button his shirt, the major snatched the baby and settled her into the crook of his arm.

Ella tensed. Gaby did not appreciate being flung about like a sack of potatoes. Every time one of the children tried it, there was an eruption of sound and tears. Instead, she took a deep breath, let it out on a contented sigh and closed her eyes.

Ella blinked. "How did you do that?"

"What?"

"She went to sleep."

"Isn't that what you wanted?"

"Well, yes, but—"

"Shh, you'll wake her."

Effectively silenced, Ella had nothing to do but watch the baby sleep, which led to watching the major's chest rise and fall.

Why did seeing him with his shirt open and unbuttoned

entice her more than his bare skin had? Because now she knew what lay beneath the white cotton, and she could imagine it all night long.

Ella shook her head. What was the matter with her? He was a Yankee. The enemy. And he was leaving, just as soon as she could get rid of him.

However, the picture he made with Gaby in his arms tugged at her. The baby adored him. Whenever he came near, she laughed and waved her hands, kicked her feet. If she cried, only his arms could quiet her. It was infuriating. Sometimes Ella wanted to scream, she was so jealous. But she also had to wonder what the baby sensed in him that she did not.

"Come here," he whispered.

Ella jumped. "What? Why?"

He tossed her a mildly annoyed glance. "Must you question everything? Come here and look."

He tilted his arms, tipping the baby forward as if to show Ella something. Concerned, she came closer.

"Is that the cutest thing you've ever seen?" he murmured.

Gaby's sweetly bowed mouth puckered and released, puckered and released.

"You think she's eating in her dreams?" he asked.

"Either that or kissing you."

Their eyes met. His were so blue they reminded her of the sky on a sunny day, even in the dead of night. The air smelled of cool breezes and the fading tang of apples, at war with the scent of male heat and sultry smoke. What would he taste like if she put her lips on his, dipped her tongue inside, savored the warmth and the heat of him?

He would taste of ashes. The death of the South.

She had to remember that the demise of all she'd held

dear had begun and ended with men just like him. He was forbidden, yet she wanted him just the same.

And because of that he had to go—or she did.

Ella whirled and headed for the house.

Six

Seth watched her go, the white nightdress trailing out behind her with the wind. The baby, content and sleeping in his arms, kept him from chasing after Ella and kissing her as he wanted to.

She'd wanted the kiss, too. He'd seen it in the way her lips had parted, the way her eyes had lowered to his mouth and clung, the way her breath had quickened, making the soft, full mounds of her breasts rise and fall with a tantalizing rhythm.

She was a beautiful girl. Of course he wanted her. But why would she want him?

As Ella had said over and over again, he was the enemy. She hated him on principle, and she didn't even know the full extent of his perfidy—that he'd participated in the very battle which had killed Henry Elliot. That his family, his legacy, his wealth was based on so much death.

What would she say if she knew everything? He had a pretty good idea.

Ella was a southern woman. They were tough, loyal, and stubborn as the old mules she'd once compared him to. Even if she was attracted to him physically, that didn't mean a thing. She'd die a slow, painful death before she'd admit the feeling, let alone act upon it. She would never let him touch her, take her and make her his.

He'd been here three weeks, and the older children still looked at him as if they expected him to breathe fire from his nose or develop a sudden craving for blood.

Seth gazed down at the sleeping baby. Only Gaby was innocent enough to see the man inside the Yankee. He couldn't explain how much she meant to him, how deeply he adored her for that alone.

The cool breeze, the scent of the apple tree, the acres upon acres of land that were his soothed Seth as nothing else ever had. The pace here was slower, the countryside quieter. The loudest noises were the cries of children.

Since he'd come to Winchester, he'd had no recurrence of the frightening fits he'd endured in Boston. Even the cannon fire that lived inside his head had stilled. Perhaps this place was all that he'd needed to heal.

He had no job, no friends, no future. He didn't belong here.

So why did it feel as if he did?

When Ella reached the house, Cal stood on the porch. He contemplated her with a somber expression. Had he seen her with the major?

What if he had? Nothing had happened. Not that she hadn't wanted it to.

The thought brought her up short. She could not, would not, be attracted to this man. He wasn't going to stay.

Seth Torrance did not belong here. He might play at taking care of his friend's children and farm, but he wasn't a farmer and he never would be. Sooner or later he'd go back to where he had come from and leave his toys behind. She didn't plan to be one of them.

"I don't like him." Cal stared at the distant silhouette of a man holding a child beneath the apple tree.

Ella climbed the porch steps and put her hand on Cal's shoulder. Poor child, unable to be a child, forced too soon to be a man. But he was only one of a thousand others just the same.

He must have grown two inches in the last month. Thank goodness Seth had the money to buy Cal new clothes. What would she have done if he hadn't come to help?

Ella put that thought out of her head, too. She could not depend on Seth. She could not depend on anyone but herself. If she did, she'd only be disappointed.

"He's not for you to like or not, Cal." She pulled him closer and smiled softly when he let her. "He's your guardian, and he's here to stay until he decides to go."

"And when he does, will everything go back to the way that it was?"

Frowning, Ella tilted her head so she could see his face—eager and hopeful in the moonlight. "The way that it was when, sweetie?"

"When just the six of us were here. I liked it then. Didn't you?"

Thinking back, Ella didn't miss the time when there was barely enough food, no money to get more, carpetbaggers strolling down the lane any old time, and deserters or worse slinking about ready to take what little they had left. She'd been scared every minute before Seth showed up.

Though she'd been able to take care of them with the aid of her guns, Seth was a battle-seasoned soldier. His eyes scanned the horizon whenever he stepped outside. He wore his Colt as if he knew what to do with it, handled his rifle the same way. She hadn't realized how safe she felt just having him near.

And that scared her so badly she blurted, "Yes. I liked it then, too."

"I can make him go."

The quiet, sure statement made Ella blink. "What? What do you mean?"

"If me and the others put our heads together, we can make him hightail it all the way back to where he came from. He isn't going to stay, Ella. Better he goes now than after she gets too attached to him, don't you think?"

His gaze rested on her face so intently that for an instant Ella wondered if he could see into her thoughts. He'd put them into words so well. Somehow she didn't think Cal was just talking about Gaby when he used the word "she."

Ella glanced at the apple tree where Seth still stood with the baby. She frowned.

When had she begun to think of him as Seth rather than the major? She couldn't recall, and that in itself wasn't good. When she thought of him as the major, she could remember he was the enemy. But Seth? He seemed more and more like a friend.

She looked at Cal once more. "Yes," she murmured. "Better that he go now than later. Before she gets too attached."

As Ella went inside, she considered that it might already be too late for her.

Seth awoke to a din reminiscent of the Battle at the Wilderness. He leaped from the bed, knocked his beleaguered knee against his new nightstand, and stumbled into the hallway. A bucket of icy water hit him full in the face.

As he stood there sputtering, drowning, trying to get his breath, the noise stopped. When he opened his eyes he found the four eldest Elliot children staring at him. Predictably, Cal held the empty bucket.

"What—what—what was that for?" he managed.

"Cat fight," Cal said simply. "Only way to get 'em to stop is to toss some water on 'em."

"Cats?" Seth glanced around the hall. "What cats?"

Cal shrugged. "They were here a minute ago. Weren't they?"

Joshua, Elizabeth, and Delia all nodded, but none of them spoke. Seth narrowed his eyes, opened his mouth, and the baby began to cry.

"Never mind," he said. "Where's Ella?"

"Makin' bekfast," Elizabeth said.

"All right. Run along and eat. Tell her I'll bring Gaby."

He hurried into the baby's room, dripping all the way. As he quickly crossed to the crib, first one foot, then the other, came down on something hard, round and mobile. He scrambled for purchase, lost, and landed on his butt—hard. Gaby's crying stopped and she giggled.

Marbles were strewn across the scarred wood planks. Seth tightened his lips, got to his feet, and rubbed his bruised behind.

Ten minutes later, he and Gaby entered the kitchen. Ella glanced over her shoulder. The mere sight of her brought back everything he'd felt last night—awareness, tenderness, desire.

She appeared as beautiful in the sunlight as she had by the light of the moon. While she worked, the skirt of her dress swayed provocatively, drawing his gaze to her soft curves. The hem played hide-and-seek with her ankles. She wore no shoes, as usual. And while his mother would think this made her common, Seth only thought it made her Ella.

Meeting her, knowing her, touching her had brought color and sound and light back to his life. The inertia that had plagued him in Boston was no more.

"What was all the racket up there?" she asked, her

voice brisk, all business, as if they'd never stood half naked in the night.

Seth looked at each child. They stared back with brown-eyed innocence. "Nothing I can't handle," he answered.

Three children glanced away. Only Cal held his gaze. But then, Seth had known Cal was the one to watch all along. He'd invaded the boy's territory, just as the North had invaded the South.

Which was why the war had dragged on for four long years, despite the Union's far superior resources of money, munitions and men. When a country was invaded, the citizens were honor bound to fight back and fight back hard.

But Seth had begun to think of this as his place and these kids, despite their hostility, as his, too. He hadn't lost a fight yet. He didn't plan to lose this one.

He took his chair. Something squalled and struggled beneath him. Seth jumped up as a huge black cat shot across the room and out the open back door.

"Told you there was a cat," Cal muttered.

Ella choked, coughed, and put her napkin to her lips—no doubt to hide a smile.

Seth had to struggle not to smile back. Cal was clever and he kept a cool head. Even now, the boy ate his breakfast as if he hadn't just masterminded the morning. Still, he would have to do better than this to get rid of Seth Torrance.

"I need to go into town." Ever since he'd arrived, Seth had been meaning to stop by the attorney's office and pick up a copy of Henry's will and any other pertinent papers pertaining to the children and the farm. "Anyone want to take a ride with me?"

He figured no one would, but it didn't hurt to ask. He was surprised when Cal got slowly to his feet. "Me and Delia will go."

The boy wouldn't meet Seth's eyes. What did the little terror have planned for him now?

He considered changing into one of his suits to meet with the attorney. He'd been wearing Henry's work clothes for the past several weeks, and while they had felt odd at first, now he was more comfortable in the loose trousers and shirts that had been washed soft through years of wear than he was in his own things. Seth didn't care if he ever put on a suit again. So he plopped his wide-brimmed straw hat onto his head and herded the two children out to the wagon.

The trip into town was uneventful. Delia sang a song about a pony at the top of her lungs and just a tad short of the correct key all the way there. Since it kept her entertained, and him as well, Seth let her. Cal merely stared straight ahead and ignored him. Perhaps that was for the best, though Seth couldn't help but wonder what deviousness he was plotting behind those somber eyes.

Once in town, however, Cal spoke up. "Can I buy Delia some candy, Major? She's never had none before."

The utter joy on the little girl's face made Seth feel guilty for suspecting Cal of hatching a new plot. The poor girl had never had candy, a situation that must be rectified immediately.

"Of course. Let's get her some right away."

He stepped toward the store, but Cal laid a hand on his arm. "No need for you to go. Best you do your errand whilst I get the candy. These days it isn't a good idea to leave the women and children alone for too long."

The reminder of the still dangerous nature of the countryside cast a chill over the warm summer day. But Cal was right.

The boy had seen his share of bad things, which had forced him to grow up too quickly. Seth only hoped he could give him back some of the childhood that had been stolen away. Candy was a step in the right direction.

"I'll just head over to Mr. Blair's office, then." He reached into his pocket and handed Cal more than enough money for candy. "Get yourself a treat, too, and some for the rest at home."

In lieu of a thank-you, Cal nodded, took Delia's hand, and disappeared into the general store.

Within a half an hour they were on their way home. Delia slurped on gumdrops, which kept her from singing. Cal continued to stare.

"Don't you want to eat your candy?" Seth asked.

"No, Major. I'm gonna save mine."

Seth wanted to ask why, but he doubted Cal would tell him.

"You could call me Seth if you like," he offered.

"No, sir, I couldn't." Cal went back to contemplating the breeze.

Seth had hoped a day together and a little bit of sugar would soften the boy. He should have known better.

Seven

Seth skirted the apple tree and strolled through the blackened fields. He knelt in the dirt, sifted some through his fingers. He wished that he knew more about farming, but he didn't.

He glanced back at the house. The afternoon was proving as uneventful as the morning, which only made Seth nervous. Cal must be planning something extraordinarily devious if he was behaving himself for this long.

Ella had put Gaby down for a nap. When he'd left, she'd still been howling her displeasure, so Ella had taken the others outside for their lessons. He could see four blond heads and one dark one beneath the shade of the elm tree in the yard.

Ella had proved to be an excellent teacher. The children adored her and did things for her they wouldn't do for anyone else. As a result, they were making great progress in their studies.

Seth smiled at the picture they made. He was due to return home in one week. He didn't want to go. But he'd come to fulfill a duty. He would have to return to Boston for the same reason.

Afternoon faded to evening. Supper went smoothly. The children thanked him for the candy, though he'd seen none but Delia eating it. Everyone headed for bed without argument. Seth sat on the porch expecting . . . Lord knew what.

But nothing happened.

He heard Ella through the open window upstairs, murmuring to the baby. From the girls' room he caught traces of a whisper, from the boys' nothing at all. They must be asleep.

When all sounds ceased, he climbed the stairs, hesitated in the hall. Tempted to look in on them, he resisted. He didn't dare start treating them like his or he'd never be able to leave.

He cast one longing glance at Ella's room and forced himself to go to bed. If he touched her as he wanted to even once, he wasn't sure he'd be able to stop.

Sleep came quickly; the dreams followed. Rebs snuck into the perimeter. He heard them whispering from the tall grass, sensed them creeping ever closer, the thud of their muted footsteps a death knell.

This had happened before—another time, another place. Mayhem. Murder. Too many of his men and theirs lost forever. He hated the war, hated the necessity as well as the horrific waste. Hated the most his presence in the middle of such strife.

When the first shot sounded, Seth sat up in bed. Darkness surrounded him. He didn't know where he was; he only knew that they were coming.

With a roar, he leaped to his feet, reaching for the gun at his hip that was not there.

Another shot sounded behind him, then another to his left, to his right. He whirled, flinched, put his hands to his ears, but the shots continued. Faster, louder, they confused and terrified him.

Icy sweat dewed his skin. His belly lurched. He feared he'd disgrace himself right there on the battlefield. Where in hell were his Colts, his rifle?

A thud in the darkness made his heart pound faster. Light poured from an unknown source, illuminating his pistols. He dived for them.

Someone shouted his name, grabbed his wrist just as he reached for a gun.

Another shot was fired, this one so close the scent of gunpowder filled his nose. With a roar of fury, Seth yanked the intruder forward, and together they tumbled to the ground.

Ella fell on top of Seth. Thankfully the guns remained on the nightstand.

He struggled beneath her, shouting, "To your posts, soldiers! We're under attack."

"It's me, Ella." She tugged at her arm, but he held on too tightly. "Let me go."

Instead, he flipped over, pinning her beneath him with the long, hard, heavy length of his body, then yanking her hands over her head. One of his legs slid around hers, aligning them center to center.

Ella's eyes widened. "Oh, my," she murmured.

"Ella?" Cal's voice came from down the hall. "You all right?"

Dear God, the children! She had to keep them from seeing Seth like this. They'd be so frightened.

"Stay in your rooms," she ordered. "Don't come out no matter what you hear."

"But—"

"Don't argue, Cal! The major's ill. I'll take care of him."

Doors closed and she relaxed—at least as much as she could with Seth plastered to her. His breath was labored, as if he'd just run a mile in the heated air, the movement rubbing his chest against hers in the slow, sensuous, rhythmic manner of a forbidden dance.

Ella shook off the desire to explore such sensations further. Something was wrong with him. Now was not the time to wonder if his lips were as soft as they looked, his kiss as seductive as his chest.

She peered into Seth's face. His gaze darted around the room, searching for something. But what?

The loud pops that had awakened her even before his shouts had sounded like gunfire. But when she'd entered the room, he'd just been reaching for his gun. If someone had shot from outside, they'd be inside by now. So what had happened?

"Are you all right?" she whispered.

He was trembling. Sweat beaded his brow. The hands that held hers prisoner were ice cold.

Ella frowned. He was scared half to death.

She knew what to do about that. The children had nightmares all the time and woke very much like this.

"Hush," she murmured. "You're safe. Nothing will hurt you now."

Her gentle tone must have reached him, for he blinked, then shifted his gaze from the shadows to hers. He still did not seem to know her. His eyes remained cloudy, in another time, another place. But he let go of her wrists, so she touched his face.

Stubble scraped her fingertips as she caressed his jaw. She ran her hands through his shaggy, soft hair, kneaded the tense cords of his neck, whispered, "You're all right, you're all right," ten times before he kissed her.

Boys had stolen kisses behind the barn, at a dance. She'd rapped every one with her knuckles or her fan and put a stop to such familiarity in an instant.

Jamie had always said good night in a chaste and proper manner. They'd had a lifetime for intimate embraces, or so they had thought.

Of course, if Jamie had ever kissed her as if he were ice

cold and she was a flame, if he had ever nibbled her lips, sucked her tongue, explored her mouth with his body pressed to the length of hers, she might have fainted.

Or begged for more.

Her fingers tangled in Seth's hair, holding him close. Her mouth opened; her tongue danced with his. Desperate whimpers clawed at the back of her throat. Her breasts, beneath the light cotton of her nightdress, ached and throbbed, wanting, needing his touch. Where he was pressed against her down low felt too good to abandon, so she arched against him, and bright lights flared behind her closed eyes.

What was happening to her?

A moment later he ended the kiss and his forehead dropped to hers. His hair brushed her cheek. She held him as his heart slowed, and his breathing evened out along with hers.

"Did I hurt you?"

His hoarse voice startled her. She recalled hating Seth's voice when he had first come here. Now she missed the strong yet gentle tones, lost to terrors she could not even imagine.

"Of course not," she said briskly, though it was hard to be so nonchalant with him still pressed intimately against her. "You would never hurt me."

He sighed and rolled away, sitting up with his back against the bed. Feeling foolish, Ella did the same. He inched away from her just a bit, as if afraid she would touch him. That hurt after what they had just shared.

What hurt even more was the guilt that flared to life as the passion thrumming in her blood dissipated. She had never felt such things for Jamie—the man she had sworn to marry, the man whose children she had promised to bear. How could she feel them for the enemy?

"I don't know what I might do when I'm like this,"

Seth muttered. "I'd hoped the spells were gone, but I guess not."

"This has happened before?"

"Ever since the war. But usually it's a loud noise that makes me forget where I am. I must be worse instead of better to have lost my place in the middle of a peaceful night."

"No." Ella shook her head. "There *was* a loud noise. Several, in fact. They woke me, too."

She stood and lit the lamp. Scattered across the floor were the remnants of several firecrackers. Their eyes met.

"Cal," they said together.

Ella sighed. The boy had gone too far.

"I'll talk to him," she muttered. "This is my fault."

"Why?" He shoved his fingers through his damp hair, mussing it more than she already had. "Did you declare war? Send me off to fight it? Make me so weak I couldn't take the death and the destruction?"

"You think you're weak because the war haunts you? If it didn't, I'd be worried."

His lips twitched but he didn't smile. "Then why is this your fault?"

"I encouraged Cal to harass you." Ella looked away. "I wanted you to leave. It wasn't very adult of me. I'm sorry. But I never suspected he'd do something like this."

"Even if you had, how could you know gunfire would make me lose my senses?" He snorted. "Hell, I still can't believe it."

She should say good night, pretend the kiss had never happened, then escape to her room, but she couldn't. She'd held Seth in her arms as he trembled, touched her mouth to his as he shook. She could not just walk away and leave him alone. So Ella sat on the floor once more, closer this time, and he did not move away.

"I'm sure these spells will fade with time," she offered.

"I thought so, too."

"The war's been over only a few months. You can't expect to forget four years of horror so quickly."

"What if—" He stopped.

"What?"

"What if I never forget? What if I'm always like this?"

"What if you are? There are worse things, Seth. Much worse."

It was the first time she'd called him by his given name out loud. She discovered that she liked the sound of it on her lips nearly as much as she liked his lips. Would she ever stop thinking about that kiss? Not likely.

"Do you know where I get all my money?"

She blinked at the sudden change of subject. "What?"

"My money. My family is the proud owner of Torrance Munitions. We're very well off. But then, there's always a need for instruments of destruction."

Ella didn't know what to say. She hadn't wanted the largesse he'd brought to them because it was Yankee charity. Now, knowing the charity had been bought with money made from killing her countrymen, she wanted it even less.

However, seeing Seth in the throes of his pain had shown her a new and disturbing truth. He had suffered the same as any Confederate soldier. Death and destruction did not pick and choose. Nightmares came to them all.

"You can't help what your family does for a living. But you don't have to keep doing it."

He shook his head. "All my life it's been understood that I'd take over. I went to West Point. That's what men in my family do. The only thing I've been trained for is killing and building things made to kill. I hate it."

She didn't know what to tell him. But now that he'd begun to talk, he didn't seem to need any encouragement from her to continue.

"I was at Saylor's Creek."

Ella glanced at him. "So were a lot of people."

"For all I know, I might have been the one to kill Henry."

"And you might not have been."

He glanced at her in surprise, and she made a sound of derision.

"Did you think I was going to pick up a stone, or maybe that gun? Seems to me you're a doing a fine job of flaying yourself alive over something you couldn't stop." Ella spread her hands. "You think if you hadn't picked up a gun they wouldn't have fought? You think if your family wasn't making munitions they'd have all laid down their weapons and shaken hands?"

"No." He sighed. "Of course not. But—" He rubbed his face. His palm scraped over the stubble on his chin. "What shall I tell the children?"

"Nothing. What possible good would it do to tell them? Henry was . . . well, I'm sure you know. If it weren't Saylor's Creek, it would have been another battle. If not the war, then something else. Henry was like a falling star—bright, brilliant, and set to burn out very young."

He didn't answer, but he didn't argue, either. Ella wasn't sure why she felt the need to comfort him. Perhaps because, as she'd said, he was doing such a good job of torturing himself.

"I want to make sure everything will be all right here before I go," he said quietly. "But you don't have to worry. I *will* go."

Suddenly his leaving held very little appeal. Unable to stop herself, Ella reached for Seth's hand and laced her fingers with his. "But not yet," she whispered.

He hesitated an instant. Then his hand tightened on hers. "No, not yet."

Eight

When Seth arose with the dawn, he felt good. Remarkable, in fact, in the face of what had happened last night. But if he'd come out of every other spell with Ella in his arms, he would never have needed to drown his fears with a bottle. He hadn't touched whiskey since he'd arrived in Winchester, and he hadn't missed it.

As Seth dressed, his mind went back to the previous night. He couldn't believe that he'd kissed Ella, or that she'd let him. In times past, his behavior would have earned him a shotgun wedding. The prospect wasn't as unappealing as it should have been.

From the front porch, he enjoyed the sight of a cool mist hovering over the fields. Soon the heat of the sun would wash the fog away, but right now it appeared as if heaven had come to Virginia.

Seth took a deep breath of the damp morning air. What if he stayed? Married Ella, raised these children, and had a few more?

They'd all starve, that's what. The only way to keep them alive was for him to return to Boston and an existence he loathed.

The door opened, and Cal stepped out. The boy looked as if he hadn't slept a wink. *Good.* He needed to learn that actions had consequences. Always.

Cal joined him at the porch rail, and together they watched the mist disappear.

"Where did you get them?" Seth asked.

"I didn't buy candy yesterday—'cept for Delia."

"Hmm." Seth had paid for his own torture. He couldn't fault the boy's cleverness. "You lied to me."

"Yes, sir."

"I understand that you want me off your place. I'd feel the same way."

Cal glanced at Seth quickly from beneath his overgrown bangs. "You would?"

"Sure. You were handling things just fine without me. Then a stranger, and a Yankee to boot, shows up and starts taking over. Hard for a man to just sit back and let that go."

Out of the corner of his eye, Seth saw Cal straighten, throw his shoulders back, nod. He stifled a smile.

"So while I can understand what you did, even applaud it, I can't let the lying pass. When I leave, you'll be the man here again, and you have to set a good example. Honorable men don't lie or cheat."

"No, sir."

"I think a day digging holes in the field behind the apple tree ought to make you think twice about lying again, don't you?"

"Sure will."

Seth let his smile break free. "Have breakfast and get started, then."

Cal paused at the door. "I didn't mean to scare you with the firecrackers."

Seth's smile faded. "You heard?"

Cal hung his head, nodded. "When you came I only saw you as the enemy. You were alive and my father was dead. It made me mad."

"Me, too."

The boy shot him another quick glance. "I've seen our soldiers come back all pale and jumpy. But I never thought about Yanks havin' the same troubles."

"We do."

"I guess that would follow. Anyway, I'm sorry I did what I did."

Cal disappeared into the house. Seth felt as if he'd turned a corner, though he wasn't sure to where.

The weeks that followed were the happiest Ella could recall. Seth and Cal had come to an understanding. Not that they'd suddenly become pals and gone fishing, but Cal no longer plotted tricks and Seth no longer avoided him.

With the lessening of tension between the two "men" of the house, the other children relaxed, as well. Joshua followed Seth around like a newborn fawn after its mother, the girls climbed into his lap whenever he sat down, and Gaby continued to adore him. The baby had known from the beginning that Seth was someone special.

Ella found herself humming as she worked, dreaming simple dreams of a prosperous farm and children of her own. Several times while she watched Seth repairing the barn or the corral fence, she slipped into delicious fantasies of clandestine meetings and midnight kisses.

Seth had been with them for over five weeks, and Ella could barely recall what it had been like when he was not. She didn't want to contemplate what it would be like when he left.

"Let's all go on a picnic," Seth announced one heated Saturday afternoon.

The children jumped up and down, clamoring their agreement. Seth swept Delia, then Elizabeth into his arms, put one on each hip and twirled them round and round in a circle of sunshine. Their giggles punctuated his laughter, and Ella's heart filled with love. She turned away as tears sparked in her eyes.

He was no longer the enemy. He'd become something much more dangerous indeed.

"All right," she said briskly to hide her softer emotions. "I'll pack a basket. We'll eat by the creek. The children can go wading afterward."

Within the hour, all seven of them lounged beneath the shade of an ancient dogwood tree. Water gurgled over smooth stones and a lukewarm breeze stirred the branches above them. Contentment flowed through Ella's soul.

"I love it here," she murmured, watching the children stick their toes into the creek, then shriek with laughter.

"Me, too," Seth whispered as he rubbed Gaby's back. The baby was nearly asleep on the blanket between them.

Their eyes met. Ella leaned forward. So did he.

"Ella!" Cal shouted. "Delia fell in."

They pulled back with a guilty gasp. Ella glanced at the children. Cal had his hand on a dripping Delia's shoulder as he marched her toward them. No one stared at Ella in reproach. No one had seen anything amiss.

She looked at Seth. His eyes promised a repeat of their one-time embrace. Her body tingled in anticipation.

The next several minutes were spent undressing the little girl and hanging her clothes up to dry. Then she fell asleep beside her sister, wearing nothing but a damp shimmy. Elizabeth soon joined them. The boys chased tiny flitting fish through the shallows.

"I'm going to follow the creek aways," Seth said. "I won't be long."

Ella nodded, then lay down next to the girls.

A shadow passed over the sun. Had she fallen asleep?

Confused, Ella opened her eyes. The silhouette of a man blocked the light. At first she thought Seth had returned and she smiled in welcome. Then a second man joined the other and her smile froze.

"Howdy do, pretty lady."

Alarmed, Ella sat up. She blinked quickly to make the dancing stars of sunlight fade. When her vision cleared, she saw three men in a circle around her and the girls.

They were rough and dirty, desperate from all appearances. From the sound of the man's voice and the tattered remnants of their uniforms, they were desperate Yankees—either former soldiers who'd gone home to find nothing left for them there, or deserters fled south to pick over the dead. They were nothing she hadn't encountered before, many times.

Ella's hand crept to her pocket and her heart gave a painful thud. Of course, she'd never encountered any before without a gun.

She cursed the feminine impulse that had made her change to a more attractive dress before they left. Her derringer still rested in the pocket of her blue gown, which hung on a peg in her room.

Her gaze drifted to the creek. The boys were headed in their direction at a run. She shook her head, but that only served to make the intruders turn that way.

"Well, whatta we got here? More of ya. You just come on over and sit down next to yer ma."

"That's right," Ella said brightly. "Come sit by me."

The boys did as they were told, but they didn't look happy.

Ella cut a glance back to the creek, hoping, praying to see Seth return. Nothing was there but the wind across the water.

"We've come a long way," the first man said.

His companions appeared tongue tied or mute. Ella didn't care for the way that they stared.

"You must be hungry." Ella shoved the picnic basket forward with her toe. "Help yourself."

"Oh, we intend to." He grinned, exposing several gaps where teeth ought to be. "To more than the food."

Cal tensed at her side. Ella laid her hand on his arm. Nothing would be gained by fighting. Not only were these men desperate, they were armed. Or at least the one with the big mouth was.

The three fell on the remnants of the picnic like wild animals. Their smacking lips and magnificent belches awoke all the children but Gaby. Ella gathered them behind her and waited. Where on earth had Seth gone?

When they were done, the leader crooked his finger at her. "Come with me."

"I don't think that I will."

"Think again." He drew his pistol and pointed it at the baby. Ella leaped to her feet.

"Cal," she said, her eyes on the gun. "You keep everyone here, all right?"

He didn't answer. She glanced at him, but he was looking at the creek. She did, too. And nearly fainted with relief.

Seth had returned.

As the situation grew clear, Seth's fury became so great he could barely control his need to shoot all three of the men dead where they stood. But he wouldn't do so in front of the children—unless he had no choice.

He'd heard there were those who preyed on the South, believed it, too, but he was still shocked to see former Union soldiers behaving like pigs.

As if they sensed him, the three turned. The one with

the gun grabbed Ella and put the barrel against her forehead. Seth's fury boiled, but he forced himself to remain calm. One thing he'd learned in the war: emotion got people killed.

"Soldier, I hope you have a damned good reason for your behavior," Seth snapped.

The man blinked at Seth's tone. Perhaps used to following orders, he hesitated, but only for an instant. "I'm not a soldier no more."

Seth's lip curled. "Obviously."

The stranger's face darkened at the insult. "Who the hell are you?"

"Major Seth Torrance. And you're on my land."

"You don't sound like no Reb to me."

"There aren't any more Rebs. Or haven't you heard?"

"I've got me one right here," he sneered. "And a passel of little ones, too. They'll be Rebs until they die. They don't change just because a piece of paper says that they do."

Seth took a few steps closer, and the man pressed the gun more firmly against Ella's head. "Hold on there, *Major.* Drop them Colts."

Seth's eyes met Ella's. She was afraid, though not as terrified as one might expect. She'd been taking care of herself and the children for quite a while now. No doubt she'd met men like this before. He'd respected her strength and her courage from the first. Seeing her calm in the face of this danger only made Seth admire her more.

He reached for the buckle on his gun belt and Ella frowned. But Seth would never take any chances with her life.

He dropped the weapons, spread his hands wide. "Now what?"

"Now we take the lady off for a little private party, and you stay here with the brats."

"I don't think so."

"You don't get to think."

"But I just can't help myself. Gaby, wake up," he shouted.

His sharp, loud voice roused the baby from a sound slumber. As always, she woke up howling.

The sudden noise made all three men glance at the baby. The gun came away from Ella's head for an instant, and she slammed her elbow into her captor's belly. He released her.

Seth grabbed the gun and they struggled, but not for long. At West Point he'd learned to be honorable, dutiful, an officer. But in the war he'd learned something equally valuable. How to fight hand to hand and dirty.

Seth's knee hit the stranger's privates so hard he fell to the ground and appeared to choke on them.

A scream from the second man made Seth spin that way, only to find Elizabeth had bitten his ankle. Ella punched him square on the jaw and down he went. He didn't move. The third tried to run away and tripped. Cal and Joshua landed on his back and went to work.

Seth smiled. They made a pretty good team.

Nine

While Seth drove the ruffians into town, hogtied and gagged in the back of the wagon, Ella brought the children home. Fearing they'd be upset, crying, and unable to rest, she was surprised when they excitedly discussed the afternoon's activities like an adventure.

No one seemed the worse for their exploits. After taking baths and eating supper, they went to sleep without a quiver. Perhaps taking part in the downfall of what had frightened them had allowed the children to get past it more easily.

Such was not the case for Ella. She sat on the porch with the shotgun across her lap and trembled. She'd been terrified that something would happen to one of the children or to Seth.

The echo of a horse's hooves rambled down the lane ahead of the horse. Ella's hands tightened on the weapon until she saw the familiar outline of Seth's horse, her wagon, his head. She stood and waited for him to come to her.

After unhitching the animal and taking care of its needs, Seth joined Ella on the porch. "Everyone asleep?" he murmured.

"Yes. As soon as their heads hit the pillows, I think."

"Too much excitement."

"Absolutely."

Ella released her death grip on the gun. Her fingers ached with the force she had applied. She didn't know if she'd ever be able to leave the house again without it.

The leering face of the soldier flashed before her eyes; she felt again the chill of the pistol against her temple and shivered.

Then again, maybe she shouldn't.

"Are you all right, Ella?"

She glanced up to find Seth staring at her hands, which had somehow crept back to the gun and locked there. She snatched them away, then sighed. "I'm scared."

"You're never scared. Not even when that fool had the gun against your head. I've never met anyone braver than you, Gabriella Fontaine."

She laughed, and the sound was a bit crazed. "I'm only brave when I have a gun and I'm sure that I can win."

"Which just makes you smart, too."

Ella shook her head. "Seth, I was so scared this afternoon I thought my heart would burst out of my chest."

"Anyone would be with a pistol pressed to their head."

"I wasn't afraid for me, but for the children and—"

She hesitated. But the events of the day had convinced her of one thing. Somewhere along the line she'd fallen in love with the enemy.

When had that happened? Perhaps the first time he'd held Gaby and the baby had stopped crying, then fallen asleep against his broad, strong chest.

Then again, it could have been the morning he'd taught Joshua how to whittle, his soft, gentle voice and infinite patience a balm to the child's troubled heart. The sight of the boy's brilliant smile after he'd mastered the task had tugged at Ella's troubled heart, too.

Or had it been when he'd forgiven Cal without a qualm, punishing the child like a fond father, then letting the matter fade into the past?

Maybe she'd tumbled into love when he'd played hide-and-seek with the girls until the sun went down, then collapsed with them in a heap on the cool grass and showed them the stars.

It could *not* have been when he trembled in her arms, then kissed her until she forgot who she was, who he was, who they'd both once been.

The war had taught her many things, the chief of which guided her now. Life was too short to hide what she felt. Even if Seth left tomorrow, at least they would have tonight.

Ella looked into his face. "I was scared for you."

"Me?" He grinned. "You've been trying to get rid of me since I got here. Seems having a bunch of renegade Yankees shoot me would have worked right into your plans."

"Don't joke about such things."

His smile faded. "Hey." He came closer, put his fingertips to her chin, and lifted it so he could peer into her eyes. "You were really scared, weren't you?" His voice held a note of wonder. "For me?"

She stood, put the shotgun aside and went into his arms. "For you," she agreed. "Hold me, Seth. Make me forget them. Make me feel safe again."

She offered him her lips, and without hesitation he took them. The kiss was gentle at first, different from the one they had shared before, yet somehow the same.

He tasted like the night, midnight blue and cool. His arms strong at her back pressed her close, kept her safe. Images of him with no shirt and the smooth supple sheen of his skin in the moonlight made her want to touch him as she'd never touched any man before.

What she wanted was dangerous—as forbidden as he was. But nevertheless she wanted it. She might never have another chance to discover the secrets between a man and a woman. If she was to learn them, she would learn them with him.

Ella broke the kiss. His mouth followed hers—damp, seeking—then his eyes slowly opened. He touched her face. "You're the most amazing woman I've ever known."

She didn't know what to say to that. No one had ever called her amazing before. She was who she was—a product of centuries of women who had loved this land, their men, their children. She did what she had to do. But having Seth call her amazing made Ella feel amazing, too. Still she wanted to know what he saw in her that no one else ever had.

"Why?" she asked.

"Why are you amazing? Why aren't you? You work from sunup until sundown with no complaint. You've taken on the responsibility of someone else's children, and you love it. Love them. I wish . . ."

He stared over her head into the night. A wistful, yearning expression crossed his face.

"What do you wish?" she whispered, hoping against hope it would be what she wished for, too.

"Nothing. Never mind. You're just . . . special."

"Like you?" His startled, confused glance made her smile. "Everything you've said about me is the same of you. I think you're pretty amazing, too, Seth Torrance."

"For an enemy."

"For anyone."

Ella recalled when she'd seen every conversation, every encounter as a battle in her own personal war with him. But the war was no longer. The time had come for peace, love, and understanding.

Taking Seth's hand, Ella led him to the door. Together they climbed the stairs. At his room she stopped and he kissed her again. Sweetly, gently, a brush of his lips and he was gone.

"Good night," he murmured.

She took a deep breath and dived. "May I come in?"

He blinked. "Pardon me?"

"Your room. May I come in?"

"Why?"

"Why do you think, Seth?"

"Um, well, I, uh—"

It amused her to hear the smooth, in-charge Yankee major stutter. That she could do this to him with a mere kiss made her feel powerful, stronger just by being near him, and some of the pulsing, paralyzing fear that had consumed her all day faded.

She reached out, put her palm against his chest, and pushed him into the room. He stood there with his hands at his sides, clenching, unclenching, confused, uncertain.

Ella shut the door quietly, then propped a chair beneath the knob. "We don't want any surprise visitors."

He continued to stare at her as if she were a stranger. "This isn't a good idea, Ella."

"On the contrary," she murmured as she lit the lamp, "it's the best idea I've had in a long, long while."

She crossed the room quickly, lest he come up with more excuses to keep them from being together tonight. Her hands worked at the buttons of his shirt, needing to feel the warmth and strength of him beneath her palms. When at last she did, he groaned a surrender and kissed her, exploring her mouth as she explored his body.

But touching wasn't enough. She wanted to see in the flare of the lamplight what had enticed her beneath the moon. So she pulled her mouth away, shoved the shirt from his shoulders, and gazed at his smooth, sun-gilded skin sprinkled with fine, dark hair.

Curious, she twirled her finger around a curl, then spread her palms flat. A finger grazed a nipple, and the nub hardened beneath her touch. More curious still, she flicked both nipples with her thumbs, once, twice, again. Mumbling a curse that sounded like an endearment, he picked her up and carried her to the bed, then followed her down.

His fingers shook as he undressed her, but no more than hers shook as she undressed him. She had never been naked in front of a man—never been naked in front of anyone, in truth, not even herself. Such things were not done. In her world, women even bathed in their shimmies. However, being naked with Seth was not only arousing, but acceptable—more right than anything she had ever known.

His large, newly work-roughened hands caressed her belly. Then his fingertips stepped up each rib until they cupped her breasts. His thumbs flicked over her nipples, once, twice, again, and she understood why he had cursed. Instead she moaned, and when his dark head dipped and his heated mouth replaced his thumb she arched beneath him, then pulled him ever closer.

"We shouldn't."

His whisper against her skin made her shiver. She tangled her fingers in his hair and lifted his head so she could see his face.

"We should. Make love to me, Seth. Show me something good can happen after so much bad."

He stared into her eyes, and she saw love reflected there. Hers alone, or his as well? She wasn't sure, but it no longer mattered. She needed to be one with him in a way she'd never needed anything else.

He hesitated no longer, teaching her with gentle strokes and whispered endearments the joys of physical love. She smoldered, and when he probed at the source of the fire, she gasped. Their gazes held, as mouth against mouth, flesh against flesh, they found a perfect peace with the joining of their bodies.

The pain she'd expected for her first time was lost in a relief of the fiery ache. Having him inside of her eased the anguish in her soul. If her suspicion was correct and this was the only night they had, at least she'd held him as close as possible for a few moments in time.

A near unbearable tension built at her center whenever he left the shelter of her body. Then he was back, filling her so completely, so wonderfully she tried to hold him forever within by will alone. At last he pulsed deep inside and the pressure broke on wave after wave of sensation.

She stroked his hair and caressed his back while they trembled together. Having Seth there with her made the ever-present fear abate. Foolish. He wasn't going to stay. She couldn't depend on him to keep her safe forever. But for now it was nice to have someone to share the burden of the children, the house, the farm, herself.

Seth shifted, and she clutched him to her. "Don't go."

"I'm too heavy, Ella."

"No. No, you're not. Please, I want to have you near me for a little while longer."

He didn't answer, but he didn't move away, either. She held him and tried not to think of what would happen when he left first her body and then her life. But she couldn't stop those thoughts from coming; she was, above all else, a practical woman.

She would go on just as she always had. It wasn't as if she didn't have plenty to do, those who depended on her. Twenty years from now, she'd look back on this night fondly. But it wouldn't pain her as much as it did now. At least she hoped not.

Seth raised his head and stared into her face. When he brushed Ella's hair from her brow, she caught his hand and pulled it to her cheek, nuzzling his palm.

His eyes heated, and he stirred anew within her. She

moved her hips upward, desiring once again the closeness they had shared. He muttered her name, then rolled to the side where he lay staring at the ceiling.

For a moment she felt cold, alone, abandoned. Then his hand groped for hers and their fingers entwined.

What would it be like to have him with her for always?

Ten

Seth lay with Ella in his arms and understood that the home he'd been searching for was here. The thought of leaving her or any of the children made him physically ache. However, if he stayed, what would he do to support them?

The problem gnawed at him so deeply he couldn't sleep. Instead he stared at her beautiful face and contemplated the future. What if he married Ella and took her and the children to Boston?

Seth winced, and Ella shifted in his arms, murmuring and turning toward him with a sigh. Her hand lay above his heart. His chest tightened. He loved her so much. He wouldn't do that to her.

He could imagine the life she'd live in the North so soon after the war. Snubs, sneers, a deep down coldness that rivaled the winter air. She wouldn't be happy there, where she couldn't walk through the fields barefoot or spend her evenings on the porch gazing at the land she loved.

The thought of returning to Boston and spending his days making instruments meant to kill in a place full of loud noises and stifling air didn't appeal to Seth, either. Despite the money he'd make, all the things he could give them, he'd be miserable and so would they.

Honor and duty tugged him both to the North and to

the South. Confused, uncertain, Seth untangled himself from Ella's warm embrace and went to the window.

Dawn burst over the horizon, spreading orange, pink, and red fingers of light across the land. The apple tree on the far side of the field stretched, strong and full, toward the sun.

And suddenly he knew what he had to do.

Ella awoke in her own bed alone. Vaguely she recalled Seth carrying her there. She'd been sleepy, happy, content. He'd kissed her on the forehead and murmured—

"Good-bye?" She sat up, scowling.

Gaby's cries had Ella scrambling to get into her nightdress before one of the children walked in. Her mind still puzzling over the memory of Seth, she changed the baby and walked down the hall to his room.

The door was open. She could see his bed—empty. Her heart began to thud with fear. He'd touched her, loved her, then left her. She shouldn't be surprised. Had she truly expected Seth to stay?

From the ache in her chest, Ella guessed that she had. Still, she stepped into the room and checked his closet and the dresser drawers. Also empty. Her eyes burned with tears.

The sound of the other children moving about had her blinking the tears away. She would not let them see how Seth's desertion pained her. There would no doubt be tears once they knew he was gone, but none of them could be hers. At least not where anyone could see.

She hurried downstairs and fed Gaby before she raised the roof with her howls. The child was doing so much better—had been since Seth arrived. For him she drank her bottles and took her naps. She'd begun to gain weight as a baby should. Ella pushed aside the thought that Gaby would suffer the most without her favorite man in the house.

Thunder on the stairs made her straighten, pat her cheeks to ensure they were not damp, and force a cheery morning smile onto her face before the children streamed in for breakfast.

No one asked the inevitable question until they'd eaten and cleared the table. As the others filed outside to do their chores, then play, Cal hesitated. "Where's Seth?"

Ella turned away. Sooner or later she had to tell them, but right now she could barely breathe.

"Ella?" Cal stood at her elbow, concerned dark eyes intent on her face. "What's the matter?"

She hesitated again, sadness and guilt nearly overcoming her. If she hadn't been selfish, if she hadn't needed his strength, desired his touch, maybe he wouldn't have left. Or at least he would have stayed a little while longer. Ella swallowed the thickness in her throat and plunged ahead.

"He's gone, Cal."

Surprise replaced the confusion, immediately followed by anger. Ella braced herself to hear horrible insults hurled on Seth's lying, Yankee head.

"You're wrong!" he shouted. "He wouldn't leave without saying good-bye. He wouldn't leave at all. I don't believe you!"

Ella blinked. "I thought you wanted him to go?"

"Not anymore. He's not like everyone else."

"What's everyone else like?" He hunched his shoulders and looked away. "Tell me, Cal."

For an instant she didn't think he'd answer, then the words came tumbling out. "I loved my pa, but he was . . ." His voice trailed off as he struggled with a way to impart the truth, yet keep from being disloyal.

"Your father was who he was," Ella said gently.

Cal sighed, nodded. "He was a friend. He loved me. But he didn't try to make me a better person. He never punished me. He'd laugh when I acted up and pat me on the back."

Ella resisted the urge to roll her eyes. That sounded just like Henry Elliot. She found it interesting that Cal understood what he needed better than his own father had.

"But Seth . . ." Cal shrugged. "Even though he's a Yankee, he knows what's right and wrong, and he wanted me to know, too. I thought he'd live here and keep us safe for always. He'd marry you. Then you'd be our ma and he'd be our pa. We could stay here, and things would be the way they were before."

Ella put her hand on the boy's shoulder. "Nothing's ever going to be the way it was before, Cal. I'm sorry. Those days are gone."

"Mama always said that when morning comes things look brighter. And things were startin' to look brighter with Seth around. He came after the dark times. He's our morning, Ella."

She smiled at the poetry in a young boy's heart and tried to draw him to her. But he pulled away and ran upstairs. She let him go. What could she say?

Truth was truth and Seth was gone.

Exhaustion weighted Ella's shoulders and she leaned against the stove. Not only had she been selfish to welcome Seth's embrace, but foolish, too. What if she were with child?

A small sob escaped her lips—not of fear, but of joy. Seth's child would be a gift. A living, breathing memory of the one and only time she'd known love. She'd cherish the gift and care for the child as she'd care for the others in her charge.

Gaby, left too long in her basket on the table, began to wail. Ella ran the heels of her hands over her eyes to blot the tears. Before she could turn and get the baby, someone stepped through the door. Gaby immediately stopped crying and giggled.

Ella forgot to breathe. The baby never stopped crying like that unless—

She spun about. Seth held the little girl aloft, grinning at her as the sun through the kitchen window caught in her hair and turned it gold.

"Seth!" she cried, and he glanced at her.

"Morning."

Ella had to sit down. When that didn't help, she put her head on the table and forced herself to breathe.

"What's the matter?"

"I—I—I thought you were gone."

"I was. To town. I had things to do."

Ella laughed and the sound was a bit hysterical. "Things to do? Like what?"

"Send a few wires. Talk to a man."

Cal skidded into the room, took one look at Seth, and threw his arms around Seth's waist. "I knew it wasn't true. I knew it."

Seth's face creased in confusion. "What wasn't true?"

"Ella said you left us." Cal glared at her. "But she was wrong."

"Left you?" Seth echoed and frowned at her over the boy's head. "Why would you think that?"

"I woke up and—" Ella went silent and glanced at Cal.

"Cal." Seth brushed a hand over the child's unruly hair. "Run outside and round up your brother and sisters, please."

"Sure." Cal ran out, banging the door behind him.

Seth raised an eyebrow and waited for an explanation.

"You were gone," Ella blurted. "Your clothes, too. What was I supposed to think, Seth?"

"Not that I'd had my way with you and disappeared into the wilderness. What do you take me for, Ella?" He held up his hand, jiggling the baby with the other. "Don't answer that. I'm a no-account Yankee. A carpetbagger. The enemy. Will you ever trust me?"

"I want to. I'm sorry. But you have to admit, it looked bad. Where are your clothes?"

"In my suitcase."

"Aha!"

"In your room."

She blinked. "What?"

Sighing, Seth kissed Gaby and put her into the basket. Then he crossed the short distance between them and brushed the loose hair away from the nape of Ella's neck. She shivered at the memories his gentle touch invoked.

"I was hoping to hang them in your closet. After you marry me."

"Marry you? But—"

"I had to go to town and see a man about a wedding. I figured I'd be back before you woke up. But while I was there, folks kept stopping me on the street to thank me for bringing in those deserters. I hear they've been causing trouble up and down the border. People were downright cordial to me today. Not that they kissed me and welcomed me into their homes but—" He shrugged. "Maybe someday I might fit in. Anyway, I brought the pastor home with me. I hope you won't have me carting him back without earning his pay."

Ella opened her mouth, shut it again, frowned.

"Is that a no?"

"No. I mean—" She didn't know what she meant.

"I'm not doing this right." Seth got down on his knees, took her hand, kissed her palm. "I love you, Ella. Say you'll marry me. Today."

Still she hesitated. Marrying Seth was a dream come

true, but there were other people to consider besides herself.

His smiled faded. "Was I wrong in thinking that you love me, too?"

"Of course not. I do love you, Seth, but—"

"No buts. That's all that matters."

"No, it isn't. What about the children? This farm? My farm? Your life in Boston? Your job? All the other things that matter make my head spin."

"I've taken care of them. Don't worry. You always worry."

"Someone has to."

"From now on we'll worry together. And I have to admit, life might get rough."

She snorted. "Rougher than it's been?"

"Good point." His hand tightened on hers. "Maybe if we're together, rough won't seem so . . . rough. And in answer to your questions, the children will be ours. The two farms will become one. Like us." He winked and Ella blushed. "As for your other questions, I sent two wires this morning. One to my mother informing her I wasn't coming home."

"Oh, Seth, that's not the way to tell her."

He shrugged. "It's done now."

"You got a reply?"

"Yes. And here's where things get disagreeable. She disinherited me."

Ella gasped. "Because of us?"

"Because I refused to take my proper place in society." He grimaced. "I loathe society. I loathe Boston and the job she had planned and the wife she had picked out."

"Wife?" This was the first she'd heard of one.

He waved away her question and the wife as if they were no more important than a fly. "Her choice, not mine. I barely knew the woman."

"Oh, well, that explains it then."

He raised an eyebrow at her tone, but let the matter drop. Ella decided to do the same.

"I was raised to do my duty to my country and my family. I was confused and torn, until last night. My family is here. So is my home. I can't do the job my father did. Hell, I'm not sure I can do this one, either."

"Which job is that?"

"Do you know anything about apple orchards?"

"Apples?" Confused, Ella shrugged. "A bit."

"Good. Because the other wire I sent was to buy as many apple trees as I could get my hands on. I think they'll grow very well here, and there's going to be a demand for Southern fruit products now that the war's over."

"I thought you'd been disinherited. How will we pay for the apple trees?"

He grinned. "I do have a little money of my own. Soldiering doesn't pay much, but what it paid, I put aside. Enough to get us started. Then we work."

She'd once thought he wasn't a farmer and he never would be. Yet here he was becoming one. Of course, she'd thought she would never marry, never have children of her own.

Ella's heart fluttered with hope. Life would never again be the way it had once been. It would be better.

"Marry me?" he repeated.

"Please."

Ella put her hand in Seth's. Together they left the house, gathered their children, and promised forever beneath the apple tree.

And Cal was right. When morning came, everything did look brighter.

HER KILT-CLAD ROGUE

Julie Moffett

For the guys in the RFE/RL newsroom:
Oleh Zwadiuk
Kevin Foley (may you rest in peace
in that great newsroom in the sky)
Bob Lyle
Frank Csongos
Chris Champagne (production)

My gratitude to you all for teaching me the true
meaning of professionalism,
giving me solid writing advice, and, of course,
sharing the secret of a good lead.
You're the best!

One

Aberdour
Scottish Highlands
May 1790

The magnificence of spring in the Scottish Highlands splashed across the countryside, covering the meadows in a riotous patchwork of yellow, green, and purple. Genevieve Fitzsimmons peered curiously at the sight through the dusty carriage window, thinking Scotland didn't seem all that barbaric in the bright sunlight. But it wasn't the scenery that had her worried.

It was *him.*

She narrowed her eyes and squinted in the distance, waiting for the famed twin turrets of *Caisteal na Mara* or Castle by the Sea to appear. The castle would soon be her new home, at least temporarily. The idea both terrified and intrigued her. For years her grandfather had spun delightful and frightening tales about the legendary castle. Genevieve had learned that for centuries the castle inhabitants had been blessed with extraordinary fortune, but also plagued by treachery, betrayal, and murder.

Swallowing her nervousness, Genevieve huddled in one corner of the otherwise empty carriage, peering out the window and clinging desperately to the seat to keep her body from flinging about. The carriage rocked so badly, she was certain a spill was imminent. Her stomach dropped as the road wound around a steep hill, revealing a precipitous rocky cliff on one side. Daring a glance down the cliff, Genevieve could see waves crashing against a boulder-strewn beach. Seagulls screeched in the sky as they circled, almost as if crying out a warning to her.

The carriage continued its dangerous trek around the tor until suddenly the castle loomed ahead. It was truly a castle by the sea. Genevieve's breath caught in her throat at the sight of the imposing stone fortress. Surrounded by a thick, high wall on one side and the natural defense of the cliffs on the other, the only clearly visible edifices she could see were the jutting twin turret towers in the northeast and southeast corners.

The carriage unexpectedly hit a sizable bump and Genevieve rapped her head hard against the carriage top. Her hands trembled as she loosened the gray velvet ribbons that held her bonnet securely beneath her chin. Several strands of her flyaway brown hair had escaped from the clip. With a sigh, she tucked them back in. It wouldn't do to present herself in such a disheveled manner. She only hoped she would have time to refresh herself a bit before being summoned by her new employer.

At the thought of him, her stomach fluttered anxiously. Connor Douglas. She'd met him ten years ago at her home in Alnwick when he'd come with his father for most of the summer to work out a business arrangement with her grandfather. Not a woman at the estate had been able to keep her eyes off the shockingly handsome young man. Connor had charmed her within the first few minutes they spoke.

At the beginning they'd been cautious friends—an

odd match, indeed. A bold, Scottish Highlander and a shy, proper English girl. But as the sweet lazy days of summer passed, they'd surprisingly discovered they had many common interests. When he kissed her for the first time, she realized she'd fallen deeply in love. Months later, when she heard of his betrothal to a young Scottish noblewoman, she grieved for the loss of her first love and innocence. From that moment on, she put the memory of Connor Douglas behind her.

But Fate was oft cruel, and now she'd soon have to face him again. Only this time she was no longer so innocent and they wouldn't share the carefree days of summer. Instead, she'd be in his employ—governess to his eight-year-old son. It might have been wildly amusing had it not been true and happening to her.

Genevieve's stomach dived to her toes and back up again, whether from the violent sway of the carriage or the mere thought of seeing Connor again, she wasn't certain.

At last the carriage lurched to a stop and Genevieve peered anxiously out the window. They were about to cross a bridge leading to the imposing castle. She craned her neck, looking up at the impressive structure just as the driver pulled forward across the bridge and into the bumpy courtyard.

The carriage door opened and the grizzled driver held out his hand. "I hope the ride wasna too rough for ye, miss," he said with a rolling burr as she alighted. "Welcome to *Caisteal na Mara.*"

She wanted to drop to her knees and kiss the ground, thankful she was yet alive. But instead she smiled graciously. "I thank you, sir," she replied, placing her bonnet firmly back on her head and tying it under her chin.

A middle-aged woman with a starched apron and white cap on her hair appeared at the doorway to the castle. She waved her hand at Genevieve. "Miss Fitzsimmons?" she called out cheerfully.

Genevieve quickly moved toward her. "Yes. Are you Mrs. MacDougal?"

"Aye, I am," the housekeeper answered. She had a round, friendly face, and Genevieve liked her instantly. "I trust the journey wasna too difficult."

Genevieve resisted the urge to rub her aching bum. "Actually, we stayed last night in the village, so the trip this morning was quite brief." She couldn't help but stare up at the castle, feeling small in its shadow. "'Tis quite an impressive structure," she breathed.

"Aye, 'tis so," the housekeeper said proudly. "And we welcome ye warmly."

"Do you really?" Genevieve murmured.

The housekeeper must have heard her for she smiled. "Dinna fret, lass. Ye'll be treated fairly here. Although for many o' us, 'twas quite a surprise to hear Mr. Douglas had hired an Englishwoman. Sometimes I fear the world has gone mad, I do."

Genevieve didn't sense any hostility behind the words, but something in her tone seemed odd. "You don't approve?"

"'Tis no' my station to approve or disapprove. 'Tis simply unusual, that is. After all, 'twas the English who stole our land, forbid us to own a dirk and play the pipes. Yet here comes an English lassie ready to learn the young master. Canna blame me for thinking 'tis a bit odd."

Genevieve sighed. "I don't blame you. It's just that my family has been friends with the Douglases for years. Not to mention that the war ended forty-five years ago."

"No' around here, it didna," the woman said softly, but then smiled. "Come, ye must be quite weary. I'll show ye to your room." She stepped through the doorway.

Genevieve followed the woman into the castle. Although she thought it most unladylike, she couldn't help but gawk at the furnishings as they traipsed down a long, echoing hallway. Heavy, ornate, and expensive furniture lined the hall—elegant chairs with velvet cushions, beautiful wooden lowboys and sidebars. Candles flickered along the walls, lighting the dim corridor and held in place by gleaming golden sconces. Thick woven tapestries adorned the walls, accompanied by a few enormous oil paintings of important-looking people Genevieve presumed were past inhabitants of the castle.

A gorgeous tapestry depicting some fierce battle caught her eye, and she paused to study it. Barbarians half dressed in blue and green plaid skirts, stockings, and no shirts, swung swords and dirks in close proximity. She caught her breath as her eyes fell on one of the figures. Wild black hair, blazing blue eyes, and a bare muscular chest—the man had been frozen in time, his dirk clutched above his head in a fist, his face a mask of anger and violence. Her heart stumbled in her chest. He was the exact image of Connor Douglas.

"Genevieve Fitzsimmons!" a voice boomed out and Genevieve nearly jumped out of her shoes as she whirled around.

Malcom Douglas, the patriarch of the Douglas family, shuffled out from a room behind her, leaning heavily on an ornate wooden cane. His hair had gone white since she'd last seen him five years ago during a visit he'd made to Alnwick without Connor. His eyes still shone with a fierce intelligence and kindness. Upon seeing him, Mrs. MacDougal nodded and then disappeared down the corridor, leaving the two of them alone.

"Genevieve," he said, taking her hand and clasping it warmly with his gnarled fingers. "How fare ye, lass?"

For a moment he reminded her of her own beloved

grandfather, and a wave of grief hit her. Swallowing hard, she managed a smile.

"As well as can be expected under the circumstances."

Malcom nodded. "'Twas my great sadness that I couldn't attend Randall's funeral," he said, pointing ruefully at his leg. "My leg pains me so much, I didn't think 'twould take the agony o' such a long journey. I hope his end was peaceful, was it no'?"

Genevieve felt another stab of pain, his passing still too recent. "Thank you for inquiring. He died peacefully in his sleep. He indeed lived a happy and fulfilling life. I can't thank you enough for offering me the position here. Grandfather's debts were quite unexpected."

She saw pity and sadness in his eyes. "Our business was no' as profitable as we had hoped," he said with a sigh. "I didna know he had invested everything in our venture, or I would have warned him otherwise."

"I'm not certain it would have made a difference," Genevieve said. "Grandfather could be quite stubborn sometimes."

Malcom looked away, but not before Genevieve saw a flash of grief cross his face. Despite their vastly different backgrounds, the men had been close friends. "He was a good man," he said softly.

Another stab of pain to her heart. "Yes, he was." They fell silent a moment before Genevieve spoke up again. "I wanted to let you know that I'm honored you feel me qualified to serve in your household. I am well educated in all subjects, including letters, sums, geography and literature. I can—"

Malcom cut her off with a wave of his hand. "Genevieve, lass, I have no doubts as to your abilities. Ye have impressed me more than once wi' your keen wit. But I should mention that *Caisteal na Mara* is no longer *my* household. Connor now rules the household here, wi' what some o' us fondly refer to as an iron fist. And just 'tween us, he is welcome to it. My days as a laird are thankfully o'er and 'twas my great pleasure to pass it into such capable hands. But I know he's glad to have ye here, too, lass. He thinks quite fondly o' ye."

Unbidden, heat rushed to her cheeks, and she hated herself for the show of emotion. "I'm not at all certain he'll even remember me," she said quickly.

"Och, but he does think kindly o' ye, lass. I assure ye, he does."

Inadvertently her gaze strayed back to the painting and the brutish man with the dirk. Malcom followed her gaze.

"'Tis Gavin Douglas, one of the Douglases who once lived in this castle," he explained. "A fierce man, he was, and sadly no' one o' much honor. Instead o' siding wi' his clansmen in the fight against the English in the fifteenth century, he instead allied himself wi' the crown against his own kind. At first, he acquired himself much o' the forfeited Douglas property and became a mighty rich man. But he sold his soul to the devil to acquire it. When he was but thirty-seven years old, one o' the few surviving Douglases hunted him down. Hanged him from the very bridge ye crossed coming into this castle. Gavin had no legitimate male heirs, so 'twas his bastard who eventually avenged him, bringing the castle back under our control again. Black Gavin is our direct ancestor. Looks a wee bit like Connor now, doesna he?"

Appalled by the story and yet nonetheless fascinated, Genevieve could only nod, although she thought Black Gavin looked more than just a *wee* bit like Connor.

"I can see I have a lot to learn about the Douglas family," she said.

He laughed. "Aye, and ye will. I'm verra glad to have ye here, lass. I canno' think o' anyone more qualified to help Connor. A sensible and sturdy lass is just what he needs to help him teach his son properly."

Genevieve tried not to wince at his rather unflattering description of her. "I am sorry to hear about the death of Connor's wife. It must be a very difficult time for all of you."

Malcom cast his eyes down. "I'll admit it has no' been the best o' times for us. The hearsay has been especially difficult for Connor."

Genevieve blinked. "Hearsay?"

"Surely ye know o' what I speak. All o' Scotland has heard the gossip."

"Need I remind you that I'm from England?" she said pointedly. "Besides, Grandfather and I haven't heard from you in months. I truly don't know of what you speak."

Malcom studied her face and then sighed when he realized she was telling the truth. "Ye dinna know then. Well, I might as well be the one to tell ye. Connor was accused o' killing Janet."

Genevieve took a step back, stunned. "Killing her?" she stammered.

Malcom harrumphed. "'Twas naught but idle talk. Truth is she threw herself out o' the tower window in a moment o' madness. Left him alone and wi' a young lad to raise, she did, the foolish lass."

Genevieve simply stared at him in horror. She'd simply assumed that Connor's wife had died of natural causes.

"Suicide?" she stammered. "Why?"

Malcom shrugged. "Who really knows except the woman herself? I've no wish to speak ill o' the dead, but Janet was no' right in her head, I'd say."

"That's simply dreadful. I'm sorry for your loss."

"'Tis been the most difficult for the lad."

"Understandably so."

Malcom ran a hand across his brow and she noticed it trembled slightly. "I willna lie to ye, Genevieve. Ewan is a strong-willed lad. We've no' been able to keep a governess here for more than a few weeks. But I'm certain your presence here will change all that."

Genevieve felt a flutter of worry. "I'll certainly do what I can to help. When will I have the opportunity to meet Ewan?"

"At supper. I do hope ye'll join us."

"I'd be delighted," Genevieve said, although she wanted nothing more than to lie in her bed and take time to absorb all the unsettling things he'd just told her.

"Well then, I'll just deliver ye into Mrs. MacDougal's verra capable hands," he said bowing slightly.

As if by magic, the kindly housekeeper suddenly appeared. After parting ways with the elder Douglas, Genevieve dutifully followed the portly woman up a wide set of stone stairs and down a long, dim hallway before she stopped in front of a wooden door.

"This is your room," the housekeeper said, opening the door. "It attaches to the schoolroom. Ewan's room is on the other side."

Genevieve stepped inside, surprised by what she saw. She'd assumed she would be relegated to a small and functional room. She couldn't have been more wrong.

This chamber was huge and bright, with three leaded windows above padded window seats flanked by dark blue velvet drapes. A large hearth took up nearly one side of the room, and someone had thoughtfully lit the fire. A cheery blaze now emanated warmth. A big, comfortable-looking canopied bed occupied the center of the room, covered with a heavy quilt of blue and white stripes. Strategically positioned near the fire was a leather armchair and next to it sat a small side table.

Against another wall sat a tall wooden wardrobe, in front of which her three valises already sat. Next to that was an elaborately carved lowboy, which held a chamber pot, a pitcher of water, a few folded linen cloths, and a small round looking glass.

The walls were covered with small tapestries. But instead of depicting battle scenes as the ones downstairs had, these showed young women frolicking happily in a garden. All in all, it was a very elegant and comfortable room.

"It's a lovely chamber," Genevieve breathed.

Mrs. MacDougal beamed, pointing to a door beside the hearth. "I'll send up Lucinda to help ye unpack your valises if ye'd like, miss."

"No, thank you," Genevieve said. "I'm quite capable of doing that myself."

"As ye wish. Supper is promptly at five o'clock. I'll have someone fetch you."

"I'd appreciate that."

After Mrs. MacDougal left, Genevieve removed her bonnet, left her valises where they were, and, curious, went to examine the schoolroom. Carefully she opened the door and stepped across the threshold, her gaze sweeping approvingly across the three small desks, the comfortable window seats, and a long trundle table covered with numerous scratches and errant splashes of ink. She spied a child's reader, a sum book, and an exercise book. She picked up the third one and examined Ewan's handwriting skills. Clearly the boy needed much work in this area.

"Are ye the new governess?"

Genevieve nearly dropped the book, she was so startled. Turning around, she saw a young boy with a mop of unruly black hair and piercing blue eyes. He was rather tall and thin, she thought, and at this moment, completely filthy.

She set the exercise book down. "Hello. My name is Genevieve Fitzsimmons. You must be Ewan."

His eyes widened in surprise. "Ye're English," he said before his lips curled in distaste. "No one told me the new governess was goin' to be English."

Genevieve swallowed her irritation that no one had thought it necessary to prepare the boy. She smiled, despite sensing a brewing problem. "Did you know our families have been friends for many years?"

He snorted, clearly unimpressed. "I'm no' goin' to be learned by an Englishwoman. Why do ye think I'd care to learn anything the English have to teach me?"

Genevieve was stunned by the hatred in the boy's voice. Taken aback, she searched for calm words. "Because I am quite proficient in reading, sums, and handwriting, among other things. And from what I just saw in your primer, it looks like the last is an area where we have much work to do."

He stared at her for a moment longer and then shrugged. "Doesna matter what ye say, ye'll no' be here for long. I've already decided I dinna like ye."

With those words, he strode across the schoolroom into his room and slammed the door shut behind him. For a moment, she could only stare, shocked by his ill manners. Was he truly going to be her charge?

Anger mingled with fear. What would happen to her if she failed? What if Connor dismissed her for being unable to manage his son? Where would she go? Her carefully laid plans for building a reputation as a reliable governess would be ruined. Somehow, in the blink of a moment, her entire future seemed to rest on this one difficult child.

Sighing, she returned to her own room, exhaustion from her journey starting to overcome her. She would rest a bit, unpack, and then prepare herself for supper. It seemed she would need more strength than expected to handle this young Scottish boy.

Genevieve had rested little more than an hour when a young servant named Lucinda unexpectedly awakened her.

"I'm sorry, miss," the young woman said as Genevieve opened the door. "But the master has requested your presence in the library at once."

Genevieve wasn't anywhere near prepared to meet Connor, either mentally or physically. But the girl stood in the corridor, looking at her expectantly and nervously enough that Genevieve got the distinct impression one did not simply say no to Connor Douglas. What was it Malcom had said about Connor running the castle with an iron fist?

Sighing, Genevieve quickly smoothed down her skirts and ran a comb through her unruly brown hair. She might have taken a few moments to rebraid it, but Lucinda hovered anxiously by the door, her body language clearly indicating that Genevieve should not tarry long.

Genevieve swallowed her irritation. Had Connor not the decency to permit her a suitable period of respite from her journey? What could be so important that he could not wait to see her until supper?

The hand holding the brush faltered and then stopped completely in mid stroke. What if Ewan had already gone to his father to complain of her? A sense of dread crept over her. Would her position here be over before it had even started? If it was, what would she do, and where would she go? Pressing her lips tightly together, she yanked her hair back and pinned it loose at the nape of her neck. At this point, the condition of her hair and gown was the least of her worries.

"I'm ready," she said as calmly as she could manage.

"This way, miss," the girl said, practically running down the hallway.

Genevieve lifted her skirts and hastened after her. Her heart was pounding hard, whether from the anticipation of meeting Connor again or from the exertion of keeping up with the young girl, she did not know. She wondered what she would do if he decided her unsuitable on the spot, and then dismissed the thought, believing that even *he* would have to give her an opportunity to prove herself.

Lifting her chin, she strode forward, stopping as Lucinda lifted her hand and knocked on the wooden door.

"Enter," came the deep voice from behind the door.

Lucinda pushed open the door, but did not cross the threshold. Instead she motioned with her head that Genevieve was to enter. Calmly, she entered the room, trying not to wince as Lucinda shut the door so quickly it rapped her on the bum.

Connor sat behind a desk, examining what appeared to be a ledger. Her first impression was that ten years had changed him little. He was still as breathtakingly handsome as she remembered, his presence somehow imposing even from a sitting position. When he looked up, she noticed at once that his long, thick hair remained as black as the night and his eyes the same piercing blue. His face had matured into hard angles and lines, and yet was softened by what she could only call a careless, dangerous sensuality. He wore a dark brown waistcoat atop a crisp white linen shirt, but his neckcloth had been removed and his throat was bare. Tension hummed in the air as his cool, aloof gaze raked over her.

"Miss Fitzsimmons," he said, rising from his chair and addressing her formally. The intimacy of many summers past was clearly gone, not that she had expected otherwise. Still, the politeness in his voice hurt.

"'Tis my great fortune to once again have the pleasure o' your company," he continued. "It has been some time since we last met. Ten years if I recall correctly."

If he recalled correctly. The cad.

She, on the other hand, remembered every detail of their last time together—the golden moon, the way the warm summer breeze blew through his dark devil hair as he leaned down to kiss her. The memory rushed at her now like a fire through her mind, spreading quickly and sending a blazing heat through her veins.

"Miss Fitzsimmons?"

His voice was still as deep and rich as ever, tempered only by the peculiar and sensual roll of his words in his soft Scottish burr. Even now her senses tingled.

"Yes? I . . . I am here," she said finally managing to find her voice and then feeling like a child for stating the obvious.

He said nothing, but walked toward her, almost sleekly, as if he were a big cat stretching his long limbs. He was far taller than she remembered, his presence seeming too daunting for the small confines of the room. It seemed unfair that age had not made him any less attractive, but instead had deepened his allure, casting his eyes with dark and knowing shadows and providing small and interesting lines around his mouth. For a moment she simply stared at him in disbelief, unable to accept the irony that God had created such a magnificent specimen in the form of a Scotsman.

"Come in, please," he urged again, this time his voice softening. "No need to linger by the door. I willna bite. No' much, anyway."

She saw a flicker of amusement in his eyes. Pride made her lift her chin high and confidently stride into the room.

"I'm not lingering," she said crisply. "You wished to see me?"

His mouth curved into a smile. "I did. It's good to see ye again. Ye're all . . . well, grown up."

His gaze swept across her quickly and Genevieve tried not to flinch, knowing he looked at her only to remind himself of her glaring faults. She stiffened when his perusal lingered on her hastily combed hair, her wrinkled gown, and her plain, ordinary features. He, of course, would know her grandfather had provided a lavish Season for her in London and that she had turned down her one and only suitor. He would now remind himself the reasons why no man, except for him during a summer amusement, had ever sent her more than a passing glance.

Nevertheless, pride kept Genevieve standing sternly. She kept her chin raised high, refusing to let him unnerve her further.

"I'm sorry to hear about your grandda," he finally said, surprising her with the genuine sincerity in his voice. "He was an honorable man wi' an even hand and a keen sense o' business. He was a good friend to my family, and I liked him as well."

"Thank you," Genevieve said her voice catching slightly.

"I heard ye had to sell the estate to pay off his debts. I'm sorry to hear that as well. 'Twas a fine house ye had in Alnwick."

She felt an unnerving flush of guilt, knowing she could have saved the estate had she accepted old Herbert Young's offer of marriage. She felt a lump rise in her throat. "Yes, it was a beautiful home."

His gaze softened. "I'm sorry about your misfortune, but I am grateful that ye've accepted our request to come here." He straightened and pulled out a chair for her. "Please, have a seat. I'd like to talk to ye about my son."

Genevieve complied, and as she swept past him, they brushed arms. She jerked back as if she'd been burned, heat streaking all the way up her arm and down to her toes. Horrified, she dared a glance at him and saw he looked at her intently. Ignoring him, she perched on the chair and waited. After a moment, he walked around the desk and sat down, the leather of his chair creaking as he lowered himself into it.

"Had ye the opportunity to meet Ewan yet?" he asked.

"I have," Genevieve said, relieved that at least the boy hadn't yet come running to his father complaining of her.

"And what did ye think o' him?"

"We had a brief and informal introduction," she said carefully. "He seems rather . . . strong willed."

Connor laughed. "'Tis kind o' ye to say it that way. The truth is the lad is in need o' proper instruction in the ways o' manners and learning. I'm oft away and need someone that I can trust to see to him."

Trust? She thought that an odd choice of words, coming from a man who had so carelessly treated her feelings. "He seemed rather shocked that I am English," she said dryly.

He looked amused, but not surprised. "Well, is he, now? The lad hasna ever met an Englishwoman. 'Twill be a good experience for him, then."

"In what way do you mean?"

"I mean, that the English seem to have a way with . . . well, subjugation."

Genevieve bristled. "I find that remark quite improper."

He laughed, revealing a row of gleaming white teeth. "Now that's the lass I remember—all prickly and proper. Do ye remember how many times ye berated me for what ye called my 'insolent' humor?"

She did remember, and even now could picture him needling her just to see her frown. And after he'd manage to coax a rise out her, he'd very ably kiss away that disapproval from her lips.

"You need not remind me," she said looking away. "And I'm not prickly."

He laughed again, a deep, rich sound. "If I offended ye, I offer my sincere apology. I meant only to suggest that ye are quite capable of handling a firebrand such as Ewan. I'll be the first to admit the lad is no' easy to manage."

"Ewan is just a child."

"A very willful and disobedient child."

"No doubt aggravated by the sudden loss of his mother."

Connor paused and then sighed. "Aye, it has been difficult for him."

"And for you?" She had no idea how that slipped out of her mouth. Mortified, she clamped her lips together and wished the floor would swallow her whole.

He looked away. "A lad needs his mother," he said softly. Surprised, Genevieve heard no trace of sorrow or regret in his voice.

"I've been told what happened," she said tentatively. "I'm sorry."

He waved a hand dismissively. " 'Tis a matter that is over. Ewan is the one who concerns me."

Genevieve nodded, understanding that the matter was now closed. "Have you no system of discipline in place for the boy?"

He shrugged. "Since I'm no' around much, I'm no' always able to provide a firm or consistent hand. He minds me well enough when I am here. But 'tis no' enough. That's why we hired ye. Consistency and firmness. Qualities I've seen for myself that ye possess."

Not exactly the words every woman wanted to hear, but it indicated he had faith in her. Given her present circumstances, that, above all, was important.

"Thank you. But discipline is only a small part of instruction. What about his letters and sums?"

"Aye, that, too, is most important. The other governesses report that the boy is a bit dim-witted. As a result, I fear 'twill be most difficult to encourage him to attend to his studies in the first place."

She thought about this for a moment. "Will you then support my efforts to impose some sort of organized discipline with him?"

He raised a dark eyebrow. "Organized discipline?"

"Punishment. Withdrawal of privileges, confinement to his room, and so on."

"Does this include floggings?"

Genevieve gasped. "Certainly not."

Again amusement flashed in his eyes. "Why no'?"

"Because it won't be necessary."

"Ye dinna know Ewan verra well."

"It doesn't matter how well I know him. I will not whip any child."

"Ye seem certain about a great many things."

"Well, I'm quite positive about that."

His mouth curved into a smile so dazzling she felt warm from it. "Then ye have my full support, o' course."

"I'm grateful for that," she said. Perhaps this wouldn't be as difficult as she had anticipated. Now the question that she wanted, no, *needed* to hear the answer to.

"May I be so bold as to inquire why you requested me?" she asked. "Given your position and status, certainly you had many more . . . let's say . . . *suitable* choices."

He seemed surprised by the question and leaned back, threading his long, tapered fingers together and looking at her thoughtfully. "Only if I may first ask why ye chose to become a governess. 'Twas no' your only choice. I heard ye turned down a suitor."

So he *had* heard. Her cheeks flamed. "I . . . I thought it best at the time." Of course, she hadn't known then that the old man would be the only person to ask for her hand. "Nevertheless, I enjoy learning, so given my present circumstances, the post of governess seemed a proper, even enjoyable choice for me. Your offer came at just the right time." Of course, it had been her *only* offer under very dire circumstances, but he didn't need to know that.

Again his gaze raked over her and she felt her face grow warmer. But to her great relief, he said nothing more.

"Well, because ye asked, I'll tell ye why I invited ye here to assume the post o' governess. I remember ye as an able young lass with a discerning eye, quick wit, and easy smile. Ye challenged me, and I liked that. Now, I hope ye'll do the same for my son."

An able young lass. So that's how he remembered her.

She didn't know why his words should hurt, but they did. Of course, just because that summer with him had been the most incredible, sensual, wonderful experience of her life didn't mean that it had been of the slightest importance to a man like Connor Douglas. He'd likely created dozens of similar memories for many more naive, unsuspecting women like her. She had been nothing to him but a pleasant summer diversion. She'd likely been invited here to Scotland because Connor's father had heard of her plight and took pity on her. Connor, desperate for any help to manage his unwieldy son, had agreed. As a result, she would do best to perform her duties adequately and move on as soon as possible.

"Well, I appreciate your frankness," she said, a strange

tight feeling constricting her chest. "I shall endeavor to fully meet your expectations."

"I appreciate that," he said lightly. "Ye are quite the responsible lass."

Responsible lass. Able lass. Prickly and proper.

God's mercy, her pride could not take much more. Standing, she decided to end the conversation before she humiliated herself any further. "Well, if that will be all, Mr. Douglas . . ."

He rose as well, and again the elegance of his movements reminded her of a sleek, predatory animal. "Before ye leave, I would request a favor o' ye," he said.

Genevieve felt a flicker of apprehension. "And what might that be?"

He graced her with one of his bone-melting smiles, and for a moment the years faded away and she saw the young man with whom she'd fallen in love. "I'd ask that ye address me by my Christian name when we are in private," he said. The request came easily and without embarrassment, as if he asked women to do this all the time. "And I would ask your permission to do the same. 'Twas how we were wi' each other the last time we were together, and somehow it feels unnatural to be so formal when it is just the two o' us . . . alone."

He paused as if remembering something. For a breathtaking moment, Genevieve thought he might say something about the last night they had been together, sitting under the big oak tree behind her grandfather's stables, gazing up at a glittering array of stars. That night he had told her she was beautiful, and she had believed him. He had kissed her tenderly and passionately, all the while murmuring sweet words of endearment in Gaelic in his soft Scottish burr. She had been so in love with him.

"Well, what say ye . . . Genevieve?" he asked softly.

Her heart stumbled . . . weakened. The way her name rolled off his tongue in his deep, sensual voice stirred up memories she had long ago buried. He'd always been able to do that, to say her name in a way that made it seem as though she were the most cherished person in the world.

"I suppose there is no harm in that," she said, surprising herself as the words slipped from her lips. God's mercy, what had happened to her resolve to keep a proper distance from him?

The corners of his slowly mouth turned up. "I'd hoped ye'd agree," he said softly.

She thought to leave, but he came around the desk and unexpectedly took her hands in his. A quiver surged through her veins at his touch, an immediate, instinctive response.

His expression softened. "There is yet one more matter to discuss 'tween us," he said quietly. "A matter of an apology."

Emotion clutched at Genevieve's heart and squeezed. "An apology for what?"

He shifted uneasily on his feet. "For leaving Alnwick as I did ten years ago. For no' saying good-bye. For no' telling ye how much that summer meant to me."

"That summer took place a long time ago, and I've long considered it completely forgotten," she said stiffly. It was unquestionably the most bold-faced lie she had ever told, and she amazed herself by the sheer audacity of it.

"I didna forget it, nor have I forgotten ye," he said softly.

She laughed, mostly in self-defense. "We were young and foolish," she said lightly. "It was a pleasant enough time, I suppose, but a mistake nonetheless."

He frowned, his dark brows knitting together. "'Twas no' a mistake. I didna regret it then, and I still dinna."

To Genevieve's shock, all the hurt and anger arose afresh in her throat, as raw and painful as if that summer had happened last night.

"Of course, you don't regret it," she said, shrugging. "After all, a man of your reputation must be quite well versed in stealing kisses and heated embraces from young ladies in the moonlight."

For a moment, she saw a flash of anger in his eyes, and then it disappeared. "Were they truly stolen kisses, Genevieve?"

A well-aimed barb directed at her heart . . . and her pride. "Perhaps not," she reluctantly admitted. "Although now you likely expect me to say how impressed I was by your admirable restraint in taking it no further."

"'Twas admirable restraint," he growled, so softly that had she not been standing so close to him she wouldn't have heard it.

Her emotions torn asunder and feeling ridiculously close to tears, she pulled her hands from his and took a step back toward the door. Connor made no move to stop her.

"Well, if that will finally be all, I shall take my leave and return to my duties," she said, devastated that after all these years he still had the power to hurt her.

"That will be all," he said quietly.

Without another word Genevieve left him, feeling deeply unsettled by the turn of their conversation. While she always thought she deserved an apology from him, now that she had it, it sat heavy on her heart.

When she reached her room, she immediately went to the small basin of water on the lowboy and dipped a linen cloth into it, applying it to her heated cheeks. Seeing Connor again had been more difficult than she had expected. Life here at *Caisteal na Mara* would be challenging, perhaps even dangerous, in ways that she had never anticipated.

Especially for her heart.

Two

As soon as Genevieve left the library, Connor turned and slammed his fist against the mantel. A vase tumbled to the floor and shattered into a dozen pieces. Furious at himself for mishandling his first encounter with her, he kicked a jagged piece of the vase with his boot, feeling a savage rush of satisfaction when it slammed into the stone hearth and disintegrated into mostly dust.

He had never expected it from her—not from his sweet Genevieve. She had been so cool, so aloof. He had been certain that she would still harbor at least *some* feeling for him, but he couldn't have been more wrong. She had looked at him with such disdain, such derision, that his heart squeezed in pain.

"Hell and damnation," he swore, stalking over to the highboy and yanking out a bottle of whiskey. He poured himself a generous helping and then took a long, steadying swallow.

Women were going to be the death of him.

How could he have been so utterly wrong about her reaction? He'd been prepared if she had said she'd been angry at his abrupt departure ten years earlier. He'd been ready to hear how much of a cad he'd been to hurt her so. But she had simply acted as if what had happened between them that summer hadn't mattered one whit. He hadn't been prepared for that.

It was a pleasurable enough time, she had said.

"A pleasurable enough time?" he said aloud, his ire rising. "What the devil is that supposed to mean?"

Her reaction changed everything now. His plans, his thoughts, his dreams. He'd never imagined that he would have to win her back. Not the one woman who knew him better than he knew himself. Not the woman who had once told him that she loved him.

The anger dissipated and he sank into his chair, the whiskey glass still in his hand. He rested a finger atop the rim and circled, reconsidering his approach. Perhaps he'd been wrong about their summer together. She had been young, sixteen, and perhaps he'd only imagined they were soul mates. Or mayhap he'd only wished for them to be so exceedingly like-minded that he could forget about what lay ahead for him.

He'd expected anger, hurt, and disbelief from her, but never disinterest and disdain. It utterly baffled him.

When he looked back to that summer, he'd be the first to admit he'd been selfish. He should have told her about his betrothal. But once he'd fallen for her, he didn't dare. He'd wanted their time together to last for as long as it could. And then it had been over all too soon. He hadn't even been able to say good-bye.

God, how he had missed her all these years. His little English sprite. When she'd walked into the room today, he felt his throat close, his breath quicken. She looked nearly the same as she had that summer ten years ago, with her impossible-to-tame brown hair, wide mouth quick to smile and short, pert nose. Her brown eyes held the same intelligence and wit that he remembered, only now they held a hint of refinement, maturity, and coolness.

Perhaps they had both grown up too much to still be meant for each other.

He sighed. His plan had gone badly awry. The longer

she stayed at the castle, the more she would learn about him, and the further away she would slip from his reach. Once again he'd acted selfishly and brought her here in his employ—but the timing had been right, and he had so longed to see her again. Besides, he feared if she had disappeared to London as a governess, he might never see her again. But pairing her with Ewan could result in disaster. It had been a calculated risk, but one he'd decided to take.

Her coolness now forced him to reconsider. But he had to try. He'd be damned if he'd just let her slip away again.

Except he knew that if she left of her own volition, there would be little else he could do.

Genevieve decided to spend some quiet time alone in her room before supper. She needed time to settle her nerves and regain her composure. She intended to look calm and refreshed, the way a proper governess should appear, not shaken and unsettled like an untried girl of sixteen.

Resolutely, she took her time, changing into a clean chemise and stockings and brushing her brown hair until it gleamed. So as to not crease her gown before supper, she pulled on a light dressing gown and sat in the padded window seat, looking out at the castle grounds. Her room had a splendid view of the front courtyard, the gardens, and an old stone gatehouse that apparently had once protected the entrance to the castle.

She shifted on the seat to get a better view of the gardens. They were beautiful and well-kept, and a warm spring had caused many of the flowers and shrubs to thrive, creating a lovely display of red, yellow, and purple. Thinking of the flowers made her miss her own garden in Alnwick, and for a moment, her heart ached to be at home among familiar people and blooms. But that life was no more. With a sad sigh, she hoped the new owner of her home would tend to the garden with the same loving care she and her grandfather once had.

A knock at the door startled her and she rose, clutching the dressing gown tighter to her chest.

"Who is it?" she called out.

"'Tis just me. Mrs. MacDougal."

Genevieve quickly crossed the room and opened the door. The kindly housekeeper stood balancing a tray with tea in one hand. "I thought ye might be in need o' a warm drink before supper," she said.

"How very thoughtful of you," Genevieve said, holding the door open.

The middle-aged housekeeper entered, placing the tray on the table next to the armchair. She gave Genevieve a smile. "Well, if that will be all, miss . . ."

"Would you like to stay and have a cup with me?" Genevieve asked. "I mean, that is, if you have the time to indulge me."

The housekeeper looked flattered at the suggestion. "Me? Are ye certain?"

"I could use the company," Genevieve admitted. "I do I feel a bit homesick at the moment."

"Well then, I suppose in the interest o' providing a bit o' comfort for a new arrival, I could join ye for a few minutes," the housekeeper said and went off to fetch another teacup. She soon returned carrying not only a cup, but a small plate of sweet biscuits and, to Genevieve's surprise, a bottle of spirits.

"I dinna normally take a nip so early in the afternoon, but seeing as how ye are a wee bit homesick, I canna see how a small splash would hurt." She poured the tea and then added a more-than-generous dollop of the spirits to each cup.

Genevieve took a sip, the liquid searing a fiery trail down her throat. The housekeeper drank the tea without incident, making Genevieve wonder just how often she engaged in these afternoon nips.

"I thank you for indulging me," Genevieve said. "You've made me feel quite welcome."

"Now isn't that sweet o' ye to say so? A good heart ye have, even if ye are English."

"A sentiment I hope many others here will share."

The housekeeper clucked her tongue. "Dinna ye fash yourself. No one at this castle would hold ye personally accountable for the actions o' the English. Besides, 'tis well known that the elder Mr. Douglas was quite fond of yer grandda. They were friends for a long time, were they no'?"

"Yes, they were. They were fortunate that their mutual interests in trade bridged the more obvious divisions of politics."

"How did they meet?"

"It's quite an odd story, actually. Mr. Douglas needed a place to sell his lumber, and my grandfather was more than happy to sell it to the shipyards in southern England. Our mutual locations near the sea made it convenient to transport the wood." She took another sip of the tea and this time, it went down smoothly. "Looking back, I think my grandfather's biggest mistake was not investing in a wider variety of goods. Fortunately, the Douglases did not make the same error."

The housekeeper cradled the cup and saucer in her lap. "Well, it may be a wee bold o' me to say, but 'twas a bit o' a surprise when Connor told the staff that he'd invited ye here."

"Connor invited me?" Genevieve said in surprise, and

then blushed when she realized she had inadvertently used his Christian name. It was one thing for the housekeeper, who had probably known Connor since he was an infant, to call him that, but it was utterly improper for the new governess to address him as such. Trying to cover her mortifying slip, she hastily added, "I thought it had been the elder Mr. Douglas's idea."

The housekeeper shrugged, either not noticing or not caring about her slip. "I dinna know for sure. Mr. Douglas certainly took it hard when he heard your grandda had passed on. But 'twas Connor himself who made it known that he intended to bring ye here for Ewan's sake. But it caused quite a stir, it did."

"Why is that?" Genevieve asked curiously.

"Because 'tis one matter to have English acquaintances, but 'tis another to bring one in to teach the young master. No' that I mean any offense to ye personally by that."

Genevieve took a bite of her biscuit, considering the housekeeper's words. "None taken. I understand that emotions over the war still run high in Scotland. I just hope everyone knows that I have no quarrel with them."

"I think they do, and those that don't will have pity on you. Especially since many o' them do no' envy your task."

"My task?"

"Managing Ewan. It has been a verra difficult time for him."

"Well, that is certainly understandable, especially since his mother's death was so sudden."

"Aye, 'twas a real tragedy."

"For both Mr. Douglas and Ewan, of course."

Genevieve saw a moment of distress in the woman's eyes before she lowered her gaze. "Aye, for all," she said softly.

The conversation lulled, and Genevieve had a feeling

that there was something the housekeeper wished to tell her, but could not. Genevieve thought that if she asked the right question, something significant might be revealed. But she knew so very little of the situation and had no desire to appear too eager, even if she desperately wanted to know.

But Mrs. MacDougal, bless her heart, apparently had a burning need to share the information anyway, for she took another sip of her tea and leaned forward. "Seeing as how ye are a part o' the household now, I dinna see the harm in telling ye what happened. I figure ye'd hear it soon enough, if ye dinna know already. Janet fell out of the tower window."

Genevieve nodded sadly, already beginning to feel a bit light-headed from the spirits. "The elder Mr. Douglas informed me of such. But why would she do such a thing? Certainly she had everything she could want—a lovely home, a child, and a husband."

Mrs. MacDougal shrugged. "I'm no' privy to what happens 'tween a man and his wife. But I do know they used to argue quite fiercely. 'Twas an ill-fated match made for naught more than coin between the Douglas and MacIntyre clans. 'Tis said Connor had his eye on another young beauty, Catherine Graham. But his da wouldna hear o' it."

"But the Douglases were quite well off," Genevieve objected. "Surely Mr. Douglas could not have been forced into a loveless match if he had strongly objected."

"Wealth is fleeting," Mrs. MacDougal said lowering her voice. "And these are precarious times for the Scots. Young Connor had a duty to his family to ensure their position and power."

"True," Genevieve murmured, remembering how quickly her grandfather's wealth had disappeared.

"Anyway, on the night she died, I heard them arguing," the housekeeper continued. "Janet ran from their room and up to the tower. I was in the corridor when she passed me, nearly knocking me over in her haste. Connor followed, looking mighty angry."

She paused for a moment, whether to catch her breath or for dramatic effect, Genevieve didn't know. "Soon after that, Janet was found dead in the courtyard," she finished with a flourish.

"That's truly a tragedy," Genevieve said at a loss for words to describe such a dreadful happenstance.

The housekeeper took a sip of tea. "'Tis a wee odd that no one heard her scream, though."

A chill crept up Genevieve's spine. "Surely you don't think Mr. Douglas had anything to do with her death. I heard there was some kind of investigation."

"Aye, there was, but mostly because Janet's da outright accused Connor o' pushing her. An accusation o' murder is no' so easily dismissed, so Connor agreed to the investigation to clear his name."

"A sensible thing to do."

The housekeeper opened her mouth to say something more, then closed it. Perhaps feeling she had already said too much, she stood.

"Well, I thank ye, miss, for inviting me to share tea and your company," Mrs. MacDougal said, gathering the cups and plates. "Ye are the first governess to do so, and an Englishwoman, no less. 'Tis a mad world sometimes, is it no'?"

Indeed, Genevieve had lately been thinking the same thing herself. Never in a hundred years had she pictured herself impoverished and at the mercy of a man who had once broken her heart and had now been accused of murdering his wife.

"It is," Genevieve said with a sigh. With that she rose and held the door open for the housekeeper.

"Lucinda will be by soon to fetch ye for supper," Mrs. MacDougal said, balancing the tray on her hand. "I'll bring a fresh pot o' washing water for ye, if ye'd like."

"That would be most kind of you," Genevieve said, closing the door behind her.

For a moment she leaned against the back of the door, thinking about the strange things she had learned about Connor and his life at *Caisteal na Mara*. Suicide, murder, and intrigue. Hadn't her grandfather once told her such tales of the castle when she sat at his feet and listened with rapt attention? Now she was living in one of those tales and was not at all certain it was a place she wanted to be.

Feeling a sudden chill, she walked to the wooden wardrobe. She pulled open the door, musing as to which gown would be most suitable for her first supper at the castle. Suddenly she felt something drop onto her foot. Startled, she jumped and let out a shriek as a small snake writhed across the floor and disappeared out of sight under the bed. She took at least two more steps back, watching the bed warily in case the reptile reappeared. Then she heard a muffled giggle from behind the door that led to the schoolroom, and her eyes narrowed. Before she could move, a knock sounded on her door. Mrs. MacDougal's worried voice carried through the wood.

"Are ye all right in there, miss?" she asked.

Genevieve walked across the room and took a deep breath before opening the door.

"I'm fine, Mrs. MacDougal," she said. "I just . . . ah, dropped something on my foot."

The housekeeper looked at her curiously, holding a tray with a clean chamber pot and a pitcher of fresh water. "Well, if ye are certain . . ."

"I am," Genevieve said, intending to handle the matter by herself.

With a shrug, the housekeeper replaced the pot and pitcher and left. Genevieve quickly dropped to her knees and gingerly lifted the bedcovers to peer underneath the bed where the snake had escaped. She could see nothing. For all she knew, the snake would rest there until she slept and then venture out under the cover of darkness. Furious, she stood and stalked across the room, throwing open the door to the schoolroom. The room was now empty.

She crossed the schoolroom in four steps and knocked on the door to Ewan's chamber. There was no answer, but she heard muffled movements from inside.

She leaned against the door, raising her voice. "Ewan, I wanted to thank you for your small welcoming gift. And seeing how you are so fond of snakes, we shall start our lessons tomorrow with a thorough study of the reptile."

Turning on her heel, she marched back toward her room, when the door to Ewan's room abruptly flew open. Hands on her hips, she turned to face him.

"It didna bite ye, did it?" he asked, his eyes glinting with triumph.

"I didn't give it the opportunity to do so."

"Then why are ye fashing so?"

"Did I say I was upset?" she said raising an eyebrow. "I do, however, recall saying that you gave me an excellent idea for our science lesson tomorrow."

"Ye were frightened."

"I don't frighten so easily."

"Ye will next time," he said softly. "And if ye tell my da about this, I'll deny it."

"I don't intend to tell him anything," she said calmly, "as long as you are in the schoolroom bright and early in the morning."

He snorted. "Blackmail? Is that the best ye can do? I willna come. Ye canno' make me."

She nodded agreeably. "You're right. I can't make you

attend your lessons. But your father can. And he told me he intends to stay at the castle for some time until he's convinced you are working hard at your lessons. It seems that you tend to perform in a more satisfactory manner when he is in residence."

Genevieve noticed he flinched at the mention of his father, and she wondered if the reaction was motivated by fear or anger. Yet as soon as he opened his mouth to speak, she saw she was wrong on both points.

"Da is staying?" he said softly and she saw unmistakable excitement in his eyes. "Did he say for how long?"

Surprised, Genevieve realized the boy had just inadvertently revealed his weak spot. Ewan desperately loved his father.

She shrugged, careful not to seem too interested. "He didn't say exactly, but it is my understanding that it will be for at least a few weeks."

She watched as a shadow descended over his eyes. "Or mayhap longer if I tell him I dinna like ye or that ye aren't learning me proper. And if I dinna learn proper, he'll have to find a new governess. And next time she willna be English."

Genevieve stiffened, surprised by the venom in his voice. "I'm afraid it's not going to be so easy, Ewan. I have no place else to go, and your father has extended me his full support in regard to you. Whether you like it or not, we are going to work together. I'll expect you in the schoolroom tomorrow."

He gave her a malicious look. "Just see if ye can find me. This is my home, English, no' yours. Mark my words, ye'll be gone before ye've been here a fortnight."

Genevieve crossed her arms against her chest, refusing to be worried or intimidated by his threats, despite the fact that he could very well be correct. "No, you mark *my* words, Ewan Douglas. You *will* learn and eventually come to enjoy it. I will not give up. And I warn you, we English are a very stubborn people, perhaps even as much as the Scottish."

"Go away," he shouted, slamming his door on her.

Genevieve took a deep breath and returned to her room, more shaken than she cared to admit by the encounter. How in the world would she breach the hatred this boy had for her and her heritage? And if she failed, where would she go? The alternatives were too frightening to contemplate. She couldn't fail. She *wouldn't.*

Nonetheless, she had no plan what to do if the boy failed to show up for his lessons. Ewan was right. This was his castle. She did not know her way around here and could hardly be expected to spend the day looking for him. She felt assured she could count on Connor to help her the first few days, but after that, he'd certainly begin to be annoyed by her inability to manage the boy. She'd have to use her wits to figure this out.

Well, she had no time to dwell on it now. Lucinda would be coming momentarily to lead her to supper, and she had yet to dress. Quickly she made her way back to the wardrobe, taking care to notice where she walked. Finding the snake and doing a quick look about the room for any other assorted "gifts" from Ewan would be a priority after supper.

She chose a dark green gown from the wardrobe and gingerly took it down, shaking it out, just to be certain the folds of material held no further unexpected guests. She donned it and smoothed out the skirts. Leaning over, she carefully examined her shoes and put them on just as Lucinda knocked at the door, announcing that supper was ready.

Standing, Genevieve followed Lucinda downstairs. She was surprised when the girl led her to the Great Hall, where Connor sat talking softly with his father in front of a blazing fire. One end of a long trundle table had been covered with a white tablecloth with four places set, and candles flickered merrily. Both men rose when they saw her, and she summoned a confident smile she did not feel and walked toward them.

"You are prompt," Connor said approvingly, offering her his elbow. Genevieve hesitated a moment before she took it, acutely aware of the strength in his forearm as her fingertips lightly touched the soft material of his coat. Although it was all very proper, Genevieve couldn't stop the way her pulse jumped just at being close to him.

"O' course, she's prompt," Malcom said with a twinkle in his eye. "She's English, is she no'? 'Tis one thing ye can say about the English, they are ne'er late for supper."

Genevieve smiled good-naturedly and Connor chuckled as he helped her into her seat. As the small talk dwindled, the mood at the table soured. After the servants had filled their wine cups for a second time, Connor began drumming his fingers impatiently on the table.

"Where in the devil is Ewan?" he said irritably. " I'll no' have that lad delaying our supper again."

Clearly annoyed, Malcom summoned a young servant and ordered him to find the boy. The servant looked visibly upset at the request, but scurried off to try. Genevieve got the distinct impression that this kind of thing happened often with the boy.

Again the conversation lulled, and Genevieve sipped her wine slowly, wondering how much longer they would wait before starting dinner. After a few minutes, Malcom pulled out his pocket watch and looked at it, grumbling softy under his breath. The scowl deepened on Connor's face before he threw back the rest of his wine and stood up.

"I'll go find the lad myself," he said shortly.

"Wait," Genevieve said quickly. "I know it's rather presumptuous to make a suggestion on my first day, but if you would indulge me, I have an idea that might help in this matter."

Connor leaned forward, placing both hands on the table. "Please do grace us wi' your suggestion, Miss Fitzsimmons," he said, his fathomless blue eyes studying her intently.

"Aye, please do," Malcom said, interest flickering in his eyes as he placed his elbows on the table.

Even the servant who stood motionless by the door that separated the Great Hall from the cooking area looked interested in what she had to say.

Genevieve swallowed hard, the taste of wine suddenly bitter in her mouth. "I would suggest removing Ewan's plate from the table," she said quietly. "If he cannot bring it upon himself to arrive at supper in a timely fashion, then he should go without."

"Go without supper?" Malcom said, looking slightly shocked.

"Yes. And the servants and those in the kitchen should be warned not to provide him any food—not even a scrap of bread," she continued.

"Surely ye canna mean to starve the lad?" Connor said with a trace of exasperation in his voice.

"I assure you, he'll not starve. But I do think it will cause him to reconsider his decision to make us wait for our supper. The rule should be consistent. If he is not at the table, washed and ready to eat, by five o'clock, then his plate will be removed and there will be no food until morning."

"'Tis a bit harsh, is it no'?" Malcom said doubtfully.

"If we do not set limits with him, then he will not know how to behave properly."

Malcom stroked his beard, looking at her thoughtfully. "Ye understand that by doing this, ye declare war wi' the boy, then? 'Tis a risky strategy wi' him, ye know."

"I know," she said. Seeing how she stood on shaky ground with Ewan as it was, this directive would certainly not endear her to him, and she had no doubt he would figure out who had issued it. Frankly, it would have been much safer to let Connor deal with this particular behavior problem and hold her tongue. She was certain she'd have enough matters to deal with as soon as they started their lessons tomorrow. But she had followed her instincts with the boy and now simply prayed for the best.

"He cannot be allowed to direct the course of the activities in this castle," she continued with a firmness she didn't feel. "This should hold true whether or not you are in the castle," she said looking at Connor. "But it will not work without your support and authority."

Connor gazed at her for a moment longer with his penetrating blue stare and then abruptly raised his hand. The servant was instantly at his side.

"Remove Ewan's plate from the table and inform the staff that they are not to provide even a small morsel o' food for him tonight," he said shortly. "If I find out that anyone has disobeyed my orders, they will lose a week's pay. Do ye understand?"

The servant swallowed, his Adam's apple bobbing nervously in his throat. "Aye, sir."

"Excellent. Then bring us our supper."

The mood of the evening ruined, Genevieve ate her soup quietly, nearly finishing before Ewan deigned to appear. To his credit, he had washed and changed his shirt, but his breeches and boots were still filthy. He ignored her as he slid into his seat.

"Da, ye should o' seen what happened in the chicken

coop today," he said breathlessly. "The rooster went mad, chasing the hens about and sending feathers flying in the air. Old Mr. McKay chased him about, cursing and falling twice on his arse. Me and Jamie jumped in and chased the rooster until it simply wore out. Mr. McKay took the bird and said he intended to wring its neck, but Mrs. McKay said 'twas no one else loud enough to wake him from sleep, so the rooster would have to stay."

He reached for a cup, then frowned when he realized it was missing. "Where is my cup?" he said looking around. "And my plate?"

Connor took a sip of his wine and regarded the boy over his cup. "If ye canna make it to supper on time, then ye willna eat."

A look of stunned disbelief crossed Ewan's face. "What? But, Da, I . . ."

"Ye heard what I said, Ewan," Connor said quietly. "I've had enough o' your excuses these past few months since your mum died."

Ewan looked imploringly at his grandfather. "Grandda, surely *ye* canna let me go hungry?"

Malcom shrugged, focusing his attention on his dinner. Genevieve watched as the boy's gaze finally landed on her and his blue eyes grew hard.

"This is your doing," he said angrily, pushing away from the table and coming to his feet. "Ye told them to starve me, didna ye, English? Ye probably told him about the snake, too. Well, I shouldna be surprised. Ye think ye're in charge here, but ye're no'."

Connor stood abruptly, his knife clattering to the table. A deathly silence suddenly fell over the room. Genevieve realized she was holding her breath.

"That is quite enough, Ewan," he said very softly. "First, ye will apologize to Miss Fitzsimmons, and then ye will go to your room. I believe ye now understand what ye must do in order to receive your meals. I suggest ye think hard and well before ye decide to disobey again."

Ewan stood, still glaring at her, bristling with hostility, his fists at his side. "Sorry," he said to her between clenched teeth, and then stalked away from the table.

After a moment, Connor sat back down and calmly resumed eating. Genevieve's appetite had fled, and she could only push the food around on her plate. Malcom, trying valiantly to revive the dinner conversation, began speaking about the lovely spring weather. Genevieve appreciated the effort and did her best to seem interested, but was thankful when Connor inquired if everyone had finished the meal. Genevieve practically leaped from her chair, wishing for nothing more than to retire to her chamber and end this horrid day.

Both men immediately stood, and Connor came around the table and offered Genevieve his arm, saying that he intended to escort her back to her room. She protested, but he insisted. Hesitantly she took his arm, her elbow linking with his, her fingers resting lightly atop his forearm. She marveled at how tall he stood and yet how completely he carried his height with a graceful elegance. Standing next to him, she could feel him radiating heat, the warmth of him beckoning her nearer.

She bid Malcom good night, and he nodded graciously. Quietly they walked down the hall and climbed the stairs until arriving at her door. Connor released her arm, and she reached for the latch, but he grabbed her hand. Still holding it, he turned her around, deftly backing her up against the door.

"'Twas a bold move ye made wi' Ewan tonight," he said in his soft Scottish burr, but his voice was not disapproving. "I like that ye took a stand wi' him."

"I do think it is the right course of action," she managed to say. Oh, God, how her heart jolted and pulse pounded every time he touched her. He was so disturbing to her in every way.

"I think so, too," he said, his mouth curving into a smile. "But it willna make your task any easier."

"I never expected this position to be easy," she said honestly, pressing back against the door and wondering how she could politely extract her hand from his. But he seemed in no hurry to release it, and a traitorous part of her openly enjoyed the physical contact. "But I do believe I shall manage somehow."

"O' that I have no doubt," he said good-naturedly, and Genevieve could not help but smile. There was something warm and enchanting about his humor, reminding her of one of the traits she liked best about him.

Nay, better not to think of those things, she told herself sternly.

His mouth quirked. "Pray tell, Genevieve, why didna ye tell me o' the snake?"

"Snake?" she squeaked, pressing back against the door as if that tiny added space would give her more resolve to resist his charm. "Oh, that."

"Aye, that."

She straightened her shoulders and firmly extracted her hand, once again a governess in charge. "It was nothing, really. I happened to come across one in my room, that's all."

"Courtesy o' Ewan no doubt. Why didna ye tell me?"

"There are some matters I am quite capable of handling by myself."

Connor leaned forward, causing her to press back tighter against the door to avoid touching his body. "So I presume that means ye dinna want to me make certain it is gone from your chamber then."

"Oh, would you?" Genevieve said in a relieved rush.

He smiled and bent his dark head toward her. For a paralyzing, breathtaking moment she thought he would kiss her, but instead he reached around her waist and unfastened the latch to the door. She would have fallen backward across the threshold if not for his hand firmly at the small of her back. They stood there frozen in time, gazing into each other's eyes.

Then he politely released her and stepped back, permitting her to regain her balance and go into the room. After a moment he followed. It seemed far too intimate a place to be with him, but he did not seem the slightest bit ill at ease. Genevieve tried not to think about the other circumstances that might make him so comfortable in a woman's chamber.

"Where did ye last see it?" he asked.

"It?"

"The snake."

Her cheeks grew hot as she pointed to the bed. "Under there. It was in the wardrobe. When I opened it, the snake fell to the floor and proceeded to slither under the bed. I looked, but couldn't see it."

"Did ye get a look at it?"

She shuddered. "It was green and grey. Rather small, actually."

"Naught more than a garden snake, likely. Completely harmless."

"I'd just rather not have it under my bed, harmless or not."

He bent down to his knees by the bed and looked up at her, a glint of humor in his eyes. "There are a lot more dangerous things a lady could have in her bed, ye know."

She pursed her lips at him. Insolent humor, she had always accused him of, and he had typically obliged. Odd how that was one of the few aspects of their relationship he seemed to remember. Although when she thought about it now, she, too, had greatly enjoyed matching wits and humor.

He lifted the bedcovers and searched beneath the bed, giving her a most spectacular view of his bum. It strained against his breeches, a tight, well-formed appendage tapering off into a remarkable pair of muscular thighs and calves. Unbidden, heat rushed through her. Appalled at her thinking, Genevieve tore her gaze away and settled it on the window.

"I canna see a thing under here," Connor said in a muffled voice, his arm sweeping back and forth beneath the bed. "I didna feel anything here, either."

"Maybe it departed," she said hopefully.

"Perhaps," he agreed, rising to his feet and dusting off his breeches. "If ye'd like, I'll check the bedsheets and blankets."

For a fleeting moment, Genevieve pictured herself tangled with him in those very sheets and blankets, and she flushed even hotter. "Please, I'd appreciate it."

He lifted the covers one by one, shaking them out. Erotic images leaped to mind as she watched his hands on her bedsheets. He had the most beautiful hands she had ever seen—long fingered, tapered, and capable of great gentleness. For a moment, she remembered how it felt to have those wondrous hands pressing into her back, tangled in her hair, and stroking her cheek.

Cease this at once, she commanded herself. Her face burned so hotly she was certain he would need only one look to know exactly what she'd been thinking.

"Clean," he said, turning to face her. "Ye should be able to sleep safely."

She quickly turned away and walked to the window, staring out. "Thank you," she said without looking back. "You make me feel safe." As soon as she said it, she snapped her mouth shut in mortification. What an idiotic thing to say.

"Well, I should bid ye a good evening then."

"Yes, good night," she said emphatically, hoping to hurry him along.

But instead of walking to the door, he approached her at the window. *What in God's name was he doing now?*

Gathering her composure, she turned to him. "Is there something else . . . sir?" Better to remind them both of her position here.

"I asked ye to call me Connor," he said softly. "Dinna forget again, aye, Genevieve?"

She wanted more than anything to resist his charm and ignore the way he made her feel. But at that particular moment, standing in the intimacy of her bedroom with the only man she'd ever loved, she couldn't.

"Connor," she whispered obligingly.

Once again he stood so close she could see the faint stub of whiskers on his cheeks and the muscles that twitched in his jaw. She was acutely aware of his powerful chest and muscular shoulders, both within the reach of her fingertips if she but dared to touch him. His face was bronzed by the wind and sun, his lips firm and sensual. A hot rush of warmth swept through her, his nearness kindling long forgotten feelings of desire.

He smiled slowly, a look of both knowing and understanding in his eyes. So he was aware of his affect on her — the scoundrel!

"'Tis good to see ye again," he said softly. "Being here wi' ye, it seems as though no' much time has passed."

The emotion and longing in his voice tugged at her heart and she struggled to set her resolve against him. She had no idea why he said such things or why he toyed with her emotions, but never again would she open her heart to such pain.

"I beg to differ," she said stiffly. "Times have changed, and so have I."

"No' in the ways that matter most," he murmured. Rain started to fall outside the open window, the pattering sound soft and familiar. She froze when he reached out and twined a strand of her hair around his finger.

"Now, wi' your permission, I'll go have a talk wi' Ewan about the snake."

Shaken by the tenderness of his gesture and dismayed at how vulnerable it made her feel, she stepped away from him. "I wish you wouldn't," she said wrapping her arms around her waist. "It will only make matters worse."

"Are ye certain?" His ice blue eyes were like summer lightning, beckoning to her with an insolent inner fire.

Her body longed to return to him, but she stood her ground. "I am."

He gazed at her, considering. "As ye wish, then."

"Thank you."

He turned and walked to the door, pausing on the threshold. "Good night, lass. I wish for ye the sweetest o' dreams, for we have a custom here in Scotland that whatever ye dream on the first night in your new home will come true."

Without another word, he left, leaving her standing there with her heart hammering foolishly and her face still warm from the encounter.

The sweetest of dreams, indeed. If only he knew what she had dreamed about him.

Genevieve sank into a chair, her knees weak. She had never felt so unnerved, so completely unable to control her emotions. Horrified, she realized it was as if she *were* sixteen years old again, without either the willpower or sensibility to conduct herself in a proper manner around him. How could he still manage to have such a disturbing affect on her after all these years?

She pressed her hand to her breast as if willing her heart to slow. This was a most unfortunate turn of events. She had no intention of engaging in any sort of misconduct with him. But she couldn't seem to stop her heart from beating quicker when she saw him, nor could she manage a cold indifference. Yet for the sake of her future, she had better try harder.

She glanced at the mussed bedsheets and remembered the way he touched them, like an intimate caress. She drew in her breath sharply. His actions had been innocent, not to mention done upon her request. It was simply that men like Connor were so practiced in the art of seduction that it clung to them as second nature.

Sighing, Genevieve changed into her bedgown and sat in front of the fire. As the heat from the fire warmed her body and the sound of the rain comforted her, she began to relax, the tension of the day's events beginning to leave her. She'd manage this. She'd handle Connor Douglas despite his reputation as a rogue.

She had to.

She'd have to draw upon her internal strength to see this situation did not spiral out of control. She was strong; she was English; she was a Fitzsimmons. She would persevere.

Feeling strengthened by the thought, Genevieve retired to the bed, ignoring the mussed bedsheets. Slowly, she let her eyelids drift shut, overwhelmed by all that had happened to her this day.

As she drifted off to sleep, the scent of Connor on her bedsheets gave her an odd comfort. Sleepily, she made a vow not to dream of him during her first night at *Caisteal na Mara.*

But despite her best intentions, Connor's mocking blue eyes were exactly what she saw as the darkness reached up to pull her under.

* * *

Connor stood in front of the hearth in his bedchamber completely naked, drinking a cup of wine and staring into the fire. The room was dark except for the flickering light of the flames, which cast grotesque and eerie shadows across the wall. The darkness suited his mood at the moment.

He'd been utterly unprepared for the strength of the desire that had slammed into him as he stood so close to her, drank in her scent, and remembered the soft touch of her skin.

Christ, it had felt so good.

He still needed her, wanted her, he thought moodily. Badly. Even ten years hadn't been able to diminish the feelings and the longing he felt for her.

He was still in love with her. Except this time around, there was no one in charge of his future but himself. Since Janet's death, his financial situation had become quite secure. Now all that was left to him was to apologize to Genevieve for his past mistakes and gain her trust once again. It seemed simple enough.

Except there were a number of complications on the horizon, ones that could pose troubling and potentially damaging problems if he did not quickly and efficiently deal with them. Now he no longer had the luxury of time to lure her to his bed. Instead, he'd have to hasten his plans considerably. Damn his father for insisting that he hold a foxhunt and ball at the end of the month. But neither had foreseen the unexpected death of Genevieve's grandfather. Connor's plan had to be put into action far earlier than he would have liked.

But he would manage.

In the past he'd been manipulated, cajoled, and forced into a life he hadn't wanted. Never again. He was fully in command of his own destiny, of his own desires. He had every intention of getting what he wanted.

Genevieve Fitzsimmons would be his, and he'd use whatever methods he could to win her. But he would have to act carefully. He didn't want her to come to him bitter or trapped or deceived. He wanted her to come to him of her own free will—because she knew, like he, that they could not deny the bonds that linked them.

He took a sip of his wine. He was not the man she thought he was. He held painful secrets. How much of a difference would that make to their bond once she discovered them?

Sighing, he set his wine cup aside and sank into a chair. He didn't dare contemplate that question for too long, because he feared the answer.

He must win her back. There was simply no other way.

Three

Genevieve sat alone in the schoolroom, trying not to continually glance out the window as the sun rose and Ewan didn't appear. She fully expected him not to appear, but had foolishly nurtured a small hope that he might. She rubbed her temples wearily, having slept fitfully her first night at *Caisteal na Mara.* She dreamed of lying abed with Connor, both of them laughing and tangled in the bedsheets. He'd kissed her tenderly as moonlight streamed in through the open window, forming golden puddles across the bedsheets. She'd given herself to him shamelessly before he suddenly gathered her in his strong arms rippling with muscles. In one easy movement, he swept her from the bed. Before she could utter a word, he smiled at her gently—then tossed her out the window. She woke up screaming, her heart thundering and her body slick with sweat.

She glanced out the window, a tight ball forming in her stomach. Ewan was a half hour late now, and she knew he wasn't coming. Not of his own accord, anyway.

She stood, deciding to check his room first. To her surprise, the door was open. To her even greater astonishment, Ewan still lay abed, huddled beneath his covers. He had apparently overslept. Encouraged by this small stroke of fortune, she pulled up a chair and sat by his bedside.

"Good morning, Ewan," she said cheerfully. "It's a lovely spring day. Perhaps we can do part of our lessons outside today."

He peered out sleepily from beneath the covers. "Go away," he said, yawning at her. "I'm no' coming."

"That's all right," she said brightly. "Well just do our lessons right here. I'll go get your primer."

That got his attention. He sat up, wide awake now and pulling the covers to his chin. "Are ye mad? I'm still abed and clad in my nightclothes."

She smiled. "Did I mention that I'm quite accommodating?"

He looked at her his mouth agape. "Ye are daft."

"Just determined. Look, Ewan, I know you don't like me, which really isn't fair since we've not yet had the chance to get to know each other. But I do have this feeling that we'll get on."

He snorted. "Go have your lessons by yourself, English."

She shrugged. "It's your choice not to attend. But I feel it's my duty to mention to you that your father said he'd stop by this morning to see how the lessons are going. In fact, I'm expecting him anytime now. I'm certain your absence would greatly disappoint him."

With that Genevieve left the room, closing the door behind her and praying her words would get the reaction she wanted. After a few minutes, she heard Ewan get up and stomp around. Finally he stalked into the schoolroom, his clothes wrinkled, his hair mussed, and his eyes glinting. He flopped down in a chair, slouching.

"I canna be learned if my stomach is grumbling," he muttered.

Genevieve walked over to a lowboy where a tray with milk and sweet biscuits sat. "Isn't it fortunate that I happened to have some food on hand?" she said sweetly.

Clearly intending to annoy her, he stuffed the biscuits in his mouth, daring her to challenge him on his manners. Instead, she ignored him, readying his math primer and using the opportunity while he couldn't speak to talk to him about the day's plan. From what she had already observed of him, he was an active boy, so she decided to intersperse writing and sitting lessons with some physical exercise and a bit of fresh air.

After he finished, he sat at his desk, at first quite rude and uncooperative. But Genevieve gently persisted, keeping the lesson light and easy. Eventually he began to come around as she increased the difficulty of the material—most likely, she suspected, to prove that an Englishwoman couldn't possibly know as much as a Scot. Quickly she adapted the lesson, making it more competitive between the two of them and much harder.

To her astonishment, Ewan met her challenges. Unlike the reports she had heard from Connor, the boy was neither slow nor dim-witted and, in fact, had a curious and lively mind.

She was grateful when Connor stopped by about an hour into the lesson. He leaned against the doorjamb, clad in dark riding breeches, a white linen shirt, and boots. His magnificent black hair had been combed back and tied with a leather strip at the nape of his neck, and his intense blue eyes raked over her hungrily, as if taking in every detail of her appearance. Her breath caught in her throat at the simple sight of him, and she was barely able to tear her gaze away.

"Good morning, Miss Fitzsimmons," Connor finally said. "Ewan, lad, it warms my heart to see ye hard at your lessons."

Ewan grunted something and Genevieve realized it had fallen to her to carry on the conversation. "Are you riding this morning, Mr. Douglas?" she asked politely.

"I am. I'm preparing for the foxhunt to be held in a fortnight here at the castle."

"Here? A foxhunt?" Genevieve said in surprise and dismay.

"From the tone of your voice I get the impression that this particular activity does not sit favorably with ye." To her chagrin, his mouth twitched with amusement.

"On the contrary. I did not state my opinion in any way," she protested, annoyed he could read her so well.

"Aye, but ye showed it."

She sighed. "Well then, no use denying it. I just don't see the point in hunting down a poor defenseless animal."

He chuckled. "Defenseless, hardly. The fox has a remarkable wit."

"All the more reason not to hunt it," she retorted.

"Miss Fitzsimmons, I had no idea ye were a champion for the defenseless." He was openly teasing her now.

"I am a champion for reasonable, not barbaric, sport."

"Well, I think foxhunts are grand," Ewan interrupted excitedly. "If ye would let me come, Da, I would . . ."

"Nay," Connor said so sharply that Genevieve looked at him in surprise.

"But, Da . . ." Ewan whined until Connor cut him off with a curt wave of his hand.

"A foxhunt is no place for a bairn."

"I'm no' a bairn," Ewan huffed.

"Then show me by behaving."

Pouting, Ewan slumped back in his chair, disappointment evident on his face. Genevieve watched the interaction both with interest and dismay. Something had changed in Connor's demeanor when he spoke to the boy. His tone was cooler, almost indifferent. She sensed no warmth, no affection. How strange, she mused. She thought tragedy would have brought them closer together.

"How are the lessons going?" Connor asked, the question directed at her.

Genevieve brightened. "Quite well, actually. Ewan is an apt pupil."

"That's no' what I've heard," Connor said, his gaze turning back to Ewan.

Irritated at the thoughtlessness of the comment, Genevieve put a hand on Ewan's shoulder as if in some way to comfort him from his father's coolness.

It was a mistake. Ewan practically snarled at her and leaped from his chair so quickly he knocked it over.

"Well, I have interrupted enough," Connor said, amusement showing in his eyes. "I can see ye have your hands full, so I shall let ye return to your lessons."

With those words, he walked away, his short visit ruining all that had been accomplished between her and Ewan this morning. Her irritation at Connor grew, as did her pity for the child.

She pretended not to notice Ewan's glare and instead picked up his reader and shut it. "I think we've done enough for this morning. Would it be acceptable to you if we adjourn until after the midday meal?"

She saw surprise and then suspicion cross his face, and she realized he'd probably never been consulted on how or when he wanted to do his lessons. "Ye mean I'm done?" he asked as if he couldn't believe her.

Genevieve nodded. "You finished the first reading lesson sooner than I expected. We'll resume with your sums after the meal. Then, since it is such a lovely day, perhaps we'll take a visit to the bog to examine some of the herbs growing there."

He stared at her a moment longer, not certain what to say or do. Finally he turned on his heel and walked out of the schoolroom without a word.

Genevieve sighed, picking up the rest of the primers

and stacking them neatly on the table. She certainly hoped she knew what she was doing.

She ate her midday meal alone in her room, then returned to the schoolroom to await Ewan. She wasn't terribly surprised when the boy did not appear.

Making a conscious decision not to be angry, she wandered downstairs and outside, thinking she had the best chance of finding Ewan there. She walked past the stables, but the stable master told her he hadn't seen the boy. She decided to take a stroll through the garden and admire the colorful buttercups and poppies. Bushes were also in full bloom, and she stopped along the way to smell the fresh, pungent scents of the various flora. For a moment, she closed her eyes, imagining herself back in England surrounded by her own beloved flowers and shrubs.

A thorough examination of the gardens indicated Ewan was nowhere around. Resigned that she might not find him at all, she decided to follow the sound of barking dogs. Soon she came upon a large pen surrounded by a low fence made of rough-hewn logs roped together. Inside the fence, a man ran around with a pack of dogs, presumably the hounds that would hunt the fox. To her surprise, she spotted Ewan not far away, sitting under a tree and watching the handler work the dogs. Ewan hadn't seen her yet, so she stood quietly, catching the boy in an unguarded moment. He looked very young and dejected, his knees pulled to his chest. There was something inherently sad about him, and it tugged at her heart.

Taking a deep breath, she hitched up her skirts and walked toward him, being certain to make noise. He lifted his head and narrowed his eyes when he saw her, but he didn't move away. Silently she sat down beside him on the grass.

"I'm no' coming back for lessons," he said, still staring at the hounds.

"Actually, I thought we might work a bit outside. Not all of life's lessons are learned in the schoolroom."

He shook his head. "Why dinna ye just give up, English? 'Twould save us both a lot o' trouble, ye know."

"Why don't you give up?" she suggested. "And then we'd have a lot more time for pleasurable activities."

"I dinna want to do pleasant things wi' ye."

"Well that's too bad. Because I simply do not subscribe to the theory that schoolwork has to be hard and boring."

He curled his lips in distaste. "Ye are an odd duck. And it isna going to work if ye think this approach will make me like ye."

She sighed. "I am quite aware of the fact that I can't *make* you like me no matter what I do. What I *can* do is make learning interesting."

He snorted in disgust. "Have ye ever been a governess before?"

"No, I'm afraid you're my first charge," she admitted.

"Ye have a lot to learn about bairns."

"I suppose I do. Perhaps we'll end up teaching each other something."

He rolled his eyes and resumed staring at the hounds. Genevieve followed his gaze to where the man was being chased about by several of the dogs. They barked and growled furiously. Then she noticed the trainer held a fox pelt in his hand. She shivered involuntarily.

"What's the real reason your father doesn't want you to go on the foxhunt?" she suddenly asked.

Ewan turned to look at her, annoyed. "Dinna ye ever stop talking, English?"

"You may call me Miss Fitzsimmons. And to be truthful, I'm rarely at a loss for words."

"'Tis just my luck," he grumbled, but for the first time Genevieve noticed the underlying current of hostility had faded.

"And you have effectively avoided the question," she persisted. "Why won't your father let you come on the foxhunt?"

He blew out a breath. "Ye heard him. He thinks I'm still a bairn."

"Fathers are naturally protective."

"He's no' protective," Ewan snapped. "He's ashamed." Then, realizing he'd let something personal slip, he frowned and fell silent.

Genevieve was taken aback by his words. "I'm certain that's not true, although I'm puzzled why he'd so strongly object based solely on your age. In England, children as young as six hunt with their fathers. Perhaps he'd change his mind if he knew that."

"He willna change his mind," Ewan said morosely. "Ever."

"Perhaps it would be beneficial if I spoke with him."

Ewan looked at her in horror. "Nay!"

"Why not?"

Ewan looked away, his cheeks reddening. "Because I said so."

Just as he spoke the words, the hounds starting barking furiously. Genevieve saw that a hapless squirrel had run into the pen. The dogs began chasing it, whining when it slipped beneath the fence to safety. A large black hound that had been separated from the others and tied to a wooden pole began barking and thrashing about viciously. Shocked, Genevieve watched as the dog snapped its leash and leaped over the fence, coming directly toward them.

Ewan screamed in terror and dived behind Genevieve. She was so stunned she didn't move a muscle. The dog darted past them and into the forest in pursuit of the squirrel. It returned moments later when the trainer whistled angrily.

"I'm right sorry about that, young master," the trainer said, jumping the fence and addressing Ewan, who still cowered behind Genevieve. "I didna know Charlie had gotten so strong. I'll have to double his bindings to keep 'im under control. Are ye both all right?"

"Thank you, we are fine," Genevieve said, although her heart still pounded.

Charlie approached them at last, stopping to sniff at Genevieve's hand. She could still feel Ewan trembling behind her.

"It's all right, Ewan," she said calmly. "Charlie's actually quite friendly as long as you aren't a squirrel. Why don't you pet him?"

"Nay, I dinna want to touch him," Ewan said with genuine fear in his voice.

"Come on then, Charlie," the trainer said. "I'm sorry to have bothered ye both." The dog followed at a trot, looking back at them once over his shoulder as if amused.

As soon as the hound was safely fenced in, Ewan stood and began stalking back to the castle. Genevieve hastily rose as well, brushing off her skirts and following him.

"So that's what the problem is," she said. "You are afraid of dogs."

He stopped in his tracks, his face flushed and furious. "I'm no' afraid of dogs," he practically shouted. "Now leave me alone."

"There is nothing to be ashamed of," she said, ignoring his command. "I was once afraid of dogs myself."

Ewan began walking again, his fists clenched at his side. "O' course ye were. Ye're a lass."

Genevieve resisted the urge to roll her eyes. "Do you know how I overcame my fear?"

"I dinna care."

"My grandfather helped me by taking me down to see the dogs a little every day. Soon they got used to me, and I wasn't so afraid of them, either."

"It willna make a difference. Da knows about the dogs. . . all right?" His face flushed with shame. "He knows. So just forget about it."

Genevieve was not deterred. "Don't give up so easily. I have an idea. Let's come down here to the pen every day until the foxhunt. To start, we'll ask the trainer, Mr.—" she paused, waiting for him to fill in a name.

"Foley," he obliged grudgingly.

". . . Foley to let the dogs sniff us through the fence. Eventually, maybe you will be willing to pet them. Perhaps once your father sees you with the hounds, he might reconsider his decision to keep you from the foxhunt."

Ewan clenched his jaw. "It willna work."

"Well, what do you have to lose?" she argued. "We can consider it a part of our lessons. And it will certainly be more entertaining than a math primer. If it doesn't work out, then no one else need know besides Mr. Foley and us. What do you say?"

Ewan stopped in his tracks and looked at her, his eyes narrowing with mistrust and suspicion. Yet deep in those blue depths, Genevieve was certain she saw a faint glimmer of indecision and something more . . . hope.

"I'll think about it," he finally said.

"That's fair. Now I suggest we go down to the peat bog."

He lifted his eyebrow in a way that reminded her of Connor. "The peat bog? What about our lessons? Aren't ye going to insist we go back to the schoolroom?"

"Do you want to go back?"

"Nay."

"Then let's have our lesson at the bog."

"But there are frogs and snakes down at the bog," he said, a sly grin blossoming across his face.

"I certainly hope so," she said firmly. "All the better to examine them in their natural habitat. And by the way, I'll be watching you closely to make certain you don't slip any unsuspecting creatures under your shirt for later use."

To her astonishment, he laughed and headed toward the bog. "All right, English. Mayhap this willna be such a bad day after all."

"Mayhap, indeed," she murmured with a smile.

A week passed, and Genevieve fell into a comfortable routine. She and Ewan had declared a tentative truce of sorts. After just one more time being late to supper and receiving no food, he began to arrive promptly, washed and well-mannered, much to everyone's delight.

He also appeared on time for lessons, and in turn, she kept them lively and entertaining. But to the boy's greatest delight, the lessons were not confined solely to the schoolroom.

She also continued to have daily tea with Mrs. MacDougal in her room, gossiped with the young serving girl Lucinda, and began to feel an integral part of the castle life. That extended as well to Malcom Douglas, for they'd made a point of playing chess together in the late afternoon, an activity she had greatly enjoyed with her grandfather.

Each evening after supper, Connor walked with her back to her room, chatting in a warm, friendly manner, a complete gentleman. There was no further mention of their time together ten years earlier. No suggestion in his voice or gaze, only amiable respect and warmth. Genevieve was puzzled, suspicious even, although she continued to be flattered by his impeccable attention. How could such a handsome, charming man not affect her? Nonetheless, she took every opportunity she could to remind herself that he was being kind because he needed her to stay for Ewan's sake.

Without Connor's knowledge, she and Ewan visited the dog pen every day. While Ewan hadn't worked up enough courage yet to step into the fenced area, he had permitted the dogs to sniff him and once she even caught him giving one of the hounds a pat on the head. The boy was still frightened by them, but the fact that he was willing even to try overcoming such a deep-seated fear was testament to how much he yearned for his father's approval.

Nonetheless, the more she watched Connor and Ewan together, the more baffled she became by Connor's cool indifference to his son. He had no warm words for Ewan, no fatherly hugs or pats, just polite exchanges that left Genevieve's heart aching for both of them. No wonder the boy felt compelled to disobey. It was the only way he seemed able to get his father's attention.

This morning after lessons, she strolled through the garden, when suddenly she heard steps behind her. She turned around to see Connor clad in a pair of tan breeches, a crisp white linen shirt, and black boots. His devil-black hair had been tied at the nape of his neck, and he was freshly shaved. Her heart skipped a beat. He looked devastatingly handsome.

"I heard ye've been spending time here," he said. "Do ye like our gardens?"

"They are lovely. I hope you don't mind that I help tend to the flowers. I do so miss my own garden."

"I dinna mind at all," he said graciously. "In fact, I'm pleased ye are able to find some solace here." He pointed to a small stone bench. "Do ye have a moment to speak wi' me?"

"Of course," she said, lifting her skirts and sitting gingerly. He joined her, his thighs brushing against her skirts. Her heart stumbled. Just sitting next to him with the sun warm on their heads and shoulders caused a flood of memories to rush back.

"How is Ewan doing wi' his lessons?" he asked.

"Quite well, actually. It's my pleasure to inform you that he is not dim-witted at all. Ewan is a highly intelligent and curious boy. I feel confident he will progress rapidly."

"I'm glad to hear that, although I must say I'm a wee surprised," he said in his soft burr. "Ye are the first governess to speak so kindly o' Ewan."

"I'm not speaking kindly, I'm speaking truthfully. He has many talents I haven't yet explored to my satisfaction. Did you know he is quite an accomplished sketcher?"

"Ewan?" Connor said, clearly surprised.

"Yes. He provided me with a beautifully detailed sketch of an oak leaf. And he drew a lovely representation of the castle."

" 'Tis a talent he received from his mum, no doubt. Janet was quite an accomplished painter."

It was the first time she'd ever heard him bring up her name voluntarily. "You'll have to come by and see his efforts for yourself."

"I must, indeed."

The conversation lulled, and Genevieve felt increasingly awkward sitting so close to him. Just being near him heightened her senses to an extraordinary level. The color of the flowers seemed more vivid, the sun warmer, and the scents of the garden far more fragrant when he was near.

"There is another matter o' which I wished to inform ye," he said shielding his eyes from the sun. "The foxhunt will commence next week. I've invited several important guests, and the celebration will take place o'er a few days. I'd like ye to keep the lad out o' the way."

"I'll do my best, of course. But if I may be so bold as to inquire, why won't you permit Ewan to accompany you on the foxhunt?"

He raised an eyebrow. "I thought ye didna approve of the foxhunt."

"I don't. But that doesn't change the fact that your son wants desperately to attend."

"He's too young."

"Children as young as six years of age foxhunt in England."

"This isna England," he growled.

She looked at him intently. "Why don't you really want him to go?"

Connor sighed, realizing she intended to persist. "Ewan is afraid o' the hounds. He may think he could manage, but 'twould be a terrifying experience for him. I've no wish to upset the lad."

She shifted slightly on the bench. "What if he weren't so frightened anymore? Would that change your mind?"

He studied her for a long moment. "Just what are ye plotting, Genevieve?"

"You'll see. I ask only that you reserve judgment on your final decision about the foxhunt."

He considered it for a minute and then nodded his head. "Agreed."

She smiled. "I thank you, then."

He smiled back, a bit of the devil in his eyes, and for a moment she saw the young man he'd once been, unburdened by the responsibilities of life. A bittersweet longing filled her, and she had to look away for fear he'd see it in her eyes.

"Oh, and my da has talked me into hosting a ball to entertain our guests before the foxhunt," he added casually as if announcing a ball were no important matter. "I'm no' certain it is a good idea, but 'tis something he truly wanted to do, so I decided to indulge him."

Genevieve felt her heart flutter with dread. Balls reminded her unhappily of her failed London Season.

"I suppose you'd like Ewan to attend," she said.

"Aye. Can ye see that he is suitably prepared?"

"In what way did you have in mind?"

He seemed at a loss. "I dinna know. I would think the proper behavior for a lad at such things. I suppose he should be taught how to dance."

"In a week?" Genevieve said in shock.

"Is that no' possible?" Connor asked worriedly. He looked so panicked that she almost felt sorry for him. Men were so utterly daft when it came to such things.

"I suppose I can teach him a step or two."

Connor looked visibly relieved. "Good."

"What kind of ball is it to be?"

He shrugged. "A costume ball."

"A costume ball?" she exclaimed in exasperation. "It's not as if I can simply produce a suitable costume for him out of thin air."

"Mrs. MacDougal will take care o' it for ye," he assured her. "She'll make one for ye, too."

"For me? You wish me to attend?"

"O' course, I wish ye to attend."

She searched around for a reason to refuse, but could think of none. He had clearly tied her presence to the ball as part of her duties in monitoring Ewan. How could she say no?

"Well, if that is what you desire."

"It is," he said, and for a moment, his expression softened.

She stood, her mind racing. "Then there is much to be

done. I must see to things at once. May I have your permission to leave?"

He seemed pleased that she had asked. "As ye wish, Genevieve."

She started to walk away, then stopped and looked over her shoulder at him. He still sat on the bench watching her, smiling. The sunlight danced across his dark hair, his face illuminated with a passionate kind of beauty. Even now her memories of him remained strong and clear, as did her attraction.

He lifted a dark eyebrow questioningly. "Is there something else, lass?"

She shook her head, denying the message of her heart. "No," she said quietly. "There is nothing at all."

Four

"I think Mari will be the one to find the fox," Genevieve said, petting the sweet brown-haired hound over the wooden fence.

"No' possible; she's a lassie," Ewan said, bravely reaching over the fence to scratch her behind the ears. "'Twill be a male who leads the pack. Charlie, I think," he said, looking over at the large black dog.

Genevieve marveled at how hard Ewan had worked to overcome his fear of the dogs. While he was not yet comfortable in their presence, no longer was he terrified. In fact, he had made progress with a great many things. He showed up for his lessons, and the work had gone as well as could be expected. Ewan was still wary and not entirely cooperative, but at least he was coming along. She thanked God for small things.

Genevieve had resumed scratching Mari's hindquarters when the sound of hoofbeats caught her attention. Turning, she saw a group of six people ride in to the courtyard. Curious, she craned her neck to see who the visitors were. As the riders dismounted, Genevieve saw Connor stride out of the castle and go directly to a cloaked woman who remained seated on her mount. Connor offered her a hand and she took it, sliding down to the ground, safely ensconced in his arms. For a moment, Genevieve felt an unexpected surge of jealousy.

The hood slipped back from the woman's head, and thick black hair spilled down her back in a cascading wave. She said something to Connor and he laughed, leaning his head down toward her.

"Who's that?" Genevieve murmured.

"Lady Catherine Montclair," Ewan said.

"Montclair?" Genevieve echoed and then an unpleasant thought leaped to mind. "She wouldn't happen to have been the former Catherine Graham, would she?"

Ewan looked at her curiously. "How did ye know she was o' the Graham clan?"

"A fortunate supposition," she said, her stomach starting to churn uncomfortably. So this was the woman Connor had wished to marry before he'd been forced to wed Janet MacIntyre.

"I hate her," Ewan declared.

Genevieve gasped. "That's truly an awful thing to say," she admonished, not able to tear her eyes away from Connor and Catherine. They certainly were a handsome couple.

Catherine laughed, the tinkling sound floating toward them on the breeze. Suddenly Connor lifted his dark head, as if sensing she was watching. His gaze landed on hers, intense and thoughtful. Embarrassed she had been caught staring openly at the two of them, Genevieve flushed and turned away, but not before she saw Catherine link her arm possessively with his.

Genevieve marched over to the fence and began petting Mari again, her thoughts awhirl. Ewan followed.

"I hope she doesna want to stay long this time," he muttered unhappily.

"This time?" Genevieve said. God's mercy, just how often did Catherine visit? "Isn't she . . . well, already wed?" Not that it would matter to a rogue like Connor, but for Ewan's sake, she hoped it did.

"She was married. But old Archibald died just a month before mum."

Stunned, Genevieve fell silent. What an extraordinary coincidence that Connor's and Catherine's respective spouses had died within a month of each other.

"She's come here a lot since mum died," he said, standing on the bottom log of the fence and reaching over toward Mari.

"Oh," Genevieve said quietly, digesting that unpleasant bit of information. "Isn't it a bit odd that she is here already? The foxhunt won't take place until next week."

Ewan shrugged. "I dinna think Da minds spending time wi' her. At least it means he willna have to be wi' me." Bitterness tinged his voice, and Genevieve winced inwardly.

"Your father is simply being a gentleman, and duty requires that he spend time with his guests," she said.

Ewan looked at her curiously. "Why do ye defend him so?"

Why, indeed?

She kept her expression neutral. "I'm not defending him. I'm only stating facts."

"She doesna love Da," he said, scuffing his foot. "She just wants the treasure."

"Treasure?" Genevieve said, startled. "What treasure?"

Ewan heaved a sigh, clearly put upon to explain things as if she were a child. "The treasure of ole Black Gavin Douglas," he said patiently. "'Tis said he hid some jewels in the castle. People have been searching for centuries for the jewels without luck. But I'll find them someday. Then Da will see for himself that he doesna need Lady Catherine."

"Why would your father need Lady Catherine to find the treasure?"

"Because Lady Catherine's ancestor 'twas a friend o'

Black Gavin's. He wrote a map to the treasure, and Lady Catherine found it."

"She found a map leading to the treasure?" Genevieve said doubtfully. "Then why doesn't she just share the note with your father?"

He looked at her as if she were truly daft. "Because she wants part o' the treasure for herself."

Genevieve laughed. "That's the most ridiculous thing I've ever heard. It's a marvelous tale, Ewan, but most likely not true. Surely any hidden treasure would have been found by now, especially if such a map did exist."

Ewan shook his head stubbornly. "I dinna think so. Besides, I heard Da and Lady Catherine talking about it."

"You weren't eavesdropping, were you?" she admonished.

He grinned. "Can I help it if they speak loudly? I overheard them speaking about the treasure just before my mum died."

Now *that* was far more disquieting. "Well, I think that's enough talk of hidden treasure," she said briskly. "Let's return to the schoolroom for the rest of our lesson."

To her surprise, he didn't complain as she led him back to the room. At least that thought warmed her even as the more disturbing thoughts of Connor, Catherine, and the purported treasure of Black Gavin served to worry her considerably.

Connor sat beside Catherine in the castle arboretum, trying to seem interested in her endless chatter about her latest journey to Edinburgh. He could care less about the newest fashions, the renovation of the inn where she had stayed, and the gossip about the so-called important people she had visited.

Why in God's name had the woman come so early?

He cursed inwardly, because he already knew the answer to that. She came for him, for what she believed would happen between them. And until he'd seen Genevieve, he'd thought it was a possible future.

However, his plans had altered once he realized his feelings for Genevieve remained true. Now he had to determine the best way to win Genevieve back without excessively hurting Catherine's feelings or pride. And from what he knew of Catherine, that would not be an easy task.

Hell and damnation, women would be the death of him.

He sighed and leaned back in his chair. The plants and flowers in the arboretum were in full bloom, and he should have been enjoying their beauty and fragrance. Instead he felt his mood sour.

Catherine said something and patted him on the knee. That intimate gesture from a woman of her beauty and stature would have had most men fervently counting their blessings. He could see how easily he had fallen for her as a lad. She had a full, curvy body, and her thick black hair hung in graceful curves over her shoulders. Her skin was the color of pearls dusted with rose, her eyes an enchanting shade of green.

Yet for all that, she could also be cruel and cold, and he hadn't always liked what he'd seen. Besides, there was no compelling pull, no common interests, and no real passion beyond that of the physical between the two of them. Had it not been for Genevieve, he might have been content with that much. But now he knew better.

Now he wanted more.

It had been a lesson well learned that beauty was skin deep and did not a blissful marriage make. Just thinking about the years he'd spent with Janet caused his chest to constrict uncomfortably. But Catherine knew too much about him, about his past. If she even suspected his affection for Genevieve, she could make trouble that even he would be hard-pressed to handle.

Christ's wounds, he had to do something to extricate himself from this intolerable situation before he lost any of the gains he had made so far with Genevieve.

But how in hell's name was he going to do that with Catherine watching his every move?

Five

As the days of the costume ball and foxhunt approached, the castle whirled in a frenzy of activity. The kitchen was busy both day and night, and Mrs. MacDougal looked harried and worried every time Genevieve saw her.

Genevieve had been briefly and formally introduced to Catherine, who had barely acknowledged her existence. She'd seen the woman about the castle, ordering people to and fro as if she already lived here. Maidservants scurried about scrubbing floors, replacing rushes, and beating the rugs.

Several nights in a row, Ewan and Genevieve ate supper alone at the big table in the Great Hall since Malcom, Connor, Catherine, and her entourage apparently dined far later in the evening. Genevieve tried hard not to be jealous when she saw Connor and Catherine strolling about the castle grounds, but she was.

And she hated herself for it.

On day five of Catherine's visit, Genevieve had the unexpected opportunity to get a closer look at the woman. Catherine swept into the Great Hall with Connor and Malcom trailing close behind, apparently determined to have an early supper. Genevieve gave Ewan a discreet nod of her head and the boy reluctantly stood until Catherine was seated.

To Genevieve's dismay, unlike some women, Catherine was even more beautiful close up. Her long black hair was intertwined with threads of gold that glittered in the candlelight, complementing her stunning black velvet gown. Just being in the same room with her made Genevieve feel even more dowdy than usual.

As she had expected, Catherine barely even registered her presence, never once addressing her directly, clearly considering her as naught more than a servant. Yet during some point in the evening, she felt Catherine's interested gaze upon her and felt a distinct shift in the atmosphere.

Soon thereafter, Genevieve rose to leave, having stayed far longer than was proper for a governess. But Connor would have none of it. He insisted she stay and chat with them, after ordering a servant to fill her wine cup again. She had reluctantly taken her seat again when the conversation suddenly turned to her.

"So, ye are English," Catherine said, her voice carrying just a hint of distaste. "A Londoner?"

Genevieve smiled sweetly. "I'm from northern England, actually. Alnwick, to be exact."

"Never heard o' it," Catherine said and turned her beautiful green eyes on Connor. "An Englishwoman for a governess. I must say, Connor, this is quite . . . unusual, even for ye."

Genevieve stiffened at the woman's casual but very pointed use of his Christian name in front of both his father and son. This was clearly a woman making a public claim on her territory.

If Connor understood the implication, he didn't show it. "Miss Fitzsimmons is an old friend of the family," he said, smiling easily.

"Is that so?" Catherine said, lifting a delicate eyebrow. "Just how old a friend?"

For some unfathomable reason, Malcom unexpectedly laughed. "Well now, my dear, her grandda and I go back quite a ways. Connor and I spent most o' a summer at their estate some years ago. Miss Fitzsimmons was an impeccable host."

Genevieve flushed. Malcom was clearly baiting the woman and seeming to enjoy every moment. Even worse, Connor made no move to stop him.

"It was ten years ago," she offered, then wondered why in God's name she had volunteered the information.

"Well, well," Catherine murmured, regarding Genevieve thoughtfully over her wine cup. "How very interesting."

"Not really," Genevieve said, rising to her feet. Her cheeks were burning uncomfortably. "Well, if no one would mind, I will retire for the evening."

The men at the table rose, but before Connor could offer to escort her, she invited Ewan to do so. He looked reluctant to leave the table, but, to her surprise, agreed. Gallantly he walked her to her door, pausing only momentarily before darting back toward the Great Hall.

Why she did not simply enter her room and retire for the evening, she didn't know. One minute she had her hand on the latch, and the next, she turned and headed toward the spiral steps at the end of the corridor. Without consciously making the decision, she began climbing up the long, winding staircase that led to the north tower. At first the way was dimly lit from below, but as she ascended farther, she had to feel the way with her hands. It was a far greater climb than she had expected and she was quite out of breath by the time she reached the top. Genevieve paused as she felt the cold wood of the door beneath her fingers. Groping for the latch, she pushed down, certain it would be locked. To her astonishment, the door swung open with a groaning creak. She blinked, trying to let her eyes adjust to the bright light of the moon that spilled into the room through an open window.

Now why was the window open?

For a moment, Genevieve stood in the doorway, listening to the whistle of the wind through the empty room, her heart beating rapidly. She could see the dim shape of a single chair and, in the corner by the window, a spinning wheel. She had no idea why she had come or what she hoped to find. Yet here she stood in the very room where Janet Douglas had met her untimely death.

Compelled forward by morbid curiosity, she moved toward the window. Cautiously, she dared a glimpse down at the courtyard below.

Suddenly Genevieve heard a clatter and whirled around, shrieking as a dark form grabbed her by the upper arm. She was yanked away from the window and slammed into the stone wall, the breath rushing from her lungs with a loud whoosh.

"What in the devil are *ye* doing here?" Connor growled, his curt voice lashing out at her. In the moonlight she could see his nostrils flared with fury, his eyes cold with anger.

"I . . . I . . ." Genevieve stammered, fighting to catch her breath and slow the thunder of her heart. "I was just exploring."

"Exploring?" he said roughly. "Here?"

"I'm sorry," she said, her body shaking. "I didn't know it was forbidden."

His grip on her shoulders eased, although he still pinned her against the wall. "'Tis no' forbidden. But if ye had wished to see the room, ye could have asked."

"You are right. I apologize."

His anger seemed to fade slightly. "Why did ye open the window?"

"I didn't open the window. It was open when I arrived."

"'Twas already open?"

"Yes."

She could see he didn't believe her. "Where is your light?" he asked.

"I don't have one."

"Ye came up here in the dark?" he asked, his voice heavy with disbelief.

"I don't see yours," she said feeling ridiculously defensive.

"I dropped it when I entered the room and saw ye at the window."

"Oh," she said in a small voice, wondering why he had yet to move away from her. He still remained pressed tightly against her, his considerably large body shielding hers as if protecting her from something.

"Hell and damnation, Genevieve, ye could have been hurt up here," he finally said, his voice hoarse. "Ye could have been lost."

She thought it a curious choice of words, but before she could consider it more, he pulled her roughly, almost violently, to him, his mouth crashing against hers in a blast of heat and hunger. The careful barrier she'd erected around her heart was crushed in an instant as his mouth devoured her softness. These were not the gentle, tender kisses he had once bestowed upon her at age sixteen. These were the kisses of a man driven by hunger and untamed desire.

Her knees buckled beneath his unexpected ravishment, and she gripped his shoulders, both thrilled and shocked by the heady sensation of his burning lips and her body's welcoming response to him. He was devouring her and she was permitting it, *wanting* it more than anything she'd ever wanted before. He tangled his fingers in her hair, angling her mouth to fit his, demanding she meet him with the same reckless abandon.

She gave herself freely to the passion of his kiss, knowingly succumbing to the forceful domination of his lips. She was weak, but didn't care. She didn't want him to stop. She had never before been able to resist him, and she realized she never would.

Then, as abruptly as he had bent to kiss her, he lifted his mouth, closed his eyes, and leaned his forehead against the stone wall beside her head. She didn't dare move. The blood pounded in her brain, leaped from her heart, and clogged in her throat along with a raw and powerful emotion.

Love.

For a moment, he said nothing. Then he reached over to close the window. "Let's go," he said shortly. "Take my hand and I'll lead ye down the stairs. They can be quite treacherous in the dark."

She hesitated for a moment, not trusting herself to touch him again and deeply shaken from his passionate onslaught. He waited for her to decide, and slowly she gave him her hand. He grasped it firmly, those same hands having moments before been wound in her hair.

Connor was silent for the entire trip down the stairs and said not even a good night as he dropped her off at her room and walked away. Genevieve entered and shut the door, leaning back against it and closing her eyes.

She still loved him. It was an admission dredged from a place beyond logic and reason. And it was horribly, awfully true.

What had happened in the tower between the two of them?

She trembled, shaken deeply by the encounter. Had he followed her, and, if not, why *had* he gone to tower? And who had been there before her and opened the window?

Ignoring a sudden chill, she undressed for bed and blew out the candle. Tonight she would dream of good things, of things that were safe. But just as she drifted off to sleep, she thought she heard a soft voice whispering in her ear.

It warned her beware of Connor Douglas.

Six

Other castle guests began trickling in on Wednesday morning for the foxhunt that would take place on Saturday. Even more anticipated, it seemed, was Thursday night's costume ball. The castle bustled with servants scurrying about cleaning, baking, and preparing rooms for the numerous guests. Genevieve personally counted twelve new faces, but was certain she had missed at least a few.

In deference to all the excitement, she suspended Ewan's regular lessons and they spent their days either practicing dance steps or down with the hounds. She was amazed at his progress and could only attribute it to his deep-seated desire to please his father.

"We still have to convince your father," she warned him. "And that may not be easy."

"We can," Ewan said—so confidently that Genevieve prayed he was right.

The rest of Wednesday Genevieve spent helping Mrs. MacDougal sew her and Ewan's costumes. Once Ewan heard he would be permitted to attend the ball, he promptly announced he wished to be a pirate. Mrs. MacDougal set two girls to work sewing his, while she selected a light blue gown to serve as a costume for Genevieve.

"Who shall I be in that?" Genevieve asked the housekeeper curiously.

"Christina Douglas, wife o' Black Gavin."

"Christina Douglas?" Genevieve gasped in surprise. "Why her?"

Mrs. MacDougal shrugged. "Because Connor requested it. And because 'twill be an easy costume to sew. She haunts the tower, havena ye heard?"

"The north tower?" Genevieve asked, thinking of the open window.

"Aye, indeed. And certainly ye've heard o' the treasure Black Gavin hid in the castle."

"Ewan told me. Surely you don't really believe such rubbish."

"'Tisn't for me to believe or no'. It simply is."

Genevieve sank into a chair. "Whatever happened to Christina?"

"After Gavin was killed, she disappeared. Some believe she found the treasure and ran wi' it, but she was never found alive or dead. And no one ever revealed the treasure."

Genevieve shuddered. "It sounds like this treasure, if it really exists, brings rather ill luck."

"'Tis so. After all, the treasure came from the English, and its price was treachery and betrayal o' Gavin's own people," Mrs. MacDougal commented. "If the truth be known, ye sort o' resemble Christina Douglas."

"I do?"

"Aye, ye can see for yerself. Her portrait hangs in the Great Hall on the wall west o' the hearth. She is sitting in the garden, clad in a gown o' blue with silver threads."

"And thus your choice of the blue gown. I must have a look at her."

"Indeed, ye should," she said, lifting up Genevieve's gown and studying it. "Ye just take care o' our Ewan.

'Twill be his first ball, and certainly a night to remember. Perhaps for us all."

Genevieve nodded, unaware of just how right she would be.

"Ye shall no' escape me this time, Madame," Ewan growled, taking a step forward in the schoolroom and brandishing a wooden sword. The black patch over his right eye slid down his nose and he quickly pushed it up. "Surrender your treasure at once or face a certain death."

Genevieve held up her hands in mock terror. "I beg of you, sire, don't harm me."

Ewan laughed, and Genevieve was delighted to see the warmth actually reach his eyes for the first time since they had met.

"Well, do I look fierce enough for the ball tonight?" he asked, holding out his hands and turning around for her inspection. Truthfully, she thought he looked nothing short of adorable in a flowing shirt of white, black breeches, a red rag tied over his head, and a wooden sword attached to his waist with a strip of leather. But she knew better than to say it.

"You look positively ferocious," she said, reaching up to adjust the rag on his head. "And remember, in front of the other guests you should address me as Miss Fitzsimmons."

He gave her a boyish grin. "I never call ye that. And tonight I shall call ye Christina Douglas. Did ye know ye look just like her?"

"There is a slight resemblance, I suppose."

Genevieve looked down at herself, smoothing down the folds of her blue gown. Mrs. MacDougal had draped the bodice of her gown with a silvery gauze, undoubtedly to look similar to the one worn by the real Christina Douglas in the portrait.

"Come now," she said. "Let's practice those dance steps one last time before you put them into practice."

The musicians had already begun to play downstairs, and they could hear the lilting strains wafting in through the open door.

"Now don't forget when you ask a lady for the pleasure of a dance and she accepts, you need to offer her your arm." Genevieve held out her arm until Ewan took it. "Now lead me to the dance floor."

The boy did as told, but he looked so nervous, she thought he might wretch. Genevieve patted him on the shoulder. "This is not so terrible a thing."

"'Tis easy for ye to say," Ewan grumbled. "Ye're a lass. Ye like dancing."

She rolled her eyes, but took pity on him. "Now, take my right hand and then turn to your left. We shall both take three steps forward and then turn to face each other again."

He took her hand and immediately took three steps. Genevieve swallowed a laugh. "No, Ewan, you must wait for the lady before you take the three steps. Like this." She showed him how to proceed and he blushed bright red, scuffing his foot on the floor.

"Sorry," he mumbled.

"You're doing fine."

They practiced it a few more times until they heard a noise at the doorway. Both of them whirled around to see Connor leaning against the doorjamb. He looked stunningly resplendent in a blazing white shirt and a kilt of black and gray. A plaid in matching colors had been draped over one shoulder and fastened with a stunning red ruby brooch. His black devil hair hung loose about his shoulders, and a sheathed dirk had been fastened to his waist with a leather belt. He looked so much like the wild Black Gavin in the painting that it took her breath away.

"Well done, lad," he said. "Ye're no' bad on your feet for a pirate."

Pleased by the praise, Ewan puffed out his chest. "Dancing is easy," he proclaimed.

Genevieve stifled a laugh at the cocky boast and glanced at Connor. He stared at her, a mixture of amusement, heat, and desire on his face. They had not spoken of the kiss in the tower; in fact, had spoken very little since that night. Which suited Genevieve just fine, because she had every intention of forgetting that it ever happened.

"Christina Douglas," he murmured. "The resemblance is remarkable."

"Mrs. MacDougal said you requested it," Genevieve responded hastily. "Given that we had little time to make a costume, I agreed this was a suitable choice."

A smile spread slowly across his face. "I'm pleased that ye saw fit to indulge me. May I request the pleasure o' this dance?"

"Now?" squeaked Genevieve. "But what about your guests downstairs?"

Connor laughed, his teeth flashing white. "Ewan, go on down to the ball and take my place temporarily as host, would ye, lad? Miss Fitzsimmons and I will join ye in a minute. I'd have her instruct me in a dance step or two."

"Ye want me to host?" Ewan asked in astonishment. "Aye, Da, I can do that," he breathed and darted out into the corridor, presumably before his father changed his mind.

"He's a good lad," Connor said, turning to Genevieve and bowing slightly at the waist. "Shall we begin, my lady?"

Genevieve nodded, trying to still the hammering of her heart. Connor held out his arm, and she took it. He slid his warm hand down her arm, leaving a trail of fire in his wake before linking fingers with her. Together they began to dance, perfectly in step with each other. After a few minutes, Genevieve spoke.

"It's clear you don't need any instruction."

"'Tis only because I have an excellent partner," he replied, a bit of the devil in his blue eyes.

She couldn't help but smile. "You are quite incorrigible. And you do realize that wearing the kilt is illegal. The king has decreed it so."

"Really?" Connor said in mock surprise, pressing his palm expertly against hers, and stepped forward. "And are ye intending to enforce the king's decree?"

"Of course, not," she replied primly. "But aren't you worried that word of this will get back to the king?"

"Are ye?"

"Certainly I am. You are my employer, after all. If you are led to the gaol, who will pay my stipend?"

His warm fingers gripped hers as they stepped side by side. An air of command exuded from him, reminding her just how powerful and virile he was. "Is that all that concerns ye?" he said in amusement. "Your stipend?"

"I would worry for the effect it would have on Ewan, of course."

He laughed. "Ye worry for naught. 'Tis just a costume, Genevieve."

She looked at him doubtfully. "A costume? And just who are you supposed to be?"

"Why Black Gavin, o' course. And if 'tis necessary, I'll remind the English that he was the one and only Douglas loyal to the crown."

Genevieve stopped dancing. "You're dressed as Black Gavin?"

In one motion, he pulled her into his arms. This was not part of the dance. "Aye, and for tonight at least, it appears that makes ye my wife," he murmured, his breath hot against her ear. "What say ye o' that?"

Their eyes locked. His arms tightened around her, one hand pressing into the small of her back. She was acutely conscious of where his warm flesh touched her, and her body tingled from the contact. His stare was bold and seductive, something intense smoldering in his normally cool blue eyes. Her body responded to him with such a fierce intensity it left her reeling.

Still, she pretended indifference. "I'd say naught, of course. It is nothing but a pretense."

His gaze intensified, searching her expression for something. *But what?*

"I like your hair loose like this," he said, taking a strand and winding it around his finger. "'Tis soft and pretty."

"It is really quite ordinary and plain."

He laughed, a rich, deep sound. "Ye are far too modest, Genevieve. Ye have no idea how beautiful ye really are."

"Now you patronize me."

His expression turned serious. "Never. Ye are beautiful, and never more so than at this moment. Come now, dinna ye still believe in a wee bit o' magic?"

She had believed once, she almost said aloud. When she'd allowed a handsome Scottish rogue to kiss her under the stars and he told her she was beautiful. Never again.

She shrugged off his closeness, his words. "Magic is for the young and foolish. I am neither."

She detected a flicker in his gaze. "One is never too old for magic," he said softly. "I could make ye believe. I did once before."

Before she could speak, he kissed her, caressing her lips with his mouth in almost a reverent fashion. She quivered at the sweet tenderness of it and, unable to resist, stood on tiptoe, winding her arms around his neck and kissing him back.

He groaned at her response, his arms tightening around her, deepening the kiss. The gentle massage sent currents of desire through her, and she savored every moment, a part of her wondering if it would be their last kiss. His hands explored the hollows of her back, and she molded into the hard contours of his body. She expected hunger and urgency in his kiss, like before in the tower, but tonight his kiss was thoughtful and intimate. Achingly affectionate and dreamy. A kiss that would make even a hardened heart believe in magic.

All too soon, he lifted his head and brushed a light kiss across her forehead. "So, do ye feel it?" he breathed against her hair. "'Tis just as it was 'tween us ten years ago."

The memories rushed back then and the pain, long suppressed and buried, broke to the surface in an agonizing burst of anguish and grief.

"I'm *not* the same girl you knew," she said fiercely. "She no longer exists."

"Och, but I think she does."

The memories of his abrupt departure assailed her, jagged and hurtful. "I'll not let you do this to me again."

He raised a dark eyebrow. "Do what?"

"Take liberties with me because it amuses you. I know you sent for me because you pitied me. I . . . I had nowhere else to go. But you hired me to teach your son and nothing else. I'll not serve as an object of your entertainment because you are bored with your other dalliances."

He looked stunned by her words. "An object o' entertainment?" he repeated, anger lighting in his eyes. "That's what ye think ye are to me?"

"And why shouldn't I think that?" she snapped, furious that once again he had caused her to forget reason, exposing her deepest vulnerabilities. "I've seen you with Catherine. This time around I know that she's your intended. So I'm putting you on notice that I'll not permit myself to be ravished again by nothing more than a . . . a . . . kilt-clad rogue!" The words came out in an uncontrolled, angry rush.

Now he was angry, too, his voice cool. "Is that really what ye think o' me, Genevieve? That I'm naught more than a man who canna keep his hands off a woman? A man who cares no' who he takes to his bed?"

"That's exactly what I think," she said, the pain in her heart making her reckless with her words. "Go back to the arms of the beautiful Catherine, where you belong, and cease your roguish dalliance with me."

She turned away from him, hating the fact that her voice sounded so strained and so terribly, awfully . . . jealous. She desperately wanted him to leave before the tears fell and she humiliated herself any further.

"I thought o' all people, ye knew me better than that," he said quietly. "I hoped that ye did."

She still could not bring herself to look at him. "And just what do I know of you, Connor? That you made sweet promises to me, none of which you ever intended to keep? Or that you broke my heart when you left without a word or explanation? How do you expect me to trust a man who drove his own wife to her death?"

The minute the words slipped out she wanted to take them back. Horrified, she turned to face him, shocked at how pale his face had gone. "Connor, I'm sorry. I was angry and hurt. I didn't mean to say that."

It was too late. Shutters fell over his eyes, his expression turning distant and cool. "I suppose ye are right about me," he said stiffly. "How kind of ye to give me a most honest, if no' brutal, look at my true self. Now, I must attend to my duties and permit ye to see to yours. That will be all."

With those bitingly cold words, he left the schoolroom without a backward glance. For a moment, Genevieve simply stood there, a horrible, unbearable pain squeezing her heart.

"If only you knew how much I still love you," she whispered, trying to swallow the lump lingering in her throat. "But I'll not be your mistress, Connor. For to do so would destroy what little is left of my heart."

Seven

The ball was a smashing success. Mrs. MacDougal and the other servants had transformed the Great Hall into an elegant ballroom, with hundreds of candles illuminating the space and beautiful displays of flowers. A group of colorfully dressed musicians played in one corner, and a long trundle table groaned under the weight of dozens of plates of food.

Guests mingled, ate, and danced with appropriate merriment as Connor made his way among them, stopping to chat. He knew he appeared the impeccable host, gracious and generous, enjoying himself as much as them. But inside he felt angry, despondent, and hurt.

Now he knew what Genevieve truly thought of him.

Her accusations stung, even more so because many of them had been true. He was no saint, and he had never claimed to be. But his feelings for her were different. They *always* had been different. Nonetheless, she hadn't believed him, hadn't believed his kisses were sincere. She didn't trust him, *couldn't* trust him because of his past. And in many ways, he didn't blame her.

Damn it all to hell.

Tonight he'd intended to reveal his feelings, to apologize for his mistakes over the past years. He wanted to tell her that he did not love Catherine, that he was not intending to wed her. But he'd never been good with words, and instead thought his kisses, his passion, would convey his true feelings. It had always worked for him in the past, and so he had hoped it might work with her.

Instead, it had only made things worse. Unfortunately, his ill-famed reputation was interfering with the most important relationship he'd ever had. What in God's name had she called him?

A kilt-clad rogue.

He winced inwardly. Did she really believe that?

Unbidden, he sought her out and saw her moving among the guests. She stayed close to Ewan, but was careful not to smother the lad. She looked so lovely and pure in that simple gown of blue. Even more surprisingly, she truly resembled Christina Douglas, with her impossible-to-tame brown hair flowing loose about her shoulders. He had no right to soil her, to stain her with his reputation, but, God help him, he still wanted her.

Clenching his fists, he turned away. Catherine murmured something, and he forced a smile. He would have to hurt her, too. He had no doubt she would quickly recover once he smoothed the way with a fair amount of coin, but he wished there was another way. He had no illusions that she loved him, because he knew she didn't. But they had been friends for a long time, and a union with her would have been tolerable. Once he might have been satisfied with a future like that, but now he could no longer be.

He sighed, knowing he should have told Catherine of his change of heart as soon as she arrived, but it would have been awkward for both of them, and he had no wish to embarrass her for the duration of her stay. It had been a risky approach, but he had done so because he was truly fond of her and hoped to spare her feelings.

But now that decision had cost him more than he would have liked with Genevieve, and he'd have to work hard to repair the fragile trust that had been building between them—if he ever could.

He caught a glimpse of blue from the corner of his eye and turned in time to see Genevieve and Ewan whirling across the floor. His breath caught in his throat at the sight of her with her head thrown back in laughter, her eyes sparkling. Emotion tightened in his chest. He wanted her no matter what she thought of him, and he had to figure out a way to win her back and soon.

Determined, he waited until Catherine's attention was elsewhere and made his way over to Genevieve and Ewan. He forced himself to keep his voice light, with no trace of his earlier anger.

"Miss Fitzsimmons, I'd like a word wi' ye tomorrow before the morning meal," he said, wincing inwardly when it came out more as a demand than a request. "If it would be convenient for ye," he added hoping that softened it a bit.

"Of course," she replied politely. "In fact, Ewan and I were just about to retire for the evening."

"That's . . . well . . . I . . ." he groped for something else to say, but as usual, words failed him. "Ye dance well," he finally blurted out, feeling himself redden. Could he sound any more like a complete imbecile?

He opened his mouth, thinking to utter something witty to recover, but Ewan had begun to stare at him curiously, and Catherine had just finished her dance and started toward him.

"I'll see ye in the library on the morrow. Dinna be late," he said to her curtly, then walked away.

He strode directly outside for a breath of fresh air and to let loose a string of curses. Christ's wounds, that had been a disaster of an idea. Now she was coming to the library, and he didn't have a single thing planned to say to convince her his feelings were true.

He didn't have time to dwell on it any further, because Catherine sidled up, linking her arm with his. "Will ye dance wi' me, Connor?" she asked, leaning into him.

He took another breath to steady himself. For one more night, he'd pretend to be the man she thought she wanted. But come tomorrow, he'd tell her the truth: His heart lay with another.

Genevieve awoke to a fierce pounding on her door. Startled, she jumped out of bed, snatched a robe and wrapped it around her. A quick glance at the window showed that it was still dark. She swung open the door and was shocked to see Connor standing there, still fully dressed in his kilt and plaid.

"What time is it?" she said, her mind foggy with sleep.

"Late," he said brusquely, removing his plaid and draping it over her shoulders. "Ye must come at once. Ewan's been hurt and is asking for ye. Fetch something for your feet."

"Hurt?" She gasped as she stumbled toward the hearth and slid her feet into a pair of shoes. The wool plaid was scratchy and smelled pleasantly of Connor. "What happened?"

"I dinna know exactly. Mrs. MacDougal just summoned me, and I'm stopping to get ye on my way out. Make haste now."

Panic streaked through her. "Where is he?"

"The hound pen," Connor said grimly.

"No," she whispered in dread. "Oh, my God, no."

She had to run to keep up with Connor's hurried strides. His plaid shielded her from the cool wind, but inwardly she was chilled by fear.

They saw the bobbing torches and heard the murmur of voices near the dog pen long before they saw Ewan.

Connor pushed his way through the small crowd and easily jumped the fence. Worried, he knelt at his son's side. Ewan lay on his back, clutching his left shoulder, tears streaming down his face. He was still dressed in his pirate's costume. Genevieve felt a rush of guilt and shame. He must have slipped out after they had bid each other good night. She hadn't thought to check on him before going to sleep.

What kind of governess was she?

"Da," he cried, relief crossing his face when he saw Connor.

Connor gently took the boy's hand. "What happened, lad?"

"I . . . I was trying to climb the fence when I fell."

"What in the devil were ye doing down here at this hour?" Connor asked.

Ewan glanced at Genevieve, shamefaced. "I was too excited to sleep. I thought to see the hounds just one last time so I could show ye how well I can handle them now. But 'twas dark and I slipped."

"Are ye hurt badly?"

He tried bravely to hold back the tears. "Just my shoulder, I fear."

Genevieve felt tears dampen her cheeks. "It's going to be all right, Ewan," she called softly.

"I'm sorry," he said to her between sobs. "I've ruined everything. I'll never be able to go on the foxhunt now."

"There will be other times," Genevieve reassured him.

"Says who?" Connor snapped. "I'll no' have Ewan harmed again."

"Dinna be mad at her," Ewan said. "Miss Fitzsimmons helped me see that the hounds are no' so frightening."

It was the first time she had ever heard him call her by

her proper name, and emotion thickened in her throat at his defense.

"I've sent for the doctor," Connor said, lifting Ewan from the ground. "Ye'll rest in your room until he arrives." He handed the boy over the fence and into the arms of a man on the other side. After jumping over, he took Ewan back in his arms.

Without another word, he strode toward the castle. Genevieve followed silently, her heart heavy. She was certain she'd soon have to face the moment she'd been dreading since her arrival.

She was about to be dismissed.

After Connor had settled Ewan into bed, he motioned to Genevieve to retreat to the schoolroom. He followed her, leaving Ewan's door slightly ajar.

Instead of immediately admonishing her, he all but ignored her, pacing the schoolroom with his hands clasped behind his back. He still wore his kilt, and as he moved, she caught fascinating glimpses of his bare, muscular thighs.

"Connor, I'm sorry," she finally said. "I should have consulted with you before allowing Ewan to work with the hounds. It's just that he wanted so badly to surprise you, to make you proud."

He stopped pacing and crooked his finger. "Come here," he said, his voice low and controlled. She took several steps forward until she stood nearly toe to toe with him.

"Was this your idea or Ewan's?" he asked, a dark gleam in his eyes.

"Mine."

He laughed, but without humor. "Are ye certain Ewan

didna manipulate ye into doing this? To plan this to look like an accident so he could rid ye from the castle?"

The thought both startled and unnerved her. "No," she said quickly, then reconsidered. But when she remembered the look of sheer joy on Ewan's face when he petted the hounds for the first time, she shook her head more firmly. "No, I'm certain. This was no devious plan of Ewan's."

Connor sighed deeply. "Then 'tis ye I must blame for this mishap."

"Yes, I accept full blame." She paused and then plunged on. "And yet I feel it is my duty to point out that part of the blame is yours as well."

His eyebrows shot up. "Mine?"

Since she felt she would be dismissed by the end of the conversation anyway, she decided to be completely candid with him. "Yes, yours. If only you had shown Ewan some attention, he wouldn't have been so starved for it, and I wouldn't have been so willing to help him gain it. But you apparently couldn't bring yourself to spare that kind of affection. Instead, you have had nothing but the coolest reserve for your own son, while you spent your time arranging foxhunts and balls, dallying with widowed women, and kissing the governess."

There. It came out a bit bolder and harsher than she intended, but she'd said it. And by God's mercy, it was the truth.

For a moment he simply looked at her in surprised incredulity. Then his eyes narrowed and she saw fire flash within their depths.

"Ye dare to tell me how to act with my son?"

"Someone has to. You barely show him any fatherly interest."

He straightened, his eyes narrowing. "That isna true. I provide for him, dinna I? He has a home, a name. I've hired him a governess to teach him the ways o' the world. What more does he expect? What more do *ye* expect?"

"I expect a lot from you. But Ewan doesn't *expect* anything. He simply wants your love, your affection. You may not realize it, but you behave quite differently when you're around him. It's like you become another person—more formal, cool and aloof. Most of the time, you don't even look directly at him. It's as if you've purposely erected some kind of barrier between you and Ewan."

"That is quite enough," he growled.

She ignored his command. "Connor, I don't know what happened between you and your wife, but Ewan is innocent. Would it hurt so terribly much to lower that barrier a bit and get to know him? He's obviously hurting, and so are you. Perhaps together you can resolve the issues that are keeping you apart."

Before he could reply, they both heard a noise in the corridor. Connor strode out and Genevieve heard him greet the physician. She waited in the schoolroom, listening to the low murmur of their voices while the doctor examined Ewan. After a short time, Connor returned to the schoolroom.

"It seems we are fortunate Ewan hurt naught more than his shoulder," he said. "The doctor will bind it."

She breathed a sigh of relief. "Thank God."

His mouth tightened at the corners. "Despite what ye think, Genevieve, I know what's best for my son."

She sighed wearily. "I know you mean well, Connor, but do you really? Have you asked Ewan how he feels about the possible union between you and Catherine? It's hard enough for him to get your attention without a wife, and he's likely terrified of what will happen if he has more competition. Perhaps if you'd reassure him that everything will be fine once you're wed, he'd feel more secure about the marriage."

She paused sadly. "Now, having said my piece, I shall go pack my bags. If you would be so kind as to order me a carriage back to Alnwick on the morn, I would greatly appreciate it."

He stared at her, his mouth open. Then he snapped it shut. To her amazement, there was no longer anger in his eyes, only sadness and a deep-seated resignation.

"I'm no' dismissing ye," he said softly. "I dinna want ye to quit as Ewan's governess."

It was her turn to be surprised. "You don't?"

"Nay," he said shaking his head. "There is much I need to discuss wi' ye, but now is no' the time. I've a son in bed with a hurt shoulder and a castle full o' guests all expecting a grand foxhunt tomorrow. Just promise me that ye willna pack up and leave before I've had *my* say."

"Your say?" she repeated. "What do you mean?"

"Ye shall see," he said mysteriously. "I promise ye, ye shall see."

Eight

Genevieve sat in a chair next to Ewan's bed, reading him a story. Her eyes were gritty from a lack of sleep, but she refused to leave the boy alone. He'd slept only a few hours, then awakened in pain as the morning sun peeked through the drapery. She'd given him a tonic, and now he sat propped up, his injured shoulder bound snug in a sling made with white linen strips. A soft breeze wafted through the room, while outside the open window a light summer drizzle fell. Genevieve wondered if the rain would interfere with the foxhunt, which, as far as she knew, was still planned for tomorrow morning.

"I got ye in trouble wi' Da," Ewan said, leaning back against the pillows.

She shook her head. "No, I got myself in trouble."

"Will ye have to leave?"

"Do you want me to?" she asked curiously.

He shook his head vigorously. "Nay, I'd rather ye stayed."

"Well that certainly is a change of heart from when I first arrived," she said, her smile softening.

He plucked nervously at his bedsheets. "I'm sorry about that. Miss Fitzsimmons, there is something else I want to ask ye. Something I've been thinking about for a long time."

"You may ask me anything."

He exhaled a deep breath. "Do ye think my da is a murderer?"

A soft gasp escaped her. "What did you say?"

"Do ye think my da killed my mum?" he repeated in a rush, as if she'd forbid him to say it again.

Stunned, she groped for words. "Ewan, why ever would you think such a thing?"

His eyes filled with tears. "I saw him," he whispered. "That night. The night mum died."

Dread crawled up her spine. "You saw what?"

"They were arguing. He followed her to the tower. I crept up the stairs to listen. They were arguing. . . about me."

The pain and guilt in the boy's eyes tore at her heart. "Ewan, sometimes people argue about many things, even their children, but it doesn't mean they don't love them. It's actually quite a normal occurrence."

Ewan pressed his lips together. "M-mum was crying and Da was yelling at her. I heard him say he didn't love her and he wished he'd never wed her. Then suddenly 'twas quiet. I thought Da was coming out, so I ran downstairs and hid. A minute later, I saw him come down. I've never seen him angrier. After he passed, I climbed back up to the tower room to see Mum. I thought mayhap I could make her feel better. I opened the door, but she wasna there. 'Twas when I noticed the window was open."

Genevieve felt as if a hand were squeezing her heart. Had he told no one of this? "Oh, Ewan," she said, her voice barely a whisper.

His lower lip trembled. "I knew Mum hadna gone past me. So I walked slowly to the window and looked down. Th-there she was, just lying on the ground so verra still."

Genevieve couldn't speak, too horrified and appalled

that the boy had gone through such a traumatic experience. Instead, she reached out and pulled him into her arms, and he shook with heartbreaking sobs.

"Ewan, have you ever told anyone else about this?"

"Nay," he said in a muffled voice. "I was afraid."

"Of whom?"

"Da," he whispered. "Did I do something to make them argue so? Did I do something to make him so frightfully angry?"

"No," Genevieve said fiercely, her own eyes filling with tears. "None of this is your fault."

"Then whose fault is it?" he whispered, his eyes luminous and shimmering with wetness.

Genevieve stroked his hair. "I don't know," she said softly. "I truly don't know."

The morning turned into afternoon, and neither Genevieve nor Ewan spoke again of what the boy had seen in the castle tower the night his mother died. Instead, she had brought him his midday meal and they had a picnic in bed. She had just begun to read a new book when Connor suddenly appeared in the doorway. He was dressed in a tan colored riding suit and dark boots, clearly having been on a practice run for the foxhunt with his guests. To Genevieve's astonishment, instead of his usual brief and formal greeting from the doorway, he sat on the corner of Ewan's bed and patted the boy on the leg.

"So your secret is out," he said. "Ye've been working wi' the hounds."

Ewan nodded. "I'm sorry for what happened, Da. I just wanted to show ye that I'm no longer afraid o' them. At least no' most o' the time. Right, Miss Fitzsimmons?"

She smiled, and Connor turned his gaze on her. Something stirred in his eyes, but he said nothing.

"Ye really wished that much to go on the foxhunt?" he asked, returning his attention to Ewan.

"I'm no' a child any longer."

"Nay, ye are no'." They were no longer talking about the foxhunt. "Ye worked hard to conquer your fear. That is indeed the action o' a man."

The boy beamed with pride, and Genevieve felt tears prick her eyelids. Connor glanced at her over his shoulder. She smiled, and when he resumed speaking with Ewan, she slipped out of the room, leaving the two of them alone.

She was dabbing her eyes with the corner of her sleeve when she saw Malcom shuffling down the corridor, leaning heavily on his cane.

"How's my grandson?" he asked.

"Quite well. Connor is in speaking with him now."

"I'm relieved to hear that. I never knew Ewan was so interested in foxhunts."

"He's isn't really. He's more interested in gaining his father's approval." It slipped out before she could stop it. "I'm sorry," she apologized wearily, running a hand through her hair. "I seem to be quite adept lately at saying things I shouldn't."

Malcom sighed. "It has been a difficult time. Janet's death was hard on both o' them."

"I know. But thankfully it seems that Connor might at last be trying to rectify the past."

"Because o' ye."

"No, because I think he finally realizes how important he is to Ewan."

Malcom cleared his throat. "Dinna be so hard on Connor. There's a lot ye dinna know. A lot that could change your mind about him."

"There isn't anything that could matter more than loving his son."

Malcom ran a gnarled hand over his brow. "That's the problem, lass. Ewan isna his son."

Nine

Genevieve's mouth dropped open. "Wh-what did you say?"

Malcom motioned with his hand. "Follow me to the sitting room. The corridor is no' the place for such a discussion."

Stunned, she followed him and waited patiently while he asked Mrs. MacDougal to bring them sweet tea and biscuits. Genevieve stirred the fire to a blaze by adding another square of peat.

After the housekeeper had served them and left, Genevieve sat back in the chair and asked the question burning on her tongue. "What do you mean Ewan isn't Connor's son?"

Malcom stared sadly into the fire. "Janet had a lover."

Genevieve felt as though she'd received a blow to the chest. "My God," she murmured.

"His name was John MacDonald," Malcom continued. "Quite the charming lad, and in many ways a lot like Connor. Anyway, Janet wanted to wed John, but her family wouldn't have it. Ye see, she'd been intended for Connor since the day she was born."

"What did Connor have to say about that?"

Malcom laughed, but it was not a happy sound. "He didna have any say, lass. He knew his responsibilities to his family, and he knew them well. He married her because I told him to."

He stood heavily on his cane and shuffled over to a wooden lowboy, from which he pulled a bottle of whiskey. He brought it over to the chairs where they sat and asked whether she'd like a dollop in her tea. Genevieve nodded, and after he added in the spirits, he sat down and picked up his teacup.

"The marriage was a mistake from the start. Connor and Janet were no' suited to each other. Janet wished to entertain and travel, while Connor preferred his solitude. 'Twas also a time when he began to shoulder more o' the responsibilities for the business, including the arrangement we shared wi' your grandda."

Genevieve took a sip of the tea, barely noticing as the whiskey burnt a trail down her throat. "It must have been a trying time for him. But how do you know Ewan isn't his son?" It was an indelicate question, and her cheeks heated as she asked it. But she *had* to know.

"Connor began to travel more and more often," he said wearily. "Part o' it was a genuine interest in the business, but more oft than no', I suspect 'twas to escape from Janet, from their loveless union. On one trip, he was away for nearly four months. When he came back, she confessed that she was with child and John was the da."

Genevieve closed her eyes, imagining the pain the revelation must have cost him. "Does Ewan know?"

"Nay, no one knows for certain except me and Connor and now ye. Connor might no' have told me, except I found him one night in the library drunker than I'd ever seen him. He never drank to excess, so it frightened me. 'Twas then he told me what happened. I'd been charged wi' keeping matters at the castle safe until his return, so 'twas my fault I failed to discover that Janet had been trysting wi' John."

"You can't blame yourself," she said, her thoughts awhirl. "Nor can Connor blame himself."

"I assure ye, we both did. In many ways, 'twas a mess o' our own making."

She didn't know what to say to that. "What did Connor do?"

"He went to call out John MacDonald, o' course. But the scoundrel had departed once he'd heard from Janet o' the impending birth. He knew Connor would come around. The last I heard, he'd traveled south to catch a ship bound for America."

"And yet Connor didn't disown Ewan," she murmured.

"Nay, he didna, although he thought long and hard about it. He finally told Janet he'd provide and care for the lad as if he were his own. But the relationship 'tween him and Janet was irrevocably destroyed."

"I can understand why," she said. God in heaven, so many things were beginning to make sense now. The coolness between Connor and Ewan, the unnatural barriers in their relationship.

"Ewan has never been an easy lad to handle," Malcom said, his voice tired. "Yet he's perceptive. I think he knew from the start that something 'twasn't right 'tween him and his da."

"And he got Connor's attention the only way he knew how—through disobedience."

"Aye. But every time Connor looks at the lad, he sees Janet's betrayal."

"He must have looked at Janet the same way," Genevieve said softly.

Malcom closed his eyes and Genevieve saw how very old he looked. "And after enough times, it drove her to her death."

Genevieve suddenly felt ill to her stomach. She set her

teacup and saucer on the table and stood. "Why have you told me this?"

"Because I dinna want Connor to make the same mistake again."

"What mistake?"

"Wedding Catherine."

She felt her indignation rise on Connor's behalf. "Shouldn't he be allowed to make his own choices at last?"

"Aye, he should. And that's why, for once, I want him to follow his heart."

"I don't understand," Genevieve said frowning. "Doesn't he want to wed Catherine?"

Malcom shook his head. "Nay, lass, he wants to wed ye. 'Twas what he wanted from the very first."

Genevieve returned to her room, her thoughts spinning. She was deeply shaken by Malcom's revelation about Janet and Ewan, and, above all, Connor's supposed feelings for her. She had no idea what to think of his claim that Connor had wished to wed her. More than likely it was simply the fanciful wishing of an old man. But the knowledge of everything together disturbed her terribly.

Nonetheless, she somehow managed to sleep away the rest of the morning and into the early afternoon. She had supper with Ewan in his room, successfully avoiding Connor and the guests who were excitedly preparing for the next morning's foxhunt.

After tucking Ewan in, she slept fitfully, waking at dawn and hearing the castle already abuzz with preparations for the big event. She dressed quickly, hoping for a breath of fresh air before the festivities got started. Slipping outside, she used the servant's stairs and then headed for the garden. She was admiring the dew-wet blossoms when she heard footsteps behind her.

Quickly she turned, surprised to see Catherine. She looked lovely this morning, clad in a blue velvet riding outfit. Her thick dark hair was pinned up and a cap was positioned artfully atop her head.

"Good morn' to ye, Miss Fitzwellon," Catherine said. "'Tis a lovely morning, isna it?"

"My name is Fitzsimmons," Genevieve said, trying not to be annoyed. "And yes, it's a lovely morning."

Catherine smiled and perched on the stone bench. "Och, how careless o' me to get the governess's name wrong. I should take more care when speaking o' Connor's friends."

"That would be kind of you."

She chuckled, a deep, throaty sound. "My, my. Ye are no' as meek as ye look. Do ye mind if I ask just how close friends ye are wi' Connor?"

"Pardon me?"

She laughed outright. "Dinna play daft. I am a woman, dear, and I know Connor quite well. Ye fancy yourself in love wi' him, dinna ye? What did he do? Steal a kiss? Whisper sweet promises to ye under the stars? Well, let me tell ye something about Connor. He's a man who has a way wi' the lassies. He's handsome, brooding, charming. Every woman he meets falls hard for him. 'Tis naught but second nature to him. It means little."

"You are quite mistaken."

"Am I?" Catherine stretched on the bench like a sleek, slender cat. "Haven't ye asked yourself why he really brought ye here? Was he bored or perhaps needed an amusement to lighten his tedious routine? Ye would be naught more than a passing fancy for him, not even suitable for a long-time mistress. Why, look at ye. Ye are plain, dull, ordinary. A woman, aye, but no' a woman who would capture his fancy for verra long."

Genevieve clenched her fists together, her anger rising fast and furious. "How dare you suggest such a thing."

The sleek cat showed her claws. "I dare because Connor is mine. He intends to announce our betrothal tonight. I wanted to make that clear to ye. Ye are naught more than a governess, a servant in his employ . . . and soon to be in mine. Your fate rests as much wi' me as it does him. So tread carefully."

Genevieve felt as if she'd been slapped. Connor was going to announce their betrothal tonight? Although she'd been prepared for an eventual joining of the two, she did not anticipate the hot flash of jealously that ripped through her.

Raising her chin, Genevieve gave Catherine a cold smile of her own. "I shall tread where I please," she said, feeling a satisfied jolt as Catherine's beautiful face paled.

With that, Genevieve turned on her heel and walked away.

The foxhunt took all morning and stretched past midday before the guests returned. Genevieve stood at Ewan's window, watching as Connor rode in first, his dark hair tousled from the ride. Catherine rode in behind him, looking as beautiful and regal as ever. They complemented each other well, Genevieve thought with an ill feeling.

At that moment, she saw Connor raise his head, his gaze capturing hers at the window. Startled that he'd seen her there staring, she stepped back.

"Did ye see Da?" Ewan asked excitedly.

"Yes. Everyone is back."

"Do ye think they caught the fox?"

Genevieve approached the bed and plumped the pillows. "I would presume so."

"I hope Da comes up here soon to tell me about it."

"I'm certain he will," she said glad to see the boy in such good spirits. "I need to attend to something now, Ewan, but I'll return later."

With that, she quickly left the room, retreating to the safe haven of her own chamber. She'd been considering her situation all day and had finally come to a decision. After the guests departed, she would tell Connor of her desire to leave. She would not be welcome in a castle controlled by Lady Catherine, nor had she any wish to live under the woman's direction. She only prayed that Connor and Ewan's new and fragile bond would hold and the two of them would be able to enjoy a newfound relationship.

She sat at her desk, writing some letters of inquiry as to governess posts in London and hoping Connor would be willing to give her a letter of reference. She still had pen in hand when a knock sounded on her door. Thinking it was Mrs. MacDougal, she walked across the room and opened it.

Connor stood there, still dressed in his riding outfit, his massive shoulders filling the coat. He was so handsome with his piercing blue eyes and secret expression that her pulse quickened in response.

"Is all well with Ewan?" she asked worriedly. "I was just with him a short time ago."

"Ewan is fine. I haven't come to see ye about him. Do ye have a moment to speak privately wi' me?"

"Of course."

Without another word, he led her to the library. After she was seated, he walked around to his side of the desk and sat down, saying nothing. Instead, he tapped his fingers on his desk and stared into space as if gathering his thoughts. He was nervous, she thought in surprise. The rogue of Aberdour was visibly unsettled about something.

The silence stretched on interminably until Genevieve could no longer bear it. "Did you catch the fox?" she blurted out.

He seemed relieved she had spoken. "I'm sorry to report that we did no'. I presume the news pleases ye, knowing how ye disapprove o' such gaming."

"I am pleased on behalf of the fox."

He managed a chuckle, but it sounded pained. "Diplomatically put," he said and fell silent again.

At a loss as how to help him further, Genevieve crossed her hands in her lap and waited. She had run out of meaningless conversation, so the rest would be up to him.

"Ye've been right about me," he finally said, causing her to look up quickly.

"I have?"

"I've treated Ewan poorly. 'Twas wrong o' me. Genevieve . . . he's no' my son."

She was struck by the raw pain in his eyes. "I know," she said gently. "But in the ways it matters most, you are indeed his father. Why didn't you tell me?"

"I didna think it would have made a difference to ye with the boy. How did ye know?"

"Your father told me."

He sighed. "I thought if ye knew . . . 'twould make things worse between us."

"It might have helped me understand why you treated Ewan the way you did."

"Ewan doesna know."

"Maybe someday he should . . . when he's old enough to understand. But then it won't matter. You're the only father he'll have ever known."

He gave her a grateful look. "My dear, sensible

Genevieve. How have I managed all these years without ye? If only I could see life the practical way that ye do. There is much ye dinna know about me . . . much that I'm ashamed to reveal. That summer we were together, I knew I was about to be officially betrothed to Janet. I didna tell ye. I couldn't."

The confession was stark and simple. But even after all this time, it hurt more than she cared to admit. "Why couldn't you tell me?"

"Because I wanted naught to spoil our magic. And because I didna love her and she didna love me. She loved another, and I didna even know what love was."

"I'm sorry," Genevieve said quietly. And she was. Sorry for him, sorry for Janet, and sorry for herself.

"I tried to stand up to Da," he continued. "I told him how I felt about ye. But he made me leave the next day without even permitting me to say good-bye. And I let him."

"You had responsibilities," she said softly, even as her heart ached remembering the grief she had felt from losing him.

He pushed his fingers through his dark hair, not able to bring himself to look at her. "When Janet told me that she was wi' babe and the child was no' mine, I raged for a week. Then, after I considered, I told her I'd raise the child as mine. She was grateful. 'Twas one o' the few times I ever saw her smile."

Genevieve felt her heart clutch. "But things did not go smoothly."

"Nay, they did no'. We began to quarrel more frequently, more passionately. I should have done something . . . I should have tried harder to please her, but 'twas too late. For both o' us. We muddled along for several years more before she finally had lived the lie enough. Jumping was the easy way out. I'd be lying if I told ye I hadn't considered it myself."

Genevieve swallowed the lump in her throat. "I'm sorry, Connor. You don't owe me an explanation."

"Och, but I do. For this and a lot more. Have ye heard I was accused o' pushing her to her death?"

"I heard. But I didn't believe it."

"I didna do it. But I'm still partially responsible for her death. For making her life a dreadful hell."

"I'm sorry," she murmured numbly. It seemed all she was able to say.

"I might have followed her, except for Ewan. Now 'twas just me and him, and I had no idea how to handle him. Then there was the matter o' Catherine."

"You were free to wed her, and she was free as well."

"'Twas true. But I couldn't stop thinking o' ye . . . o' our summer together. I heard ye had turned down a suitor some years earlier. I wondered why. And I couldn't stop wondering what kind o' woman ye had become and if ye'd ever forgiven me."

She never thought she would say the words, but to her surprise they came out easily. And they were true. "I forgive you, Connor."

Their eyes met and locked. "I canna tell ye how much that means to me," he said hoarsely.

She sighed. "And now that your conscience is eased in regard to me, you are free to wed Catherine."

His eyebrows shot up. "Catherine?"

"Yes," Genevieve said patiently. "She told me you intend to announce your betrothal tonight."

"Tonight?" he repeated. "Genevieve, I'm no' going to wed Catherine."

Her breath caught in her throat. "You aren't?"

"Nay, I'm no'," he said firmly. "I dinna intend to

make the same mistake I made wi' Janet. I can't wed Catherine, because my heart lies elsewhere."

"Elsewhere?" she whispered, barely daring to trust her voice.

He leaned forward on the desk. "Wi' ye, Genevieve. I fell in love wi' ye that summer in England. I'd never met a lass so self-assured, so keen in wit, so enjoyable to be wi'. I'd found my soul mate, and I was too young and foolish to realize it. Well, I'm older now and far wiser. And I still love ye, lass."

She was so astounded by his revelation that she simply sat there in shock. "You love *me?*"

He laughed. "I tried to show ye wi' my kisses, to make ye believe in the magic again, but ye thought me too bold . . . a rogue." He paused, his mouth twitching at the corners. "I'll be the first to admit my approach wasna the most refined."

Stunned, she groped for something to say, anything. "But how can you be certain you love me?" she whispered. As if she didn't know for herself what it felt like to be in love.

He considered the question for a moment. "Because despite the years, my feelings for ye havena changed. I knew the moment I saw ye again. My heart slammed against my chest so hard I couldna breathe. And each time I've seen ye since, I'm as nervous as a lad. My palms get slick and my tongue feels heavy. I should tell ye that even before your grandda died, I was already plotting to get ye here to *Caisteal na Mara.* I am truly sorry for the loss of your grandda, but it gave me the perfect opportunity to bring ye here. I thought I only had to break through the mistrust ye had for me and make ye see that my feelings were true. Instead, 'twas ye who saved me, giving me a chance to redeem myself through the love o' my son."

He took a deep breath and looked at her with such a burning intensity that it touched her very soul. "The truth is I brought ye here, Genevieve, because I had to know. Did I really love ye or just a memory o' what once was? Now I know."

Genevieve felt ridiculously close to tears, the last of the wall she had so painstakingly built around her heart crumbling to dust with his words. "I don't know what to say."

He stood and came around the desk, pulling her up from the chair and holding her close against his muscular chest. "Then say that ye love me. Or if not that, at least that ye could learn to love me."

Emotion like she had never known before welled in her throat and broke, leaving bright unshed tears glittering in her eyes. "I do love you, Connor. I always have. You did make me believe in magic, as you're making me believe now. But I'm frightened. I was so terribly hurt when you left. I grieved for you for many years. I just couldn't bear it if you left me again or changed your mind."

"Never," he whispered fiercely against her cheek and she believed him. "Wed me, Genevieve. Be my wife and stay wi' me forever."

Without any more hesitation, she wound her arms around his neck, pulling him down toward her mouth. "You know that I will," she breathed against his cheek. "But when will you tell Catherine?"

"Tonight," he promised as his lips claimed hers in a hungry, possessive rush.

Ten

Genevieve watched the sunset from her window seat, her nerves jangling, her thoughts so scattered she could hardly think straight.

Connor loves me.

She wanted to pinch herself, yet feared waking to find it had all been a dream. But it had to be true. Her heart brimmed with so much happiness, she thought she'd burst.

She didn't dare tell a soul, not even Ewan. In fact, she was almost afraid to attend the closing feast, afraid everyone would see the joy in her eyes and know what Connor intended. But he had asked her to come, and she agreed. Now, she had only to act as normal as possible, whatever that was.

Earlier she'd begged off her afternoon tea with Mrs. MacDougal, who stared at her strangely. But bless her heart, the housekeeper said naught a word.

Now Genevieve took extra care in preparing herself for the feast, braiding her hair and choosing her best gown. She had just finished dressing when the servant girl Lucinda knocked on the door and handed her a note. Puzzled, Genevieve took it and closed the door. She unfolded the parchment and read the bold, sprawling handwriting.

Meet me in the north tower at half past six. 'Tis important.

Connor

Perplexed, Genevieve read it again. What could Connor possibly have to tell her that couldn't wait until after the feast? And why did he wish to meet her in the tower? She folded the note and sat down in the chair in front of the hearth. Her heart thumped uncomfortably. Had he changed his mind after all?

She stood and went to check her timepiece on the desk. It was nearly half past six now. Hurriedly, she left the room.

Walking down the corridor, she heard a noise coming from Ewan's room. Genevieve decided to check on him.

He smiled when he saw her, whistling approvingly. "Ye look awful fancy," he declared.

She perched on the bed beside him. "For that welcome flattery, I'll bring you some food later."

He grinned. "Hurry, would ye? I'm hungry. And bring some plum pudding."

She patted him on the cheek. "Only if you eat some venison first."

"Must I?"

"You must." She rose, walked to the door and paused at the threshold. "Ewan, does your father often go up to the tower room?"

He seemed taken aback by the question. "Sometimes. Why?"

"Well, he's invited me up there to talk."

"About what?"

She lifted her hands helplessly. "Something important that apparently can't wait until after the feast. I'll tell you about it later."

She gave him a smile before she headed toward the

tower stairs. Slowly she climbed up, thankful that Connor had lit the torches all the way to the top. When she reached the door, she pushed down on the latch and the door swung open. Standing on the threshold, she could see that Connor hadn't arrived yet, but the window was open again. The same eerie moaning noise echoed through the room, bringing to mind the legend of Christina Douglas and how she supposedly haunted the room. The hairs on the back of her neck stood up.

Deciding to wait for Connor at the bottom of the stairs, Genevieve turned to leave, when she heard a slight noise behind her. Before she could move, something hard hit her on the back of the head.

"No," she breathed as the world turned black.

Connor stood in the courtyard helping the stable master, Mac O'Donnelly, calm a restless steed. One of the guests had taken the horse out for a ride, and for some strange reason the beast had become uncontrollable. Connor always had a deft touch with the horses and had a particular fondness for this steed, so he rushed out to help Mac, even though he was already dressed in all his supper finery.

"Hell and damnation," Connor cursed as the steed nearly kicked him in the leg. "What's gotten into him this evening? He was fine during the foxhunt."

"I dinna know, sir," Mac said, barely escaping a buck to his ribs. "I've never seen him act this way."

"Did he throw a shoe?"

"No' that I can tell, sir. Seems to me his stomach is hurtin'. As if he's eaten somethin' rotten."

A small crowd had began to form around them. Connor wiped a bead of sweat from his forehead and stopped to catch his breath as the horse quieted momentarily. So much for his impeccable evening finery. He'd have to go and change again before supper.

Mac had just offered the steed a lump of sugar as a bribe when Connor suddenly noticed Ewan walking unsteadily toward him, still dressed in his nightclothes.

Connor dropped the reins and ran toward the lad. "Ewan," he cried, his heart leaping to his throat. "What are ye doing out o' bed?" He knelt in front of the boy, noticing his face was deathly white and contorted with pain.

The boy needed a moment to breathe. "I . . . I looked out my window and I saw ye in the courtyard, Da. Ye are here."

Connor looked at him puzzled. "Aye," he said slowly. "Mac needed my aid with the steed. Where else would I be?"

A trickle of sweat slipped down Ewan's temple, and Connor realized the effort it had cost the boy to personally summon him. "B-but Miss Fitzsimmons said ye wanted to meet her in the north tower. Now."

Connor felt the world stop for an instant, his heart turning over in his chest. "Stay here," he ordered the boy and dashed toward the castle at a dead run.

Genevieve came to, her head pounding, her stomach queasy. The room seemed to be spinning, so she blinked, but the movement didn't stop. It was then she realized someone had grabbed her beneath the armpits and was dragging her across the floor . . . toward the open window.

"No!" she gasped, twisting her body to the side and causing her attacker to lose balance. Genevieve dropped to the floor and rolled sideways, freeing herself from her captor's hold. The movement nearly caused her to wretch, and her vision spun so badly she could barely see. Nonetheless, she managed to come to a crouch amid her skirts.

She could see her attacker blur and then split into two figures. Genevieve closed her eyes and opened them again until it became one figure again.

"Dinna move," the form said softly, almost reassuringly. "I'm no' going to hurt ye."

Genevieve started at the familiar voice. "Mrs. MacDougal?" she whispered. "What are you doing here? Someone hit me and . . ." Her words trailed off as the housekeeper took a step closer, effectively blocking the door. The waning rays of the sun glinted off a dirk in the woman's hand.

"You," Genevieve uttered in disbelief. "You hit me. But why?"

Mrs. MacDougal took a careful step forward. "Because I'm no' goin' to let ye give Connor even one moment o' happiness. He deserves to suffer as she did."

Genevieve rose unsteadily to her feet. "You think he murdered Janet," she said, trying to ignore the wild throbbing in her head.

"He did murder her," Mrs. MacDougal said coldly. "He drove her to her death as surely as if he'd had pushed her wi' his two hands."

"It was a doomed union from the start," Genevieve said, stepping back until her back hit the cold wall. "Surely you can't put the blame solely on his shoulders."

"She was my niece . . . my baby," the housekeeper said, her voice pained and hurt. "I raised her as my own. And she took care o' me by bringing me here to run her household. But I failed her."

Genevieve's eyes widened in shock. She'd assumed Mrs. MacDougal had been in Connor's household since he was a babe. But it was Janet who had brought her to the castle, and that was where her loyalties lay.

"Janet was so verra young and frightened," Mrs. MacDougal continued. "And he didna want her."

"She didn't love him, either," Genevieve pointed out.

"She might have if he'd shown her any true affection. But she told me at night when he slept, he murmured the name o' another."

Genevieve felt the blood freeze in her veins. "Wh-who?"

"Ye, lass. He was dreaming o' ye."

Her heart squeezed in anguish. "I didn't know he was betrothed to her."

"Nevertheless, 'twill cost ye yer life."

Glancing behind the housekeeper, Genevieve noticed that the wall was at an odd angle. She blinked, but the wall stayed where it was, strangely out of alignment with the rest of the room.

"A secret passage," Genevieve gasped, suddenly understanding. "That's how you got up here without anyone seeing you. It was you who kept opening the window."

Mrs. MacDougal nodded. "'Tis one o' many passages that were sealed since the death o' Black Gavin. He used them to evade capture by his Scottish neighbors while he was shamelessly aidin' the English. After he was killed, the passages were sealed. I reopened this one wi' the aid o' John MacDonald."

"Janet's lover," Genevieve gasped.

"Aye, 'twas me who helped reunite the true lovers. This was where they met and loved, safely shielded from the prying eyes o' others at the castle. Janet was so happy."

"How could you do that to Connor?" Genevieve said, surprised her voice came out so angry. "Given time, they might have been able to make their marriage work."

She laughed coldly. "Never. And look at him now, the

heartless bastard. Janet was barely cold in her grave before he sent for ye. But I'm no' going to let his little plan work. Wi' ye gone, he'll at last turn to the poor, grieving widow Catherine Montclair. She'll make his life utterly dismal, the same as he made Janet's. Let him live the life he forced on her." Again she laughed, waving the dirk in front of her.

Genevieve desperately searched for some escape. The housekeeper had already come within two steps of her.

Summoning an inner courage she didn't know she possessed, Genevieve lunged forward and slammed her foot directly into the housekeeper's knee. She darted sideways toward the door, but Mrs. MacDougal reached out and grabbed a fistful of her skirts, yanking her backward. Genevieve let the full force of her body knock into the housekeeper, sending them both hurling to the stone floor. Genevieve managed to roll away, but Mrs. MacDougal recovered quickly and charged her again, apparently furious at her unwillingness to go meekly.

Genevieve turned and dashed for the secret passageway. She'd taken a step or two inside when Mrs. MacDougal crashed into her from behind, wielding the dirk. Genevieve wrenched her body to the side at the last moment and the blade slid into her upper right arm. White hot, searing pain enveloped her and she screamed, pushing at the housekeeper with all her strength.

With a cry of triumph, Mrs. MacDougal yanked the dirk out of Genevieve's shoulder, thrusting it at her neck. Genevieve threw herself to the side of the narrow passageway, crashing her body hard against the crumbling wall. The dirk missed her head by a hairbreadth and sent a shower of small stones sliding to the floor. A bright glint from something lodged in the wall caught her attention, but she had no time to examine it further. Mrs. MacDougal lunged, grabbing her arm and twisting it hard behind her back. Genevieve sobbed as an agonizing pain shot through her. Blood, hot and thick, ran down her arm and back. Her gown was already soaked and sticky. Her head pounded and her vision began to swim again.

"No," she whispered as the housekeeper pressed the dirk against her neck.

"Fight me no more, lass," Mrs. MacDougal said calmly. "Let me help ye end this as peacefully as possible."

Genevieve felt her legs buckle, her limbs refusing to obey her commands. The housekeeper dragged her across the stone floor. Barely conscious, Genevieve could summon no more energy to fight.

"Fare thee well, lass," Mrs. MacDougal said as she hefted Genevieve up to the windowsill.

Genevieve felt wet tears on her cheeks and hadn't even realized she was crying. She didn't want to die like this . . . like Janet. Without ever having the chance to see Connor again.

Suddenly the tower door crashed open. Mrs. MacDougal screamed in rage, and Genevieve glanced over her shoulder, seeing Connor dart toward her, his face stricken with fear.

"Connor!" she screamed and stretched out a hand just as she started to fall out the window.

Eleven

Connor felt his heart drop to his toes when he saw Genevieve balanced over the windowsill with Mrs. MacDougal ready to push. In the longest, most agonizing moment of his life, he threw himself forward, knocking the dirk from Mrs. MacDougal's hand and catching Genevieve just as she began to disappear over the side.

He braced his body against the windowsill, holding on to Genevieve's hand, grimacing as Mrs. MacDougal screeched and jumped on his back. He jabbed an elbow hard into her stomach, hearing the breath go out of her as she dropped gasping to the floor.

Sweat beading on his temples, he dragged Genevieve over the sill, back into the room. A quick glance at her indicated she was breathing, but had fainted. He carefully laid her on the floor, then rose to deal with Mrs. MacDougal, who held a dirk and came at him brandishing it.

"Ye killed Janet and drove John MacDonald away," she hissed. "Ye stole any chance at happiness she had."

Connor fought to control his rage. "Is that why ye've done this? To see me pay?"

"Why shouldn't ye suffer as she did? Janet's no' even six months in her grave and ye've already brought *her* here."

"I know ye loved Janet and I'm sorry ye lost her. We all lost her. Janet and I were young and foolish when we wed, completely unsuited to each other. And we were both in love wi' someone else. We never meant to hurt each other, but 'twas simply our lot in life."

"How could ye no' love her? She was perfect."

For some reason, he felt obliged to reply. "Matters o' the heart are more complicated than that. And ye should know Genevieve is innocent. She didna know I was betrothed to Janet."

"It doesna matter," the housekeeper retorted. "I'm no' going to let her give ye a moment o' joy or peace."

Connor looked down at his hands and saw they were sticky with blood. His temper flared again, hot and blinding. "If ye've harmed her," he said softly, dangerously, "I may just yet commit murder in this tower."

She screeched and threw herself at him, the dirk aimed at his heart. With one hard swipe of his hand, he knocked the dirk from her grasp and it went clattering across the floor, disappearing into a secret passageway he'd thought long sealed. She came at him again, pummeling and clawing his face with her bare hands. He yanked her off and cast her aside roughly. She slammed into the stone wall and crumpled unconscious to the ground.

"Connor?"

It was Genevieve lying beneath the window. He turned, his heart lodging in his throat. Quickly he knelt beside her.

"Ye're going to be fine, my love," he whispered, shrugging out of his coat and then removing his shirt. With one sharp rip, he tore the material down the middle. He took a strip and began winding it around her arm to stop the bleeding.

"How did you know I was here?" she asked weakly.

"Ewan. He told me ye'd come up here to meet me. Imagine my surprise to hear that."

Genevieve turned her head toward the passageway. "She found it."

Connor paused, holding the strip still. "I saw. I thought the passageway was long sealed."

"Mrs. MacDougal opened it years ago with the aid of John MacDonald. Connor, this is where Janet trysted with him."

His stomach clenched tight, but he resumed calmly binding her arm. "I'll have it sealed again."

"The treasure is there."

His eyebrow shot up. "Treasure?"

She nodded, biting her lower lip. "I saw it out of the corner of my eye in the stone wall. A red jewel of some sort, wrapped partially in a cloth. Mrs. MacDougal inadvertently revealed it when she tried to skewer me. I think it may be the treasure of Black Gavin. It's yours now."

He slid his arms under her body, lifting her up and holding her close to his bare chest. "My darling Genevieve, I already have the treasure of Black Gavin."

She frowned. "You do?"

He pressed a kiss on her nose. "Christina Douglas was Black Gavin's treasure. The legend is that she was more precious to him than a thousand gems. 'Tis what every Douglas man seeks. That treasure doesna lie wrapped in a cloth and hidden in a secret passageway. 'Tis lying in my arms right now."

Genevieve managed a weak smile. "That's the most romantic thing I've ever heard."

Connor grinned, a lock of hair falling across his forehead as he pressed another kiss to her lips. "I've known the jewel was there all along. It stays where it is to perpetuate the legend. Some day our son will seek out the treasure, but find his greatest reward lies in the arms o' the woman he loves."

Genevieve wound an arm around his neck, pulling his mouth back to hers. "That's a beautiful tale," she murmured against his lips.

"Indeed, it is," he replied, holding her close and showering featherlight kisses across her eyes and brow. "A tale o' true love and magic. And at last, I'm finally claiming the Douglas treasure for *my* very own."

Thrilling Romance from Lisa Jackson

__Twice Kissed	0-8217-6038-6	$5.99US/$7.99CAN
__Wishes	0-8217-6309-1	$5.99US/$7.99CAN
__Whispers	0-8217-6377-6	$5.99US/$7.99CAN
__Unspoken	0-8217-6402-0	$6.50US/$8.50CAN
__If She Only Knew	0-8217-6708-9	$6.50US/$8.50CAN
__Intimacies	0-8217-7054-3	$5.99US/$7.99CAN
__Hot Blooded	0-8217-6841-7	$6.99US/$8.99CAN